THE PHANTOM CHASE

Also by Cap Daniels

The Chase Fulton Novels Series
Book One: *The Opening Chase*
Book Two: *The Broken Chase*
Book Three: *The Stronger Chase*
Book Four: *The Unending Chase*
Book Five: *The Distant Chase*
Book Six: *The Entangled Chase*
Book Seven: *The Devil's Chase*
Book Eight: *The Angel's Chase*
Book Nine: *The Forgotten Chase*
Book Ten: *The Emerald Chase*
Book Eleven: *The Polar Chase*
Book Twelve: *The Burning Chase*
Book Thirteen: *The Poison Chase*
Book Fourteen: *The Bitter Chase*
Book Fifteen: *The Blind Chase*
Book Sixteen: *The Smuggler's Chase*
Book Seventeen: *The Hollow Chase*
Book Eighteen: *The Sunken Chase*
Book Nineteen: *The Darker Chase*
Book Twenty: *The Abandoned Chase*
Book Twenty-One: *The Gambler's Chase*
Book Twenty-Two: *The Arctic Chase*
Book Twenty-Three: *The Diamond Chase*
Book Twenty-Four: *The Phantom Chase*
Book Twenty-Five: *The Crimson Chase*

THE PHANTOM CHASE

CHASE FULTON NOVEL #24

CAP DANIELS

ANCHOR WATCH
PUBLISHING
** USA **

The Phantom Chase
Chase Fulton Novel #24
Cap Daniels

This is a work of fiction. Names, characters, places, historical events, and incidents are the product of the author's imagination or have been used fictitiously. Although many locations such as marinas, airports, hotels, restaurants, etc. used in this work actually exist, they are used fictitiously and may have been relocated, exaggerated, or otherwise modified by creative license for the purpose of this work. Although many characters are based on personalities, physical attributes, skills, or intellect of actual individuals, all the characters in this work are products of the author's imagination.

Published by:

ANCHOR WATCH
PUBLISHING
** USA **

13 Digit ISBN: 978-1-951021-53-5
Library of Congress Control Number: 2023950524
Copyright © 2023 Cap Daniels – All Rights Reserved

Cover Design: German Creative

Printed in the United States of America

The Phantom Chase

CAP DANIELS

Chapter 1
The Door

Summer 2010

"Run, Chase!"

In my thirty-six years on the planet, I had probably run more miles than I'd walked, but even when I was playing for the College World Series championship in 1996, I'd never run harder than I did when pushing myself on that muggy, Southern, summer afternoon in Birmingham, Alabama. I've always demanded more of myself—mentally, psychologically, and especially physically—than anyone else ever asked of me, but that day, the tables had turned. I wore a clumsy backpack, gym shorts, well-worn boots, and more wires, electrodes, monitors, and unidentifiable detritus of every medical gadgetry they could attach to what remained of my body.

In the previous four months of my life, I conducted quite a shopping trip at the University of Alabama at Birmingham Hospital, one of the finest hospitals anywhere on the planet. I picked up a new right wrist, in just my size, that made the fourteen-year-old outdated model look like a caveman's toy. I initially destroyed that wrist and much of my hand in a nasty train wreck at home plate during the final game of the aforementioned College World Series. We won, and I was fortunate enough to be named most valuable player of that final game. The five surgeries that began in Omaha, Nebraska, and ended at Emory Hospital in Atlanta, so long ago, resulted in the installation and fine-tuning of a mechanical wrist joint that performed relatively like the wrist God gave me the day I was born, and I'd grown fond of my mechanical joint over the years.

Although my baseball career was over, and I'd never wear catcher's gear over an Atlanta Braves uniform, another door was opened for me that led to a career and world I never knew existed. Throughout the first decade of my career, I came to think of that door as C.S. Lewis's creation in *The Lion, The Witch, and The Wardrobe*. Beyond that wardrobe door lay two worlds: one of utter and indisputable evil, and another of undeniable good. Life beyond my wardrobe wasn't as clearly delineated as was Mr. Lewis's fictional world of Narnia, into which Peter, Susan, Edmund, and Lucy Pevensie were fantastically transported in wartime England.

My Pevensie family was a team of covert operatives and support staff, and my Narnia was every inch of ground beneath my feet in every corner of the world. No, there was no wardrobe door separating reality from fantasy in my world. My team and I *were* that door separating a realm of utter chaos ruled by the never-ending battle of freedom versus oppression, security versus anarchy, good versus evil.

"Faster, Chase. Push it as hard as you can."

The last time I ran prior to that day at UAB, I was running from four Mikoyan MiG-29s of the Russian Air Force and the 500-pounders they dropped from the hardpoints beneath their wings and onto the airport at the Dashoguz near the Uzbekistan border with Turkmenistan. The resultant explosions separated my body from the previous prosthetic that had been my lower right leg and foot. I lost the particular flesh-and-blood body part during a fight aboard a ship in Western Africa.

Doctor Michael "Ham" Smithfield, one of the world's leading orthopedic research surgeons, designed, built, tested, and installed a state-of-the-art prosthetic that was nearly a miracle of modern medicine. Between the sensors, servos, and strength of that first prosthetic, I often forgot it wasn't my real leg, ankle, and foot, but the updated version took the technology even further. The new foot on which I was running that day boasted a first-ever integration with my body's central nervous system. The appendage was still in the experimental phase, so there was no FDA approval, and I was test subject número uno. Neither Dr. Ham nor I knew if there would ever be a second guinea pig.

My burdens that day were many. However, the immediate weight bearing down on me was the eighty pounds of lead in the backpack that was clearly manufactured to fit a racehorse jockey, and at well over six feet and 225 pounds, I'd never ride a thoroughbred.

"Ninety more seconds. Push it, Chase. Push it!"

The movie reel of my sprint from the hangar at Dashoguz Airport, with Russian munitions falling from the sky, played over and over in my head as inspiration to survive the next minute and a half. My boots thudded against the whizzing treadmill track, and my lungs screamed for more air. Before the explosion in Uzbekistan, I could run a sub-5-minute mile and a 4.8-second 40-yard sprint, but based on the pounding of my heart, I wasn't confident I had the gas for the ninety seconds the physical therapist demanded.

The explosions didn't come, I wasn't buried in debris, and there were no Russian fighter pilots overhead, but the same exhaustion I felt that day on the far side of the world returned as I collapsed over the frame of the treadmill, my lungs churning, and my legs burning . . . Both legs.

Between panting breaths, I managed to ask, "Should I . . . be able . . . to feel . . . the foot?"

The physical therapist looked up from her clipboard and cocked her head. "Feel it? What do you mean?"

My breathing slowed, and my heart decided to stay inside my chest. "I mean . . . I can feel it tingling. Just like my left foot."

Her eyes widened, and she turned to see Dr. Ham trotting from the monitor station, where he'd recorded more information about my body in the previous five minutes than the flight data recorder on any airliner.

He shoved his glasses on top of his head. "Did you say you feel the prosthetic tingling?"

"Yeah, it feels just like my natural foot."

"Where?"

I pointed at my boot. "On top, and where the Achilles tendon should be."

"Wiggle your toes," he ordered.

My brain sent the signal to my little piggies to go to market, but I shook my head. "I don't feel them moving."

"Look at your boot."

I followed his gaze to see the toe of my Israeli Urban Palladium commando boot rising and falling as my prosthetic toes cycled inside.

"You can't feel that?" he asked.

"No, but maybe I will after I catch my breath. I didn't expect your therapist to crack the whip quite so hard."

"She does that, and that's exactly why she works exclusively with me. Sometimes, I think she and I share a brain. Want some water?"

I nodded, and a bottle landed in my palm.

The therapist said, "See? There's that sharing-a-brain thing again."

I downed the water and tossed the bottle into the recycle bin. "So, what's next, Doc?"

He pulled down his glasses and checked his Rolex. "Lunch. Wanna join me?"

I looked down at my sweat-covered body. "I could use a shower first."

"Meet me in my office when you're finished."

Twenty minutes later, I pecked on his office door. "Doctor Ham?"

The sound of a closing drawer and a dropped pen proceeded. "Come in, Chase."

I pushed open the door to find him peering into the inner workings of a prosthetic foot just like mine. "I'm trying to figure out why you can't feel your toes. That's going to be essential for improved balance."

I tried again and focused on how mechanical toes should feel. "Sorry. I'm still not feeling them, but I can feel pressure changes in the ball of my foot and the heel."

He froze. "Oh! You do feel that?" I nodded, and he said, "That's what you should feel. Think back to your days crouched behind home plate, and give me that same crouch."

I dropped into the old familiar position with my right hand tucked behind my hip and the imaginary mitt on my left, hovering between my knees.

He said, "Now, focus on your toes and specifically your balance on the right foot."

"I still can't feel the toes moving, but I can feel the effects of them moving on the rest of my foot."

"That's what we want. As long as you can establish improved balance, that's the immediate goal. If we run out of other things to work on, perhaps we'll put some nerves in the toes of the next iteration."

"It's certainly better than the last one," I said. "And you mentioned something about lunch."

He replaced the prosthetic into a charging cradle behind his desk and pushed from his chair. "I did. How do you feel about pancakes?"

"For lunch?"

"Trust me."

We walked the few blocks from his office to the Original Pancake House in the Five Points area, dodging trash cans, parked cars, other pedestrians, and curbs. As we walked, he seemed to exaggerate his maneuvers and sidesteps, forcing me to do the same. At 11th Avenue and 20th Street, the "Don't Walk" sign turned red, and he took off in a sprint into the crosswalk.

That's when the psychologist in me put it together. I passed him a few strides from the curb. "Come on, Doc. Keep up."

We settled into a booth and ordered our lunchtime pancakes. I took a sip of water and asked, "How'd I do?"

He chuckled. "I wish all my patients were as fit as you, but not quite as smart."

"I'm not smart, Doc. I just pay attention."

"Call me Ham. And sometimes, smart and attention are interchangeable. How does it feel?"

"It's good. Different from the first one, but good. It'll take some time to get used to the sensations, but it'll come."

Our plates arrived, and we dug in.

He wiped his mouth. "Not bad, huh?"

I swallowed a mouthful of chocolate chip pancakes. "There are more calories on this plate than anybody needs in a day."

"Yeah, but they're good calories, aren't they?"

"Indeed, they are."

He laid his fork on the edge of his plate. "Is everything else okay? You seem preoccupied."

I held up my right hand and slid my right foot from beneath the table. "I'm running out of real body parts, Doc. I've got a lot on my mind."

He poured an abundance of salt onto his remaining pancakes, and I asked, "What's that about?"

"You got me thinking about the calories I don't need, so I made the rest too salty to eat."

"That's a great idea."

He said, "I don't have the willpower to stop unless the waitress takes it away or I do the salt trick. It's obvious you don't have willpower issues, but there's more going on behind those eyes than the loss of body parts. We're off the record here, Chase. What's going on?"

I drew stick figures in the syrup on my plate. "Penny, my wife, is pregnant."

When he cocked his head and let his eyes drift to the ceiling, there was no question in my mind about what was going on. He was rereading my medical history in his mind, but when he came to the page he'd been searching for, it hit him, and he stopped reading.

I nodded, pushed my plate to the edge of the table, and said, "Yep, you read it right. After my injury overseas, I'm not capable of producing children."

Chapter 2
The Talk

There are countless beautiful places on the planet, but my favorite has always been the gazebo in the backyard of my family's ancestral home, Bonaventure Plantation, on the banks of the North River in St. Marys, Georgia. The property had been a pecan and cotton plantation in centuries past but now served as my home and operation center for Tactical Team 21. The centerpiece of the gazebo was an 18th-century cannon I pulled from the mud and muck on the bottom of Cumberland Sound, just a few miles from home. The gun was a gift for my great-uncle, Judge Bernard Henry Huntsinger, before he bequeathed the property to me.

After arriving home, I spent the first hour alone in that gazebo with my feet—both mechanical and God-given—propped on the cannon carriage, communing with the ghosts and phantoms of the men still haunting the gun for having taken their lives, or, in many cases, had been the weapon of war with which they doled out death eighteen pounds at a time. The Cuban Cohiba hooked inside my index finger was one of the greatest indulgences of my life. Another was the well-aged, honey-colored bourbon in the tumbler by my left hand. With the river, gazebo, cannon, and cigar as drinking buddies for the hour, I was in pretty good company, but that was about to improve.

Just as I crushed out the stump of the cigar, my moral compass and spiritual shepherd, Jimmy "Singer" Grossmann, slid into an Adirondack directly across from me. "How'd it go up at UAB?"

"Hello, my friend. Thanks for coming."

It would be impossible to tell just by looking at Singer that he was an ordained Southern Baptist minister, choir leader, and the most devout Christian most people would ever meet, but the dichotomy of my friend is what made him even more fascinating. In years past, he'd worn the black beret of the U.S. Army Rangers on his head and the tab of a sniper on his arm. There may have been no one on Earth more qualified to lead a man gently to the saving grace of the Lord in the morning and then put a supersonic rifle round through his skull from a mile away later that afternoon. Singer was one of the world's elite snipers with a number of kills he'd never say out loud, but he would much rather lead a man to salvation than deliver him to final judgment.

He said, "You never have to thank me for coming to spend time with my friend."

I raised my glass. "Would you like some sweet tea?"

"No, thanks. I had a glass on the way over. Sure is a pretty afternoon, isn't it?"

I set my half-full glass of bourbon beneath my chair out of some misguided, self-imposed moral obligation—or perhaps respect—to Singer. He was a teetotaler but never seemed to judge me or anyone else for enjoying a libation from time to time.

I've often heard him say, "The biblical record of the first miracle Jesus performed on Earth tells us about Him making a batch of wine out of water when they ran out at a wedding party one night. If Jesus doesn't mind you having a snort, then who am I to disagree?"

I called my old friend, believing he held the answer to a question that haunted me, much like the spirits surrounding the old cannon, but his gentle manner would never allow him to bring it up until I did.

After ten minutes of watching pelicans and an eagle dive on baitfish in the river, I let my feet fall from the cannon's cradle. "I guess you're wondering what I needed to talk about, huh?"

He didn't look away from the birds. "No, sir, not wondering . . . Just waiting."

I gathered my courage—or perhaps my ignorance-based stupidity. "I'm sure you remember the extraction from the Khyber Pass when you and Clark got shot up on the mountain."

That was enough to draw his attention—and his eyes—inside the gazebo. "I'll never forget it. We would've died up there. Especially Clark, if you hadn't come to get us."

I sighed. "I can't take the credit. I had some solid help from a pair of Tajiki helicopter pilots and a Defense Intelligence officer."

He nodded in silence, and I continued. "The gunfight on the ground before we all made it to the chopper is a bit of a blur in my memory, but I ended up taking a dive onto a pile of rocks and doing a little damage"—I waved a hand over my gut—"in this area."

He let me off the hook with a well-timed chuckle. "Yeah, I remember. You broke your babymaker."

I appreciated the comic relief, but the reality of what was going on inside my head outweighed the lighthearted moment, and I stammered when I tried to continue. "It's just that . . . I mean, it's not like I . . ."

Singer motioned toward the floor of the gazebo beneath my chair. "Take a breath and a drink, Chase. I know what's going through your head, and I could give you all the reassurances of fidelity on Earth, but none of them, and not even the collection of them as a whole, would put your mind at ease."

Thankful for the distraction, I lifted my tumbler and enjoyed a third of its contents. "What I'm trying to say is—"

He held up a hand. "Let me finish."

I took another drink and closed my mouth.

"You and I believe in the same God, and we have the same faith that we'll be rewarded by that God with life eternal in a place where men like us aren't required. There will be nobody to hunt down and nobody to kill when that day comes, and that alone is reward enough for my soul, and I suspect the same is true for yours."

"I've never looked at it that way, but I guess you're right."

"That's only a small secondary point to the grander and more important point of faithfulness inside your marriage. May I speak frankly, Chase?"

That required another drink, but I said, "Of course. Please do."

He let out a chortle. "I may need one of those drinks for this."

His way of breaking up the discomfort of a terrible conversation was a skill I envied. When I saw psychological patients in my part-time practice, I often wished I could come up with brief intermissions like Singer had mastered, but I still had a lot to learn.

"Anyway," he said. "Penny is a beautiful woman who spends over half her time in a place where morality packed up and left a long time ago. The industry in which she thrives has never been heralded as a bastion of monogamy. Hollywood is only one vowel away from being Hellywood. Most of the people in that industry wouldn't bat an eye at the thought of a married woman carrying someone else's illegitimate child."

The more he spoke, the more I longed for another moment of levity, and I couldn't resist interrupting him. "Wait a minute. I think you may have the wrong idea."

He crossed his legs and relaxed his previously tense shoulders. "Perhaps I do. Why don't you tell me what we're talking about before I take this conversation someplace it should never go?"

I cleared my throat and suddenly wished for a bottle of whiskey and a long straw. "I don't question Penny's faithfulness. I never have. Believe it or not, that thought never crossed my mind."

He furrowed his brow. "Then what are we doing here?"

I never remember seeing Singer quite so baffled as I'd left him in that moment. "I fear something far more sinister than infidelity. I fear she may have been . . ."

I couldn't force the word from my lips, no matter how hard I tried, but my friend and counselor caught me before I fell. "Do you think she may have been raped?"

I stared between my boots and forced myself to swallow the bile rising in my throat. "I don't know, but short of immaculate conception, I can't come up with any other way this could've happened. She wouldn't cheat on me. She wouldn't."

"Listen to me. You don't have to keep trying to convince yourself of that, and it's clear you're trying to do exactly that. If there's a thought of infidelity in your marriage, then this is an issue far deeper than who fathered that child."

"No, not even for an instant have I thought she would willingly betray me. She's too strong and too good to stray. If she suddenly wanted someone other than me, and who wouldn't, she would come directly to me, and we'd address the issue. She's not a cheating wife."

He waved a hand through the air. "Look around. Her life ain't bad here at Bonaventure."

"Yeah, but I'm gone at least a third of the time, and she's in Hollywood more often than you and I are off playing Dirk Pitt from a Clive Cussler novel."

"You said it yourself. She's a strong woman and a good woman, and all of that couldn't be truer. Ultimately, that means if she were unhappy with the life she has here with you, she would come to you, and the two of you would deal with it."

It was his turn to pause and gather his thoughts, and my turn to say, "What's going on in that head of yours?"

He didn't look back at me for a long moment, but when he did, he wore a look of ultimate sadness, dusted with a measure of pleasure. "A baby will change everything."

"I know. I've already been wrestling with that one, but I've not brought it up with Penny yet."

"That's a conversation you can't avoid, Chase. You have to start that talk."

"You're right, but from the perspective of a psychologist, I think it's a conversation and a decision that has to be made after the baby is born. As much as I already love the child she's carrying, when I get to hold her for the first time, I may hang up my boots that day."

The look on Singer's face said he was at a crossroads, so I waited patiently as he resolved the questions floating around in that brilliant mind behind those eyes.

Finally, he said, "We're talking about two very different things that I think we have to keep separate. Let's deal with the first issue first. Is that okay with you?"

"Absolutely. I'm sorry for rabbit-holing on you. I'll try to focus."

He said, "It's okay. I'm a little ashamed for thinking this was going to be an infidelity conversation. I should've known better, but that's the carnal mind still letting the devil creep in."

"It's okay, and I can see how that would be a question, but I know Penny better than anyone on Earth, and the one flaw she has does not fall into that category."

He glanced toward the house, I assume, to make sure Penny wasn't bouncing down the stairs off the back gallery to hear me say she had a flaw.

I said, "Don't worry. She's in L.A."

"Why aren't you?"

It felt like I'd been hit in the head by a brick. "You know what? I'll be there by the time the sun goes down."

"Before you run off, let's walk through this fear of yours so you'll be well prepared to have a meaningful conversation with her tonight. Keep talking about what's going through your head."

I let an ice cube slide from my tumbler and onto my tongue. "The one flaw I mentioned has more to do with me than her. I made a grade-A jackass out of myself at a party in the Hollywood Hills one night when I watched a producer let his hand slide down Penny's back and onto a part of her only I'm allowed to touch."

He almost smiled. "Let me guess. You broke his arm."

"I didn't break it, but he'll never grab my wife's butt again."

"We're cavemen, and you can put a caveman in a tux, but you can't make him stop picking fights with sabertoothed tigers."

I chuckled. "That sounds like something Clark would say."

"What I mean is, we live in a world of violence of action and speed of response. Men like us don't always think through our actions to a logical conclusion. As far as I'm concerned, you probably should've broken his arm, but I suspect Penny was a little unhappy to be at the center of a scene like that."

"She was," I admitted, "but probably not for the reason you think. She was upset with me because I didn't have enough faith in her to know she would've likely done far worse to the guy than I did. That's what upset her. She didn't need me to run to her rescue. She had things well in hand, so to speak."

He uncrossed his legs and stared into the bare rafters of the gazebo. "Oh! So, that's what you're afraid of. You think somebody may have assaulted her, and she didn't tell you because of how she knows you'll react."

I sucked the last sliver of ice from my tumbler. "And she's justified in that fear. I'd probably go to prison."

He said, "We'd probably all go to prison."

"Probably so."

A long moment passed, and he said, "Okay, we've got that one behind us, so let's talk about hanging up your boots. None of us, except maybe Penny, wants to see that happen. You're our team leader. We'd follow you into any fight you picked—even the ones you start. I guess that makes us the six musketeers."

"I guess it does," I said. "I've been giving it a lot of thought, and I'm torn between two diametrically opposed perspectives. First, I don't know if I can jump into a fight with the real possibility of never coming back, knowing I've got a newborn baby at home."

"That one's perfectly understandable," he said. "What's the opposing view?"

"That's the one that'll make sense to you and the rest of the guys, but not to Penny. I don't know if I can resist jumping into a fight to make the world a better place for my baby to grow up in."

He rocked back and forth in his chair. "Yep, you're right about that one. She won't get it, but I do. I'll tell you what I'm going to do . . . I'm going to pray for you, and for Penny, and especially for your baby, but you have to have that conversation with her. You have to be honest, transparent, and thorough."

I cocked my head. "About quitting after the baby is born?"

He shook his head in disappointment. "No, you have to talk to her about who the father of that baby really is." He gave me a wink. "And I'm not ruling out immaculate conception."

"You wanna come to L.A. with me?"

He checked his watch. "Can't. It's Wednesday, and the choir's going to raise the roof tonight. I can't miss it, but I look forward to hearing all about it when you get back."

Chapter 3
The Real Talk

Disco, our chief pilot and retired Air Force A-10 Warthog driver, jumped at the chance to take our Gulfstream IV *Grey Ghost* across the country. He said, "How long do you plan to stay in L.A.?"

I said, "I don't know. If it goes well, I may want to stay a few days, but if it goes how I fear it's going to go, we may be heading east before dessert."

"Oh . . . It's one of those things."

"I'm afraid it is. Why do you ask?"

He suddenly took on the look of a teenage boy asking Daddy for the car keys. "Well, the *Lori Danielle* is in dry dock down in San Diego, and I haven't seen Ronda No-H since the Alaskan mission."

"I'll tell you what. You go check on our ship, and if the conversation doesn't go well with Penny, I'll catch the red-eye flight back to Atlanta tonight."

"No, I can't have you doing that. Chase Fulton doesn't fly commercial."

I gave him a slap on the back. "He does if he screws this one up, my friend. How soon will you be ready to go?"

"I'm ready now. If I need more clothes and deodorant, they have stores in San Diego."

Four hours later, we descended into smog so thick we couldn't see the skyscrapers of L.A. I hoped that wasn't an omen of how my evening would go. We touched down at Hollywood Burbank Airport and stepped off the Gulfstream into air that was thirty degrees cooler than when we left the sweltering heat and humidity of coastal Georgia. The difference was pleasant, and I considered that to be a gris-gris to ward off the previous omen of smog.

"Are you sure I don't need to wait for you?" Disco asked as we walked toward the FBO.

"I'm sure. Go spend some quality time with Ronda. You deserve it. You've got a card for fuel and hangar space, right?"

He patted his hip pocket. "I've got one. If you don't mind, shoot me a text later and let me know how it goes . . . whatever it is."

"You got it," I said. "Don't worry about me. Just enjoy yourself . . . and Ronda No-H."

The car service at the airport has always been second to none, but the stars apparently aligned against me that afternoon.

The young lady behind the counter said, "I'm so sorry, sir. The service can't get anyone here in less than an hour, but I'll be happy to call around and see if I can find an alternative service."

"How about a rental?" I asked.

"Oh, sure. We've got plenty of those. What type of vehicle would you like?"

"Do you have anything a little exotic? I'm thinking something convertible that will make Mulholland Drive feel like Mulholland Drive should feel."

She pulled her hands from her keyboard. "There's only one car for that, sir, and we don't have it. But my boyfriend does."

"Is it for sale?"

She fumbled beneath the counter and came up with her purse. After digging past lipstick, powder, and car keys, she came up with a business card and slid it across the counter. "They're all for sale, sir."

I lifted the card and saw the name "Chris Porter, Sales Mgr., Porsche Downtown L.A."

I asked, "Will you call a taxi for me?"

She said, "Of course, sir. Where would you like to go?"

I held up the card. "To see your boyfriend."

It wasn't the smile of a lady born and raised in coastal Georgia, but it was the first sincere smile I'd seen behind the counter since our arrival. "If you have a seat, I'll let you know when your car arrives. Would you care for a drink, sir?"

I held up Chris's card again and tried to imitate the flowing Southern drawl of my great-uncle, the Judge. "No, thank you, ma'am. You've done quite enough already."

If she caught it, she didn't react, and I took a seat near the window so I could watch planes bigger—and smaller—than mine arriving and departing, picking up and dropping off self-important passengers who likely believed they were owed the courtesies of temporary wealth and deserved the luxurious surrounds of their private jets. I secretly wondered how many of the jets were chartered instead of owned outright, and that led me to the ridiculous musing of how many on the ramp were purchased with taxpayer funds and used by others like me, when parts of the world—even tiny, unheard-of parts—become unruly and in need of reigning in.

Disco pulled me from my ridiculous musings. "Are you sure you're okay if I hop down to San Diego? You don't need me to wait?"

I looked up at the best pilot I knew. "Who are you, and why are you bothering me?"

He chuckled. "I'm terribly sorry, sir. I can see you're bothered enough without me piling on, but the ladies at the counter asked if I would escort you out of the building. They mentioned something about you scaring the paying customers."

I laughed. "Get out of here. I'll call if I need you, but plan to stay as long as you'd like."

"Thanks, Chase. I'll see you in a few days."

"Mr. Fulton, your car has arrived." Still not Southern, but definitely more sincere than before.

I stood and said, "Thank you, ma'am. Now, could you do something about this man? He's begging for spare change, and anything I give him will have to come out of your boyfriend's commission."

Clearly unaccustomed to jackassery in her FBO, the lady couldn't decide if she should laugh or call the airport police.

Disco exited through opposite doors, and miraculously, a black Lincoln Town Car waited curbside instead of the requested taxi, and I was pleased. We arrived at Porsche Downtown thirty-five minutes later, and I tipped well, but not from Chris's potential commission.

It wouldn't have taken a supersleuth to pick out the sales manager. He was well dressed, his hair coifed, and he wore knockoff Italian loafers that were close enough to fool most people.

He stuck out a hand. "You must be Mr. Fulton. I'm Chris Porter, the sales manager here at Porsche Downtown. Would you care for a cocktail?"

I shook the offered hand. "Call me Chase. I'd like to look at a Nine-Eleven Turbo convertible, and I'll pass on the cocktail unless you fail and I have to leave without a new Porsche."

"God forbid," he said. "I think we've got exactly what you need, Chase. Come with me."

Instead of leading me onto the showroom floor, Chris wound his way through a sea of 911s that would more than satisfy my desire to hug the curves on Mulholland Drive, but when we arrived outside a roll-up door at the back of the building, a gleaming, brand-new 911 Turbo all-wheel drive Cabriolet convertible dream sat savoring the attention of the soft, cotton towel being used to remove every spot of water before it could dry and leave its temporary mark on the flawless paint job.

"You like?" Chris asked.

"Who wouldn't?"

He grinned, no doubt in anticipation of the weight of the check he expected me to write. "She just came off the truck yesterday, and as you can see, she's fresh out of detail and ready to go. The keys are in the ignition if you'd like to go for a drive."

"Let's go."

An hour later, after the verification of my wire transfer, I drove away in Penny's new Porsche convertible, headed for Mulholland Drive. Although I've never been what could be classified as a car guy, the 911 was astonishing and felt remarkably similar to my P-51 Mustang as I climbed away from the bustling city of L.A. and accelerated through the first turns on the legendary street and into the Hollywood Hills.

After having far more fun than anyone should be allowed without going to jail, I pulled into the driveway of the single-story house we bought for Penny so she could feel just as much at home on the West Coast as she did on the coast I preferred. The timing worked out perfectly, but to my surprise, when she pulled into the drive, she wasn't alone, and my heart sank.

Had Singer been right? Was Penny living another life in Hollywood? Was I the fool?

As I tried and failed to mentally prepare for who I'd see stepping from the passenger side of Penny's Suburban, I suddenly wished I'd never left Georgia, but to my enormous relief, I'd never been happier to see anyone than the man who stepped from the passenger side door.

Mongo, our team's resident giant, married a Russian and welcomed an adopted daughter, Tatiana, into the family. The girl had danced the Bolshoi as a child before leaving Mother Russia and was now a senior at Juilliard and highly sought after by more ballet companies than I could count. Her boyfriend, Grayson Knox, also a student at the prestigious fine arts school, was a highly accomplished classical pianist and composer. Why Grayson was in Penny's Suburban was still a mystery, but at least my heart didn't have to explode.

The smile on Penny's face when she saw me leaning against the Porsche was more beautifully pure than anything I'd ever seen before that moment. "Chase, what a surprise! And it looks like you've been car shopping."

I greedily absorbed my beautiful wife into my arms and felt the baby press against my stomach. When she stepped back, I let my hand glide across her belly, and we shared a moment as if no one else existed.

Finally, she said, "What's with the convertible?"

I tossed the key fob into the air between us. "It's for you. Now that you're a big-time screenwriter, you don't need to drive that big battleship of a car."

"But I love the Suburban. I feel so big and tough when I drive it."

"Just wait until you put this thing into a few of those turns on Mulholland, and you'll forget all about the SUV."

She caught my hand and placed it back on her baby bump. "Okay, but I think I'll keep the Suburban, too."

"That's a good idea," I said and turned to Grayson and Tatiana. "What are you guys doing out here?"

Grayson couldn't contain his excitement. "I'm writing the score for a movie at Penny's studio. It's crazy. Can you believe it?"

I glanced back to my wife. "Did you set that up?"

"Nope. I just made the introductions and put Grayson in front of a piano. Half an hour later, he had a contract to score a small project being filmed in Western Canada."

"Congratulations, Grayson. That's fantastic."

He hadn't gained apparent age since I last saw him, but his newfound confidence fit him well. "Thanks, Mr. Chase. It's the coolest thing ever."

"Just Chase," I said. "You're practically family. You guys don't mind if I borrow my wife for a few hours, do you?"

"Cool with us," Tatiana said. "But are you taking the car? The Porsche, I mean."

Penny jingled the key fob. "Oh, yeah. We're taking the Porsche, and Momma's driving."

Momma was a far better driver than I expected, and I quickly came to understand that I'd never be behind the wheel again, and for some reason I can't explain, I was okay with that. We did Mulholland twice, and I was the helpless passenger both times. Dinner was at Spago, Beverly Hills, and we found our way to the Jerome C. Daniel Overlook above the Hollywood Bowl. The view was breathtaking, but my gut wasn't looking forward to the coming conversation.

I took her hand in mine and said, "We need to talk."

She laid her head on my shoulder. "I thought that's why you came all the way out here bearing gifts . . . and what a gift it is." She squeezed my hand. "I know what you're thinking, and I've been trying to think of how to start the conversation. I'm really glad you're here, Chase."

I gave her a kiss, and my mind replayed the second I first saw her on the deck of a catamaran in Charleston, South Carolina. In that moment, our first glance, our first smile, and our first desire felt so distant, and yet, in a way I could never explain, it felt as if it had happened only moments before. I was destined to screw it up, but I was determined to put it into words.

I slipped my arms around her waist, and she laced hers around my neck. We stood there with her face lying against my chest and me looking out over what had become her kingdom.

I said, "Remember that night in Charleston?"

She sighed. "I fell in love with you that night."

"I think I fell in love with you a billion years ago, and every day I pray for a billion more to spend with you."

She spun in my arms, relaxed her back against my body, and surveyed the world beneath us. "It's kind of pretty in its own way, don't you think?"

"It is, but I'll always prefer the ocean."

"Even when she's angry?"

I thought about her question as the breeze blew her hair against the skin of my face. "Sometimes, that's when she's most beautiful."

"And most terrifying."

I knew I was going to screw it up, but I didn't realize I'd do it so quickly. "Terror and passion aren't so far apart inside our brains."

She pressed herself against me. "This isn't about our brains, Chase. Did you buy that car with your brain? Did you fly all the way across the country because of your brain? I hope not." She spun again and looked up at me. "I hope you're here in this shiny new car—which I love, by the way—because of your heart . . . not your head."

I kissed my wife and felt a love most men would never taste. I had a thousand questions, but she answered them all with a kiss unlike any force I'd ever known. "The baby is yours, Chase. She's ours. I don't understand it, but I'm not going to question it. And in a couple of months, I'll be too fat to fit behind the steering wheel in this thing."

I pressed my lips against the top of her head and let her hair blow all around me. "When the baby comes, I'm finished. I'll hand the team over to Mongo and spend the rest of my life showing our baby how beautiful the world truly is."

"Can I come, too?"

I ran my fingers through her hair. "You're the reason it's so beautiful, and I'd never dream of doing it without you."

Chapter 4
We Need to Talk

By the time we made it back to the house, midnight had come and gone, and I was exhausted. I would wait until morning to touch base with Disco, and I hoped he shared my opinion that no news is good news.

"I have to be on set at ten," Penny said when we woke up in each other's arms eight hours later.

"Why do you have to be there? Don't they just shoot what you wrote? I was looking forward to spending the day together."

She giggled and pulled most of her hair into a ponytail. "That's not how it works. Sometimes the actors hit on a line that doesn't feel right, and somebody has to be there to rewrite it. It's not always the actors, though. Sometimes it's the director, and that's even more important. We're shooting a bunch of dialogue-heavy scenes today and tomorrow, so I'm sorry, but I have to work."

"I'll survive," I said. "The Porsche and I can surely find something to keep us entertained."

"I'm sure you can, but you could also come with me if you want. I know there will never be a take-your-wife-to-work day at your job, but that doesn't mean you can't come see mine."

"I've seen yours. Don't you remember? You kicked Hunter and me off the set and told us we could never come back."

"That's because you were criticizing the shot."

"We were not. We were just explaining the difference between how it really looks when somebody gets shot and when an actor pretends to get shot."

She rolled her eyes. "The truth doesn't sell tickets at the box office."

"I hope you never have to see the truth I've seen."

She laid her head against my chest. "Me, too."

We lay there in silence for a few minutes, just enjoying the time together, until she groaned. "I'm up. I'm up. I'll shower first. You make coffee."

I lifted my phone from the nightstand and dialed Disco.

He answered on the second ring. "Are you back in Georgia?"

I laughed. "No, I'm starting to like it here in Tinseltown. I think I may stay a while. I even bought a car."

"A car," he said. "Sounds serious. Why did you buy a car?"

"Well, it was originally going to be a really expensive apology, but it turns out it wasn't necessary. Everything's good. How's Ronda?"

"She's spectacular, and I'm going to check on the ship later this morning, unless you need me to pick you up."

"No, that's not necessary. I'm eager to hear how the ship's coming along. We put her through the grinder up there in the ice."

He said, "We sure did, but Ronda says it's going well and projected to be out of dry dock by the end of next week."

"Keep me posted."

"I will, but there's one more thing. Ronda said Captain Sprayberry wants to talk with me. Do you know what that might be about?"

I said, "I don't have any idea. Maybe it's got something to do with the ship's helicopter."

"Maybe so. Whatever it is, I'll let you know as soon as I see him."

"Good enough. I'll be in touch."

I finished making coffee just in time to have a front-row seat to the wrestling match between Penny and her wet hair. I'm still not sure who won, but I enjoyed the show and the coffee.

We had just enough time for breakfast together before she had to be on set, and I had a date with the Pacific Coast Highway from Santa Monica to Santa Barbara. Little did I know I was destined for a road far more challenging than anything Coastal California could serve up.

The drive was exhilarating, and the views of the Pacific were breathtaking. I immediately planned to drive the entire PCH, even if we had to do it with a baby seat on board. The Santa Barbara Shellfish Company on Stearns Wharf welcomed me for a late lunch and served up a dish that was new to me. When the fresh, pan-seared red abalone over sautéed tomato basil rice with a garlic and sherry reduction sauce landed in front of me, I wondered why we couldn't introduce the abalone to the Golden Isles and coastal Georgia. Everything about the dish was unique, and I couldn't get enough. Although the atmosphere was seaside, it felt different than the Atlantic coast, but I couldn't help wondering if perhaps it was me who was different and not the geography.

Have I fired my final shot in anger? Have I met my obligation to my fellow man to answer the call when that call comes? Am I a new man, a father who dreams of showing my daughter or son a thousand sunsets on a thousand beaches all over the world? Am I retired at thirty-six?

The longer I pondered those questions, the more the answer became yes to each of them and all of them combined. To that point, nothing in my life ever caused such a rapid and dramatic shift in my perspective of the world around me. When the ability to play baseball professionally was yanked from beneath my feet, and I was thrust into a world of international chaos, everything changed, but the new perspective was gradual. Seeing the barely noticeable bump in Penny's stomach tore away the drive I felt to put my feet back on the battlefield. In an instant, the warrior in me became a protector of another sort—a father in love with his unborn child.

Back in the Porsche, I checked the angle of the sun against my decision to turn north toward whatever lay in that direction, or back south toward L.A. The sun and my watch suggested Penny would be home soon, and I didn't want to miss a minute I could be spending with her.

Just as I pulled onto the highway with the top down and the wind tugging at my baseball cap, my phone rang, and I pulled over. Although most of my body survived a massive explosion in Central Asia only months before, my hearing did not. Thanks primarily to Dr. Celeste Mankiller's brilliance, I wore a bone conduction transmitter attached to my jawbone beneath the skin of my face. A pair of hearing aids rested behind my ears, feeding sounds to that magical device. The system worked much like a cochlear implant without the necessity of the external receivers permanently attached to my head. One of the weaknesses of the system was wind and road noise during a telephone call, but that was easily overcome with a simple exit from the highway onto another stunning overlook of the wild Pacific.

"Hello, this is Chase."

"Hey, it's Disco."

"How's the ship?"

He said, "She's coming along nicely. They'll finish up the paint today or tomorrow, and she'll be ready to float again in a few days. It turns out we didn't do as much damage as we feared. She's a good ship."

"She certainly is. Did you talk with Captain Sprayberry?"

Disco said, "That's actually why I'm calling. I think you need to hear what the captain has to say."

"Can you brief me up?"

He said, "Not on this phone."

"That sounds serious."

"Oh, it's serious, but it may be a textbook example of sticking our nose where it doesn't belong."

I watched a sailboat tack a few hundred yards offshore, and he did it ugly. I wondered if I remembered how to sail after having spent far too much of my recent life ashore.

"So, should this be a face-to-face?" I asked.

"I think so. I can either come pick you up or I can bring the captain to L.A. Which would you prefer?"

For the first time in my career, I didn't want to hear the briefing. I didn't want to know what issue had to be resolved. And I didn't care what had our ship's captain wrapped around the prop shaft. I wanted to lie in the hammock with Penny and watch the sun melt into the Pacific.

Walking away from my job wasn't as simple as clocking out and never coming back. I was responsible for hundreds of millions of dollars' worth of paramilitary equipment, not the least of which was a 500-foot covert operations vessel in dry dock just down the California coast. Although officially designated as the Research Vessel *Lori Danielle*, she was far more than a floating oceanic laboratory. Her capabilities included operation in nearly any environmental conditions, defensive capabilities rivaling those of any battleship at sea, the offensive brute of a frigate, and most impressively, she could race across the waves at nearly sixty knots on hydrofoils built into her hull. Such was the direct charge of Captain Sprayberry, so if he felt we needed to talk face-to-face, I didn't have the option of blowing him off.

"Come get me. I'll meet you at Burbank in two hours."

My next call went straight to voicemail, and I said, "Hey, Penny. It's me. Listen, I have to run down to San Diego to check on something with the *Lori Danielle*. I'll call you later and let you know when I'll be back. I love you."

The southbound leg of my brief journey on the PCH was consumed by a mental battle inside my head, and I didn't like anything about it. Whatever Disco and Captain Sprayberry had to tell me wouldn't come close to the level of importance of the baby who, against all odds, was growing inside the woman I adored.

I watched the *Grey Ghost* touch down as I pulled into the parking space at the Burbank Airport, and the brutal reality of my life struck me squarely in the face. Much like the *Lori Danielle*, the Gulfstream that I loved so much wasn't mine. She was an asset of a company that doesn't truly exist, and although I'd been financially successful in the previous decade of my life, I'd never be able to afford an aircraft of the *Ghost*'s size, luxury, or capability on my own.

As I trotted through the FBO, the lady behind the counter said, "Good afternoon, Mr. Fulton. Chris told me you bought the perfect car for Mulholland Drive."

I slowed only long enough to give her a smile. "I did, and it's fantastic. Thank you for the suggestion."

Fantastic of an entirely different kind was the interior of the Gulfstream. It seemed excessive to use the jet as a two-person means of transportation, but for the time being, I would enjoy the indulgence and think about life after covert operations later.

Chapter 5
Our SEAL Problem

Climbing out of the smog of L.A. was much more pleasant than arriving in it, and the scenery to the west could've been the view from Heaven's window. Disco did the flying while I managed the radios and watched the world grow smaller beneath our wings.

When we leveled off in cruise flight, he said, "So, I take it things are good with Penny."

"Yeah, everything is perfect. I wouldn't change a thing."

"Glad to hear it. Tell me about the car."

I glanced back out the window as if I could see the car already a hundred miles behind and five miles below us. "It's a Porsche Nine-Eleven Turbo convertible."

He let out a long, low whistle. "If you ever feel the need to apologize to me with a gift, by all means, don't resist. That sounds fantastic. What made you pick the Porsche?"

"I rented one a long time ago in another life, and even though I didn't get to drive it, I've had the bug ever since. How about giving me a little primer on what's about to happen in San Diego."

He pulled off his glasses. "It's not good, Chase, and I'm not smart enough to understand the simplicity of it."

"That sounds interesting. If it's simple, what's keeping you from understanding it?"

"You'll have to hear it from Captain Sprayberry. The short version is this. Some Navy SEALs on leave were hanging out in Cabo San Lucas doing whatever SEALs do when they're not saving the world."

I interrupted. "Eating fish and lying naked in the sun."

"Exactly," he said. "Anyway, they picked up on some chatter about some Americans being taken hostage by some drug traffickers, and that caught their attention, but when they started poking around, they got shut down by the Navy."

"That doesn't sound right."

He raised an eyebrow. "Now you know why I wanted you to hear it straight from the horse's mouth."

"Leave the horses out of this. You know how I feel about those demons."

He chuckled. "Someday, you're going to have to tell me why you hate horses so badly."

"You don't want to hear the story. You'd never be the same afterwards. But how does Barry know about the thing with the SEALs?"

He said, "The captain's mother must've still been on pain meds when she named her son Barry Sprayberry. That's just cruel."

"He's a good skipper, and he knows exactly how far he can push that ship to keep her from finding her way to the bottom."

"That he does," Disco said. "But to answer your question, I don't really know how he got the word. He was a little vague on that detail, but in his defense, I didn't really give him time to explain it. I was in over my head when he shook my hand and said, 'Have a seat.'"

"What makes you think this has anything to do with us?" I asked.

"I get the impression Captain Sprayberry wants us to put out some feelers and maybe get involved in a rescue effort."

"A rescue effort? That's not exactly our bailiwick."

He shrugged. "I'm just telling you what I think, and come on, Chase. We're not exactly a bad choice for a hostage rescue mission on foreign soil . . . or water."

"It sounds like we've got a lot more questions than anyone has answers right now, so we'll give the captain an audience and then decide where to go from there."

"That's why you're in charge, and I'm just an overpaid bus driver."

"Yep, that's you," I said. "A five-hundred-knot bus driver."

We landed in San Diego, and Ronda No-H picked up us in a crew van from the *Lori Danielle*. "Hey, Chase. How've you been?"

"Pretty great. We're having a baby."

"A baby?" Ronda almost squealed. "That's fantastic. Congratulations."

"Thank you. I'm pretty excited. How are things with you?"

She grabbed Disco's hand. "We're not having a baby. Not now, not ever. But I couldn't be happier. It's been a little boring with the ship in dry dock, but we'll be back in the water by the first of the week. I just hope we get a mission."

Disco said, "You enjoy being on the boat, don't you?"

"I really do," Ronda said. "But I like the special projects a lot more than the routine research stuff. Marine biologists are a boring lot."

I let the dichotomy of research missions versus covert tactical operations play through my head. "So, you'd rather hang out the door of the chopper and mow down bad guys with your Minigun than manage research grants from your office?"

She glanced at me in the mirror. "What can I say? I'm an action girl."

"If you're as good with a calculator as you are with a machine gun, I feel sorry for any auditor who ever tries to test you."

She made a pistol with her thumb and index finger and blew on the imaginary smoke from the imaginary muzzle.

We parked a couple hundred yards from the *Lori Danielle*, and the vessel looked enormous sitting on cradles in the dry dock.

"She looks different out of the water," I said without really meaning to say it out loud.

Ronda said, "It's even weirder to be on board and not feel it moving at all."

We climbed the gangway and found Captain Sprayberry on the bridge, poring over some blueprints. He looked up and stuck out his hand. "Hey, Chase. Good to see you. Welcome aboard, such as it is."

"Thanks, Barry. It's good to see you, too. Disco tells me we didn't do as much damage up there in the ice as we feared."

He motioned toward the blueprints. "No, the damage wasn't bad at all. We spent more time taking advantage of the dry dock to get some pesky little projects and repairs out of the way. Big Bob down in engineering had a list a mile long."

"That's good news," I said. "But I hear you've got something on your mind. Do you want to get that off your chest?"

He rolled up the blueprints and slid a rubber band around them. "Yeah, but let's have that talk back in the CIC."

The Combat Information Center was the brain and central nervous system of the ship when she was involved in an operation. Practically anything Skipper could do from the operation center back at Bonaventure could be accomplished from the CIC aboard the *Lori Danielle*. The big exception was computing power. The ship didn't have the twin supercomputers that Skipper built back in Georgia, but she was no slouch in any area, including computing muscle.

Captain Sprayberry took his seat and propped up his feet against the edge of a console. "I don't know how much Disco already told you, so I'm not sure where to start."

I said, "Let's pretend I don't know anything, and give me the whole rundown."

He glanced around as if a bit paranoid about what was on the verge of coming out of his mouth. "I know I don't really have to tell you this, but it'd be best if you didn't talk about anything I'm going to tell you once you leave the CIC."

I said, "I understand, but if it rises to the level of action, I'll have to brief the chain both up and down."

"I get that," Barry said. "I just don't want to get my buddies in a bind."

I leaned back in my chair. "Let's have it. And I promise not to burn your buddies."

He cleared his throat. "I was having a couple of beers with some guys from the teams the other night. You know, just some guys hanging out and talking. There were a few young guys hanging around, and as the night wore on, they got a little closer and more interested in our stories about the glory days back when we were young and bulletproof." He paused and took a sip of coffee. "I guess they didn't want to be outdone, so they started telling some stories of their own. Apparently, four of them were down in Cabo recently on a long weekend, just chasing skirts and drinking too much. You know how it was when we were their age."

"Don't lump me into the old timers' club with you and Disco. I'm still young, and part of me is still bulletproof."

"I guess you are," he said. "As the night went on, they started telling us about a conversation they overheard about some Americans turning up missing. That caught their ears, so they stopped drinking and started paying attention. Keep in mind, Chase, these aren't kids straight out of boot camp. They're SEALs with more than a few deployments under their tridents, if you know what I mean."

"I'm tracking," I said. "Keep talking."

"As it turned out, these guys knew some of the places the other folks were talking about, so they put together a plan to go take a look. Apparently, they saw and heard enough to convince them there really were some Americans being held against their will. They sent it up the chain of command, expecting to get immediate orders to yank the Americans out of there and repatriate them, but that's not what happened. Instead of being sent to work, the Navy recalled these guys back to Coronado and told them to shut up about the missing Americans."

A shiver ran down my spine, and I slid to the edge of my seat. "Are you telling me the Navy ordered SEALs to ignore an American hostage situation in a foreign country?"

Barry took another sip of coffee. "No, that's not what I'm telling you. What I'm saying is that I *heard* that happened. I don't have any firsthand knowledge of it."

I studied the console behind the captain and remembered the level of activity in the small room when a combat mission was in progress. It would've appeared to be chaos to anyone not directly involved in the operation, but to those of us in the know, it was a well-orchestrated dance between a dozen performers on an endless stage.

"What do you expect me to do with this information, Barry?"

He picked up his empty coffee cup and stood. "What information, Chase?"

A few seconds later, Disco and I were alone in the CIC, neither of us certain of our next step.

"Well, that was interesting," I said.

"Now you know why I wanted you to hear it from the captain. Now that we know, what are we going to do?"

I slouched in my seat. "You've been a high-ranking military officer. What are the chances of it being true?"

He huffed. "I was a tank killer. The closest I ever came to special ops was when those guys asked for help, and I just happened to be in the neighborhood. There's nothing like bringing hell from the sky when you know the real heroes are pinned down."

"I get that, but give it to me from the perspective of a colonel."

He sighed. "There's too much we don't know, but if we assume what the captain heard is true, there are a thousand reasons a senior officer would squash the information. Perhaps the DEA or even the Coast Guard is working the problem. Maybe it's an undercover op that's never supposed to make headlines. Maybe the SEALs had too much to drink and heard something they thought would be a cool mission. Who knows?"

I let out the breath I'd been holding. "You're a lot of help."

He said, "Point me toward a column of Iraqi tanks, and get out of my way, but don't ask me to think like a naval special warfare officer."

Before I realized it was coming out of my mouth, I said, "I'm retiring."

Disco laughed. "Yeah, right."

I hadn't wanted those words to see the light of day yet, but now that they were out, I rather enjoyed the relief. "I'm serious. When Penny has the baby, I'm done."

He leaned forward. "You're not messing around, are you? What'll happen to the team?"

"I don't know for sure, but I assume it'll become Mongo's team, and I'll quietly slip away."

"But Bonaventure . . . We've built the perfect training and operations base down there. Where are we supposed to go?"

I chewed my lip. "To be honest, I've not thought it through to that point. I guess I just assumed you guys would stay in the game, and Bonaventure would still be in the middle of it all."

The concern on his face spoke volumes, and he said, "But you're still in the game until the baby comes, right?"

I could almost feel Penny's tummy beneath my palm. "I don't know. It depends on what the Board says about our SEAL problem."

Disco held up a finger. "That's a good sign . . . You called it *our* SEAL problem."

Chapter 6
Shackles and Chains

Disco said, "I guess that means we're headed home, huh?"

For some reason, I checked my watch against the clock in the console that constantly updated itself to stay in time with the atomic clock in Boulder, Colorado. "How quickly would *you* want us to show up if you were one of the Americans being held hostage?"

He ducked his chin. "That escalated quickly. A minute ago, it was hearsay from potentially overzealous, drunk sailors."

"Not just sailors," I said. "SEALs. I know you want another day or two with Ronda, and I don't want to leave Penny, either, but think about how those hostages—if they exist—feel. They'd probably like to be home with their families, too."

He stood. "All right, let's go. But *you* have to tell Ronda."

I pointed toward the console. "Do we have secure coms in here while we're in dry dock?"

He said, "I don't know, but I know how to find out."

He lifted a handset and dialed Captain Sprayberry's cell. "Captain, do we have secure coms in the CIC?" He paused for the answer. "Thanks. He said all secure systems are up and running."

I rolled my chair into position in front of the primary operating station and dialed Bonaventure.

Skipper answered after several rings. "Op center, unsecured line."

"Hey, Skipper. It's Chase. Did you say unsecured?"

"Yeah, I did. I've got the phones in the op center forwarded to my cell. Do you need me on a secure line?"

"I need to know where Clark is," I said.

"He's at home, as far as I know. Did you try calling him?"

"No, I wanted to get you first. How long will it be before you're back in the op center?"

"I can be there in ten minutes. What's happening?"

"Call me in the CIC aboard the *Lori Danielle* when you get there, and I'll fill you in."

"The *Lori Danielle*?" she asked. "Is she back in the water?"

"Just hustle back to Bonaventure and give me a call."

She hung up, and nine minutes later, the line lit up.

"CIC, Chase."

"Chase, it's Skipper on a secure line."

"We're secure from here, as well. Listen up. I don't have a lot of facts. So far, it's all second- or third-hand accounts, but I need you to dig into some missing Americans near Cabo San Lucas, and I need you to keep it on the down-low. Don't get caught looking."

"Sure, I can do that, no problem. But what's it about?"

I said, "Disco and I are headed home. If you find anything that looks like it could be true about missing Americans in Cabo, I need you to get Clark to Bonaventure ASAP."

"So, what about the ship?"

"She's still in dry dock, but they'll float her tomorrow and conduct sea trials over the next couple of days. Do you have anything for me?"

"No, everything's copacetic here. I'll see you when you get home. Oh, and do you want me to call you if I find anything?"

"No, that just creates one more possibility of a leak, and we need to keep this one close to the vest. We'll see you in a few hours."

I stepped from the CIC and almost plowed into Disco.

He jumped back. "Whoa, big fella. Where you headed in such a hurry?"

"To find you."

He said, "You did it, and you're off the hook. I told Ronda."

"What did she say?"

He chuckled. "She asked if it was a mission and if she was going to get to shoot anybody."

I waved a finger. "You should be very afraid of that woman."

"Oh, I am. That's part of the fun."

* * *

When I told Penny I had to return to Bonaventure, she said, "What about the car?"

"It's parked at the FBO in Burbank, and the extra key fob is on your dresser."

She said, "I'll get Grayson and Tatiana to take me out so I can pick it up tonight. You're just going home, right? You're not leaving the country, are you?"

"For now, it's just questions, answers, and maybe a little planning, but I'll keep you posted."

"Can you tell me what it's about?"

"I'm sorry, but I can't. Maybe this will be the last time you have to ask that question."

I could almost see her smiling. "Maybe this'll be the last time you'll have to give that answer."

"Maybe so. How was filming? Did you have to rewrite anything?"

She sighed. "I had to rewrite everything. It's been quite a day."

"I'm sorry. Maybe you can take the car for a spin. I learned it's hard to be stressed with the top down."

"Looking forward to it," she said. "Call me when you make it home, okay?"

"I will. I love you and the baby."

* * *

Eastbound flights, especially at forty-one thousand feet, are far faster than the opposite direction. The winds of the jet stream gave us an extra one hundred knots, and we touched down in St. Marys less than three hours after climbing away from San Diego.

To my surprise, Clark Johnson landed two minutes behind us at our private airport that used to belong to the taxpayers of Camden County. Economics of a small Southern town can't always support the operation of an airport, but a place to launch and recover aircraft is crucial to our operation, so we wrote the check and became the proud new owners of the airfield.

The VW Microbus that was born before I was carried the three of us from the airport to Bonaventure, where Skipper already had a briefing prepared and the rest of the team assembled. I slid onto my seat and into an arena that felt more like a funeral than a briefing.

Skipper spun in her chair to face the table. "Okay, I guess the gang's all here. Let me start with this. I don't know what happened in California to put Chase and Disco on this trail, but there's definitely something going on in and around Cabo San Lucas. Take a look at this guy."

She pointed to the overhead monitor. "This is Spencer Baldwin, a reporter from the *Sacramento Bee*, the local daily newspaper. He's a UCLA grad who seems to lean slightly left of center, but for the most part, he has the reputation of a brilliant investigator and a well-respected reporter. He's got three Pulitzer nominations and one win for investigative journalism."

I tried to tie Spencer Baldwin to the SEALs' story, but it wasn't happening for me, so I held up a finger.

Skipper said, "Just wait, Chase. I'll bring it all together for you."

I let my hand fall back to the table, and I settled in to listen and take notes as she continued.

"Baldwin was apparently working on a piece about an ongoing feud between two rival drug cartels on the Baja Peninsula. He's been there for three weeks, but he apparently turned up missing six days ago."

Hunter, our former Air Force combat controller, scowled. "How do we know he's missing?"

Skipper said, "I'm glad you asked. He was supposed to be honored at a dinner in Sacramento with the governor of California and a bunch of local political types, but he didn't show."

Hunter said, "Maybe he's deep into the story and he'd rather win another Pulitzer than sit through some stuffy dinner with a bunch of politicians."

Skipper said, "Maybe, but his sister doesn't think so."

"His sister?" I asked. "In less than four hours, you found a missing newspaper reporter, ran his background, and talked with his sister. Are you serious?"

She said, "I didn't actually talk with his sister since you told me to play this one close to the vest. I dug up a series of unanswered emails from his sister, and she's clearly concerned."

Kodiak, retired Green Beret, asked, "You can read anybody's email you want?"

Skipper brushed an imaginary flake from her shoulder. "If the National Security Agency can do it, so can I."

"What did you find in the emails?" I asked.

"An increasing feeling of desperation with every new email. Baldwin and his sister, Patricia, are apparently pretty close. They have an ongoing, almost daily email trail going back for years. Most of them are benign, quick check-ins, but the last eight emails from Patricia paint a picture of a woman who's clearly worried about her brother. I sent copies of the emails to your tablets so you can read through them if you want."

I quickly scanned through three of the unanswered emails, and the concern was more obvious with every new letter. I asked, "Does the paper have anything to say about their missing reporter?"

Skipper said, "I can't find any official statements from the paper, but I didn't knock on any doors. Since you want to keep this one quiet, I tread lightly."

Mongo, our resident giant and intellectual, drummed his fingertips against the table. "Is Baldwin married?"

Skipper said, "He was, but they divorced five years ago."

"Roommate? Gym buddy? Anyone else in his life other than the sister?"

"Not that I could find," Skipper said. "What are you chasing?"

Mongo said, "I'm just trying to build a picture of the guy's life in case we have to start rattling cages. Is he the only missing American you came up with?"

"No, he's far from alone, but he's the only recent MIA."

"When was the last missing person report?" he asked.

"That's not really how it works in Cabo," she said. "Most of the people who go"—she made air quotes—"missing . . . are actually in jail as the result of a few too many tequila shots, or they're running away from something or someone. If you want to disappear, Mexico isn't a bad place for the vanishing act."

It was my turn to jump into the fray. "So that everyone will know what this is about, Captain Sprayberry from the *Lori Danielle* overheard a conversation between some naval special warfare operators about missing Americans in Cabo, and they claimed they got shut down when they reported the case to their commanding officer."

Skipper said, "I already briefed them on that before you got here, but that's okay. It never hurts to solidify the foundation."

"I just want to make sure I understand," I said. "The only recently missing American is the reporter, and the only person asking questions is his sister?"

"No, that's not exactly the case. I'm sure there are others. At least, I suspect there are others, but you tied my hands a little, so I've not been able to cast a wide net. If you take off the shackles, I'm sure I can find a busload of folks who aren't where they're supposed to be."

"We'll save that for now," I said. "But one missing reporter doesn't mesh with the story we heard . . . at least as the SEALs told it."

Skipper said, "I know this is a long shot, but is there any chance of finding at least one of the SEALs who heard the conversation? It would shed a lot of light on this thing if we could have a first-hand account."

I said, "I doubt it, and even if we had a name, it wouldn't be easy to get him to talk."

Disco said, "I know I'm just the pilot, but this is starting to sound like comparing apples to dump trucks. One missing journalist isn't the same thing as missing Americans . . . plural. Are we sure we're looking at the same case, or are these two separate, unrelated issues?"

I said, "That's just one of the things we don't know. I'm not even sure we have enough to send this one up the chain. What do you think, Clark?"

He plucked the lollipop from his mouth. "If we ran back through the history of American tourists in Mexico, I doubt we could find a one-month period in which at least one of them didn't turn up missing. This isn't exactly an isolated incident, but that's not what has me most concerned. This isn't our thing. It's not what we do. The Board hands assignments to me, and I pass them along to you. It's not designed to work in the opposite direction. Besides, what do we have to support the suspicion that the SEALs were doing anything other than trying to keep up with the old guys telling tales?"

I pushed my notepad away. "This is what we've got. A clandestine services ship captain with the best instincts I've ever seen, a few SEALs with real downrange experience, all telling the same story about a possible midlevel cover-up, and a sister who loves her missing brother. Maybe I'm way off the mark here, but that sounds like enough for us to start asking some questions."

Clark leaned back and steepled his fingers. "What's stopping you?"

I leaned in. "What do you mean?"

He shrugged. "You don't need permission from the Board to take a trip to Sacramento or Cabo. Ask all the questions you want. Surely you've heard of the golden rule. Never ask for permission when you can be safe and sorry."

I palmed my forehead. "First, that's not the golden rule. Second, you're an idiot. And third, you're a genius. Are you coming with us?"

Chapter 7
Somewhere in the Past

Being the most recent addition to our island of misfit toys, Kodiak wore the look of a man trying to distinguish the phantom voices in his head from those of the real people around him.

I asked, "You okay, Kodiak?"

"I'm just trying to figure out how this whole thing works. I've never been part of anything this loose, and I'm digging it."

"Loose?" Skipper said. "You're looking at it all wrong. What we do inside the team is tight. How we approach outside problems is open-minded."

"Oh, that's what you call it . . . open-minded."

"Exactly," she said. "We don't approach anything arrogantly believing we know the whole picture. We ask a lot of questions before we start pulling triggers. That's why we don't fail and why we bring everybody home alive."

Kodiak said, "Yeah, we're alive, but we're not always in one piece."

I took the floor. "Sacrifice is what we do. If that means we slowly turn into robots as the years and missions come and go, that's the price I'm willing to pay to do the work I believe in."

Kodiak threw up both hands. "Hey, man, I get it, and I'm all in. I just never knew teams like this existed, and I'm happy to say I've finally found me a home."

"I'm glad you feel that way," I said. "Before we run off chasing missing people who may not really be missing, let's clear up a few housekeeping issues. Hunter, let's start with you. How are you feeling?"

He took a long breath. "As much as I want to tell you I'm battle-ready, it's not true. I'm getting better every day, but my lung still isn't a hundred percent. I'll be back. It's just going to take some time."

"Thanks for being honest. I'm not ready to put you back in the trenches, but you're good to go if we're just snooping around, right?"

"As long as snooping doesn't turn into fistfights and shootouts, I'm good, but one good body blow would send me to my knees."

I turned my attention to Tony, and before I could ask, he said, "I'm done, Chase. You know I'm always up for whatever I can do to support the mission, but I can't risk putting you guys in danger because of my issues."

"I'm not expecting you to crawl into a foxhole with any of us, but you're still a valuable member of the team. With your Coast Guard experience, you have a perspective the rest of us don't, and I, for one, am glad we've got you in our corner."

A hearty round of "Me, too" followed, and Tony said, "Speaking of traumatic brain injuries . . . What's your status?"

"I'm good to go," I said, "I need to put in some hard hours working on cardio, but the head is good. I'm stuck with these hearing aids for the rest of my life unless Dr. Mankiller comes up with some new piece of technology to put me back in the hearing game. The leg is good, the hand is healed, and I'm ready to come off the bench."

Clark gave me an eye. "You heard what Tony and Hunter just said, right?"

"Yeah. What about it?"

"You could take a lesson from them. They're man enough to admit their limitations. Are you pushing yourself so hard you've forgotten how to be honest?"

"Here's the truth," I said. "If we were tasked with a mission to track down a high-value target in the mountains of Afghanistan, I'd bow out because I'm not ready for that, but if we're playing detective in California and maybe Cabo, put me in, coach. I'm ready to play."

Clark nodded. "Okay, that's good enough for me. Is there anything else?"

Skipper spoke up. "Are my hands still tied, or can I start throwing the big net?"

"For now, stick with the covert net. Find Patricia Baldwin, and start looking for the last time her brother's credit cards were used. Surely, he's got a cell phone, too, so find out where it pinged last. In the meantime, the rest of us have to pack."

It felt strange packing for an operation with no rifles or C-4, but we still loaded our pistols and sharpened our knives.

I said, "If this thing turns into a fight in Mexico, I want to be well-equipped, so let's load-out for a fight in the desert, just in case."

Singer stepped beside me. "Samson or Methuselah?"

I'd probably never know the whole story behind why our sniper named his two heaviest rifles after Old Testament characters, but his .338 Lapua Magnum and Barrett 50-cal wore the monikers well. "Bring 'em both. You just never know."

With the *Grey Ghost* packed, we piled into the op center for one final briefing from our analyst before we blasted off for Sacramento.

She said, "I just sent a full dossier on Patricia Baldwin to each of your tablets. And while I was running down the last known position of Spencer Baldwin's cell phone, I discovered that it's still active and pinging."

"Did you try calling it?"

She huffed. "What do you think? Of course, I called from a dozen different untraceable numbers, but it went straight to a voicemail notification that hadn't been set up."

"What does that mean?" Hunter asked.

Skipper said, "To be honest, I'm not sure. It could be something to do with international roaming, or it could be that he never set up his voicemail, but that would be weird for a journalist."

"That'd be weird for anybody," Clark said, "not just a journalist."

She said, "I can't explain it, but I'll stay on it. How soon will you guys be airborne?"

I said, "How soon can you find us a place to sleep in Sacramento?"

She rolled her eyes. "Oh, ye of little faith, you're booked at the Sterling, and there are three SUVs waiting for you with Modern Aviation at Sacramento Mather Airport."

"I should've known," I said. "Thank you, Skipper. You're the best."

She waved a dismissive hand. "I know, now get out of my op center and get to work."

My third trip between coasts in one week went more smoothly than expected. The forecast called for severe thunderstorms over Oklahoma, but the *Ghost* had more than enough muscle to carry us over the top with the storms raging a few thousand feet beneath us.

There's nothing quite like watching a thunderstorm from the cockpit. The experience is even more fascinating—and sometimes horrifying—at night, when it's impossible to know how far away the lightning, treacherous wind, and extreme turbulence are. Fortunately, our magic carpet was well equipped with a panel full of electronics to not only allow us to see the storms, but also to ensure that we avoided them. Watching the lightning flashing a mile beneath us made me question the self-imposed mission we'd assigned and accepted, knowing little more than rumors and suppositions about what lay ahead. I prayed the storm into which we were throwing ourselves was nothing more than a rain shower of misunderstanding.

As always, Skipper had every detail managed to the letter, including a forklift to offload our gear from the *Grey Ghost* and onto the spotless concrete floor of our private hangar. It took less than an hour to offload what we needed and pack each Suburban.

Driving away from the airport, Kodiak said, "That analyst doesn't mess around."

I chuckled. "*That* analyst is *your* analyst now, and you're right. She's one of the best. Believe it or not, she's the daughter of my college baseball coach. She's always been like a little sister to me."

He said, "I knew there had to be a connection there besides the obvious, but I would've never put that together."

"She made some bad decisions that put her in the hands of some pretty nasty guys down in Miami about a dozen years ago. Back then, it was just me and Clark. We didn't even have an airplane of our own. We yanked her out of there and got a former Russian SVR officer shot through the back."

"Did he make it?"

"She wasn't a he," I said.

Kodiak snapped his fingers. "Oh, her. I'd like to hear the story about her sometime."

I patted the steering wheel. "She's a long story, my friend, and maybe it's best if we just leave her where she is . . . somewhere in the past."

We pulled into the Sterling, and I was astonished. The beautiful Victorian mansion could've been right at home on a square in Savannah, but she was still the belle of the ball, even in California. A pair of bellmen more than earned their tips by moving what must've looked like the Donner Party from the parking lot and into our suites.

Dinner was as exquisite as the gorgeous hotel, and I couldn't stop thinking how much Penny would enjoy the experience. Perhaps we could include Sacramento in our Pacific Coast Highway adventure to come.

Mongo stared down at a bite-sized morsel in the center of a plate that should've held more than enough to feed the giant. "Is this some kind of joke?"

That drew a hearty round of laughter, but before the meal ended, our behemoth was more than satisfied with quality and especially quantity. He wiped his mouth and tossed the napkin onto his barren plate. "This is nice, and I could get used to it, but do we have a plan for getting started on this . . . whatever it is?"

I checked across my shoulder to find a mostly empty dining room before saying, "I'll touch base with Skipper first thing tomorrow morning, but I plan to put eyes on Patricia Baldwin tonight."

Napkins hit the table, and chairs slid across the carpeted floor. "Let's do it," Singer said.

We paired off into the three SUVs. Mongo and Singer took the lead, Disco and Kodiak trailed, and Hunter and I brought up the rear. The GPS took us to Patricia's address in the Poverty Ridge neighborhood of Sacramento.

Hunter kept one eye on the road and one eye on the upper-middle-class homes. "Why do they call this place Poverty Ridge? It's pretty swanky from where I'm sitting."

I said, "I read a little bit about that. Apparently, when the gold rush was happening out here, they had a terrible flood, and the miners scampered to the only high ground in the area to survive. This was that high ground. The name came from the fact that this is where the poverty-stricken miners ended up. It's obviously changed a little since the eighteen fifties."

He motioned to a two-story house on a large corner lot. "That must be the place."

I checked the number beside the door as we passed. "Yep, that's it."

I wasn't the only team member with one of Dr. Mankiller's bone conduction transceivers attached to his jawbone. Each of us had one that was electronically connected to the particular method of coms we happened to be using. In an operational environment, we most often used satellite communications gear, but for the night's simple reconnaissance operation, we paired our bone conduction devices to our cell phones and initiated a conference call between all three vehicles and the op center back at Bonaventure.

Eyeing the front of the house carefully, I was pleased to see nearly every window lit up from inside. "Good news, boys. She's got all the lights on."

Singer, with his sniper's eye, said, "There's a figure in the first window on the right on the second story. No other signs of life, but we're moving to the east side to get a better angle."

Forgetting he was on open coms, Hunter said, "Man, that guy's got some eyes."

Singer said, "Thanks, but they're no better than yours. Just trained to be different."

Hunter laughed. "I'm sticking with better. We're making the block to see if there's a line of sight from the rear."

Lights seemed to be the standard on Poverty Ridge. Nearly every house was lit up like a parade route. That played to our advantage since the interior lights would make it difficult for people inside to see us or any traffic on the street. Every neighborhood has one resident who sees and hears everything.

Kodiak said, "We just got a lot more attention than we wanted. There's a guy walking two little dogs on the northwest corner. He stopped to check us out, and he got a good long look at our license plate."

"Keep driving," I said. "Let him see you leave the neighborhood."

Three black SUVs in one small neighborhood weren't easy to hide, but we had one advantage: Singer's eyes.

The sniper said, "I'm on foot with the dog walker in sight. I'll report his turns."

That's when dumb luck smiled on us.

From behind Patricia's house, I stared straight up a beautiful sight. "You'll never believe it, but there's a concrete drainage way leading directly from the house. It's at least three feet deep and four feet wide."

Singer said, "Our dog walker made a turn to the north. Stay on the south side."

Hunter and I held our position on the opposite side of the house, but Mongo was caught.

He said, "I made the turn to the north just before you warned me off. I'm busted."

Skipper said, "Ask for directions."

Although we couldn't see the engagement, every sound played through the cell phone. A pair of yapping dogs filled the air with high-pitched chirps, and Mongo's baritone almost got lost in the tornado of ear-splitting chaos. "Sorry to bother you, sir, but I'm looking for Sacramento City College, and I seem to have gotten lost. Can you point me in the right direction?"

The man said, "Hush, now. That's enough. Quiet!" The dogs obeyed. "Why would you be looking for the City College at this hour?"

The sounds of Mongo opening the door clicked in my head, and I froze in fear of him throwing the man in the back of the Suburban for being nosey, but his plan soon became obvious.

"I'm the new strength and conditioning coach for the football team, and tomorrow is my first day. I wanted to make sure I knew how to get there so I wouldn't be late."

I could almost see the dog walker staring up at Mongo. "Oh, that makes sense. Just go up here and turn south on Nineteenth. Follow that underneath the highway, and it'll become Freeport Boulevard. That will take you straight to City College."

Mongo said, "Thank you, sir. If you're a football fan—"

The man laughed. "Oh, my goodness, no. I don't go in for violent sports. Good night."

Apparently, our giant couldn't resist. He said, "I know exactly how you feel. I'm a pacifist, too, but a man's gotta make a living."

If the dog walker reacted, it didn't come through the coms.

"Well, that was fun," Mongo said.

I said, "Strength and conditioning coach? Really?"

"It's the first thing that popped into my head. I couldn't tell him I was the new beautician in town."

"Get out of here," I said. "Make it look like you're following his instructions. We'll grab Singer and meet you back at the hotel."

Our sniper met us a block from Patricia Baldwin's house and slid onto the back seat. He said, "I think Mongo may have a career on Broadway. Did you catch that performance he put on?"

Hunter said, "I guess three hundred pounds of human could convince anybody he was a football coach, but I still think beautician would've been funnier."

Singer said, "There are two cars in the garage. Do we have any trackers with us?"

I said, "The kit is right behind your seat."

He reached across and pulled a pair of GPS tracking devices from the bag and checked their batteries. "Drop me as close as you can, and I'll find a nice little temporary home for these babies."

We dropped Singer half a block from the house, and he disappeared into the night. Even knowing the approximate route Singer would take to the garage, I couldn't see him or any evidence of him, no matter how hard I looked. Becoming part of the environment was a skill he mastered in his earliest days as a Ranger and honed every time the opportunity arose.

Less than fifteen minutes later, Singer said, "Stop where you are, and don't shoot me."

Hunter tapped the brakes, and the back door of the Suburban sprang open.

Sneaky Snake slithered onto the back seat, and I said, "How? How do you do that?"

Singer said, "I could tell you, but then I'd have to kill you."

Chapter 8
Follow the Leader

The jetlag caught up with us, especially me, after crossing all four time zones. Everyone was ready to hit the sack minutes after returning to the Sterling, but a call to the op center couldn't wait. To my surprise, it wasn't Skipper's voice on the line.

"Op center, Tony."

"It looks like you got the graveyard shift," I said.

"Yeah, Skipper was crashing. She'd been awake a long time, so I told her I could manage anything that came up for tonight. Please tell me you're not doing something I can't handle."

"Actually," I said, "we need you to hack into the Sacramento power grid and the traffic light system. We also need the list of registered firearms owners between the ages of thirty and fifty-four who moved to California in the last seven years."

He vapor-locked. "Uh . . . I mean, maybe . . ."

"Relax, Tony. I'm just messing with you. I just need to activate a pair of GPS trackers. They're numbers Tango-zero-one and Tango-zero-two."

The relief in his voice was enormous. "That's something I can handle. I don't know if I was more afraid of waking up Skipper or trying to take control of the traffic lights three thousand miles away."

"For the record," I said, "she would've had all of that done be-fore I finished the request."

He chuckled. "Yeah, but let's see if she can paint eighteenth-century warships in battle."

"We all have our talents. We're off to bed, but I need you to set both trackers to report to my cell phone. You can do that, right?"

"No problem. Anything else?"

"That does it. We'll check in tomorrow morning."

"It's already tomorrow morning here on the East Coast."

I checked my watch. "In that case, we'll check in later today. Get some rest. We won't need the op center until Patricia is on the move."

* * *

Breakfast came early, but I'm not sure why. I made a circular motion with my hand above the table. "Coffee all around, please."

Biscuits and gravy weren't an option, but apparently, the chef had some sort of bizarre love affair with avocado. Kodiak and Disco opted for the avocado French toast, and I finally convinced the server to bring out an omelet without the ubiquitous green fruit. California might be good at making movies and wine, but I'd stick with the South when breakfast time rolled around.

Three cups of coffee into the avocado festival, my phone chirped, and Tango-zero-one was on the move.

I caught the server by the arm. "We have to run, but charge it to my suite, and your tip is on the table."

Skipper answered as if she'd been holding her waiting hand over the phone. "Op center."

"We're on the road," I said. "Are you tracking Tango-zero-one?"

"You keep asking stupid questions. Of course I'm tracking. She made a two-minute stop at the post office, and she's headed downtown now. Do you want it on your tablet instead of your phone?"

"That would be great. I had to deal with unqualified help last night," I said. "It's good to have a pro at the helm this morning."

"I heard that!" Tony said in the background.

Skipper ignored the jab. "She's pulling into Starbucks on Nineteenth. Stand by, and I'll tell you if she's hitting the drive-through." A few seconds later, she said, "Our girl just parked. What's your plan?"

"If it's a get-and-go, we'll keep following at a comfortable distance, but if she curls up in a booth, I may introduce myself."

She said, "I'm working on the camera system inside the building. Give me just a couple of minutes."

I spun in my seat. "Can anybody think of a reason not to approach her?"

Hunter said, "What are you going to say? 'Hi, we're a special operations team here to find your brother'?"

I shrugged. "That sounds like a pretty good opening line to me, but I'll just play it by ear and see what happens. It's a Starbucks. Nothing bad happens at Starbucks."

Mongo rolled his eyes. "That's what we call foreshadowing. God only knows what's going to happen now."

Skipper said, "Who's your girl? I'm in! She's not exactly curled up in a booth, but she is in a corner with her laptop on the table."

I said, "Send me her picture so I don't scare the wrong sister to death. Something tells me she won't be the only woman inside with coffee and a laptop."

My tablet came to life with a live camera feed from inside the building, and Skipper said, "That's her in the upper right."

I zoomed in. "I'm glad we didn't bring Clark. He'd hit on her."

"I heard that!" came Clark's voice from somewhere near Tony's.

"You've got an audience this morning," I said.

Skipper groaned. "Tell me about it. I'm trying everything I can think of to get those two to go anywhere other than here, but they're stubborn."

We pulled into the parking lot of the Starbucks and tried in vain to find a spot big enough for the Suburban.

Finally, I said, "Just drop me and get in the drive-through lane. That'd be a lot less suspicious than hovering by the front door."

Hunter pulled to a stop near the door, and I slid from the seat. Once inside, I ordered a coffee after decoding the tall, grande, venti sizing chart. My Italian isn't great, but I seemed to remember *venti* meaning wind. Nothing about that made sense, but I survived the ordeal.

As nonchalantly as possible, I waited for my windy coffee and studied Patricia Baldwin. She appeared to be engrossed in something on her laptop screen, but my angle wouldn't let me see it. The cup arrived a few inches from my waiting hand, and the barista yelled, "Chase!"

No one in the room seemed to notice, but I was shocked. Her shrill voice reverberated inside my head. I was tempted to yell, "Thank you," but I held my tongue.

Although far from Mongo's size, I'm a bit of an imposing figure, so instead of towering over Patricia, I slid onto a seat opposite her and asked, "May I join you?"

Her eyes shot from the screen and directly into mine. "Who are you?"

Trying to sound nonthreatening, I said, "My name is Chase." I made a show of reading her name from her cup. "And you're Patti."

She recoiled and slipped a hand into her purse. "What do you want?"

I couldn't resist following her hand into the bag. "There's no need to spray me. I'm not a threat. I want to talk about your brother, Spencer."

Instead of relaxing as I'd hoped, the muscles in her neck and shoulders drew tighter.

I tried to defuse her anxiety. "It's okay, Patti. I just want to drink my coffee and talk with you."

She withdrew her hand from the purse with her fingers wrapped tightly around a red and white can of pepper spray. "You're from the government, aren't you? I'm going to scream and spray you if you don't leave now. I'm not afraid of you people."

I tried to shrink in my chair. "What people?"

"You people!" Her voice cracked, and she slammed her laptop closed.

"I'm not with the government, Patti. My name is Chase Fulton, and I'm sort of in the private security business."

"Sort of? What does that mean?"

I pushed my coffee aside and leaned in. "What did you mean when you said 'you people'? Has someone been harassing you?"

She squeezed her threatening little aerosol can. "Look, Chase. Or whatever your real name is. This isn't going to work. You're not going to stop me."

"I'm not here to stop you from doing anything. I simply want to talk with you. I might be able to help."

"How did you find me?"

The truth wasn't a great idea in that moment, so I told some of the truth. "Some colleagues of mine happened to be in Cabo San Lucas and overheard a conversation about some missing Americans. When they told me about it, I started doing some digging and discovered that your brother might be one of them."

She loosened her death grip on the pepper spray. "I want to see some identification."

I moved very slowly. "Don't spray me. I'm reaching for my wallet."

She raised the spray above the table. "Give me your wallet . . . the whole thing. I know the trick about having a fake ID. You'd better hope all of your cards have the same name on them."

I made no effort to hide my smile. "I like your style, Patti. Here's the wallet. Dig all you want. I really am who I say I am."

She pulled my Georgia driver's license from its spot. "When's your birthday?"

"January first, nineteen seventy-four. It's two thousand ten now, so that makes me thirty-six." I quoted my address and recited the details of my pilot's license that lived just behind the slot for the driver's license.

She laid the card on the closed laptop, lifted her phone with her non-spray hand, and snapped a picture. Before I could react, she took a picture of me sitting across the table. "I'm sending these to my girlfriend, so if anything happens to me, they'll know you did it."

I softened my posture even more. "The world would be a lot safer if everyone were as vigilant as you. I'm impressed."

She lowered the phone and slid my wallet back across the table. "You have no idea what it's like for a single woman."

"You might be surprised. I already told you I'm in the security business, but the truth is, we know more about real threats than most people. So far, everything you've done has been spot-on perfect. You should teach a class."

"Why are you really here?" she asked.

I laid my palms flat on the table as a sign of submission. "The friends of mine who overheard the conversation in Cabo were in the military, and they're not prone to making up stories like that. I believe them, but the military does not."

"So, is that what you are? Are you military police or something?"

"No, Patti. I'm a civilian security specialist."

"Like Blackwater and companies like that?"

"Not exactly, but something like that. We're an extremely small company, and we don't show up on the evening news."

"I don't have any money. So, I can't afford to hire you to find my brother if that's what this is about."

"That's not what this is about. I want you to tell me everything you can about what your brother was doing in Mexico, how long he's been missing, and anything else you think is important. I can't promise to find him, but I suspect everyone you've reached out to for help has shot you down."

She nodded, and a tear formed at the corner of her eye. "Do you really think you can find him?"

I wanted to take her hands in mine, but instead, I said, "I don't know, but if he can be found, we're as good or better than any-body else in the world at this sort of thing. If you give us enough details about what's going on, and you tell me the truth about ev-erything, I promise to do my best to get not only your brother, but also the other missing Americans safely home. Can you do that, Ms. Baldwin?"

Skepticism loomed in her eyes. "But I don't know anything about the other Americans. There's nothing I can tell you about them."

"That's okay as long as you tell us all the details about your brother's disappearance. You're not responsible for the others."

She ducked her chin and raised both eyebrows. "I'm not responsible for Spencer's disappearance either."

"I'm sorry. I didn't mean to imply that you were. What I meant was, you're only responsible for telling us everything you know about Spencer's trip and disappearance."

"You'll have to forgive me. All of this sounds crazy to me. You're willing to go to Mexico, deal with the drug cartels, and bring Spencer home, and you're doing all of this for free? Surely you can understand why that sounds ridiculous to me."

I checked over my shoulder for prying ears. "You've heard of attorneys doing pro bono legal work, right?"

"Sure."

"Well, think of this as pro bono security work. We've been blessed with the means to do this sort of thing when we believe the cause is just, and recovering innocent Americans when the authorities refuse to get involved sounds exactly like a just cause to me."

Chapter 9
The Whole Truth

Patricia Baldwin dropped her can of pepper spray back into her purse, and I took advantage of a moment to build trust.

"Do you remember when I first sat down?"

She said, "Sure."

"What was the first thing you did?"

She played through the moment in her head. "I grabbed my pepper spray."

"Not exactly. You stuck your hand in your purse and began *searching* for your pepper spray. That's not the same thing. If I may, I'd like to suggest that you designate a precise position in your purse where you always, without fail, carry your pepper spray. That way, you'll be able to retrieve it in an instant instead of digging through everything else in there to get to your defensive weapon."

"Weapon? It's not a weapon. It's a can of pepper spray."

"Like a lot of people, you've been conditioned to think of weapons as exclusively knives and guns. If you picked up your laptop and fought me off with it by swinging it like a baseball bat, wouldn't you consider the laptop a weapon? Being on the receiving end, it would certainly feel like a weapon to me."

Her posture continued to relax as she came to believe I had her best interest in mind.

I asked, "Do you own a handgun?"

The tension returned, and she recoiled. "No!"

"That's okay. It simply means we need to teach you to use other things in your environment, like your pepper spray, more effectively. When we first began talking, you said you weren't scared of *you people*. Who did you mean?"

Instead of answering, she said, "You keep using the word *we*. Who do you mean?"

"Now we're getting somewhere. You're reacting out of logic and curiosity instead of fear. When we react out of fear, especially fear for our lives, we do some pretty caveman stuff. A lot of things happen in our brains and inside our bodies to protect ourselves and either defeat or escape the source of the fear."

She nodded. "Yeah, fight or flight, right?"

"Not exactly. Fight and flight are only two of the three reactions to a threat. The third and most common is freeze. People simply freeze and can't do anything. For most of us, that's the worst possible time to freeze, but it's the most common time we do. You didn't freeze when I showed up, and that's a very good thing. You chose to fight. That's why you pulled the pepper spray."

"I didn't really make that decision. It just happened."

"You still made the decision whether you realize it or not. A billion options flashed in your brain in an instant, and you picked what you thought was the best option. That means you're security-minded. The fact that you carry pepper spray is further proof of that mindset. That gives us a great foundation to build on."

She said, "It sounds like you're trying to sell me a self-defense class."

"I'm not trying to sell you anything, but some of your reactions during the first few seconds of our interaction told me a thousand things about you. First, by using the phrase *you people*, you suggested you believe there's an organized group of people trying to hurt you. Now, I need to know who you think that group is."

She glanced around the coffee shop. "Maybe we should have this conversation somewhere else."

"That's up to you. But first, I want to answer your question."

"Which question?"

"Who is we? We're a team of six operators. The other five are outside enjoying overpriced coffee and waiting for me to come out. In addition to that part of the team, we have professionals in a place we call the operation center or op center. Those people manage our operations from a safe distance, surrounded by all the tools they need to support us in the field."

"So, you're mercenaries."

"That's not the word we'd choose, but if that's how you need to think of us, then sure, we're mercenaries. What you need to understand, though, is that we're not what you see in the movies. We don't storm buildings and kill everybody inside. Well, sometimes we do that, but as a general rule, we're investigators. We find a problem, dissect it until we understand every element of it, and then solve the problem."

"With violence."

"I won't lie to you, Ms. Baldwin. Sometimes, violence is required. For example, if we find your brother is being held hostage in the Mexican desert by armed cartel fighters, do you want us to walk in there and try to negotiate his release, or do you want us to liberate Spencer, regardless of the means?"

She licked her lips and seemed to let the question roll around inside her head. "I guess you guys aren't really negotiators, huh?"

"No, ma'am. We're not. Negotiating with irrational people isn't possible, and the Mexican drug cartels certainly qualify as irrational. In cases involving people like that, we're problem solvers."

"How did you find me?"

"We didn't find you. Our analyst in the op center found you. She's very good at her job."

"And you swear you're not from the government?"

"I do. In full disclosure, though, we occasionally work as contractors for the government. That's not the case here, though. We're completely independent on this one."

"What if I say no?"

I smiled for the first time in our conversation. "Even if you say no, we're still going to find Spencer and bring him home. It'll just be a lot harder without you."

"Where can we talk privately?"

In a continued effort to gain and retain her confidence, I said, "Wherever you'd like. I want you to be comfortable."

"Nothing about this is comfortable, but I think I believe you are who you say you are. The *you people* I was referring to are the government people. They're trying to get me to shut up about my brother."

"Have they approached you?"

She nodded. "Twice. The first time, it was two of them in nice suits. They told me not to worry about Spencer. They said he was on an assignment that prevented him from contacting me and that he was perfectly safe."

"You didn't believe them?"

"No, I didn't believe them. You have to know Spencer. He's never going to work on a story about Mexican drug cartels for the government. He's a journalist, and a damned good one. He wouldn't compromise his principles like that. He's an independent investigative journalist with emphasis on the independent part."

"So, these two men in suits . . . Did they threaten you?"

She shook her head. "No. They were very polite, but the other guy . . ." She paused, and I was left hanging on every breath until she continued. "The other guy was nasty. He found me at a gas station, and I didn't have my pepper spray. It was in my purse inside the car. I only had my credit card in my hand."

"What did he say?"

"He stepped between me and the open driver's door of my car and ran his finger along the top edge of the door. It was creepy."

"What did he say, Ms. Baldwin?"

"I'll never forget it. He said, 'You're a beautiful woman, Patricia Baldwin. It would be a shame if something were to happen to you because you weren't smart enough to keep your nose out of things that aren't your business.' I told him I was going to call the police."

"What did he do when you made that threat?"

"He laughed and said, 'Go ahead. Just remember, though. We're the government, and we're not concerned about the Sacramento PD.'"

The dossier Skipper prepared on Patricia Baldwin contained a comprehensive list of everything she'd ever done professionally, but I wanted to check her honesty. "What do you do for a living?"

She ducked her head. "I don't know if you can really call it a living yet, but I'm writing a novel. I've got a journalism degree from UCLA. That doesn't exactly swing open the doors of opportunity on six-figure careers."

So far, so good.

I kept pushing. "You must have some source of income if you can afford to write full-time and drink six-dollar cappuccinos."

"Spencer and I inherited a little money from our parents when they passed. I'm living on the interest, such as it is. We got their house, too, so no house payment. Just taxes and utilities for the most part. It's not glamorous, but I can still afford decent coffee."

No attempts at deception. I liked Patti a little more every time she opened her mouth.

"You said you weren't afraid, but is that true?"

She bit her lip. "I want it to be true."

"I understand, and we can help with that."

"What? Like a bodyguard?"

"We could arrange that if you want, but I was thinking about taking you somewhere safe so you can write without worrying about being threatened while we find your brother."

"Where?" she asked.

"Anywhere you want to go. The friend you texted my picture to . . . Maybe you could stay with her."

I didn't feel good about playing games with her, but pushing her to the point of ultimate honesty was crucial. That question did the job.

"I didn't really text it to anybody. I just wanted you to believe I had. It was a ploy."

"And a very good one," I said. "Come on. Let's meet the rest of my team and continue this conversation back at the Sterling."

"You're staying at the Sterling?" I nodded, and she said, "That place is gorgeous."

"Yes, it is. Would you feel comfortable talking there?"

Instead of answering, she packed her laptop and drank the last of her coffee. I took that as a yes.

* * *

In our suite at the Sterling, Patricia pointed at Mongo. "Can that guy be my bodyguard?"

I said, "Unfortunately, we need him just in case we have to flip over a school bus or fight off a gorilla."

Introductions were made, and Patti came clean. "I was lying when I told you I wasn't afraid."

It was time for a psychologist's trick. I cocked my head and waited for her to continue. When a patient starts talking, I stop talking, and the ploy works every time. Patti was no exception.

"I am scared. I'm scared for my brother. I know something terrible has happened to him. I just know it. And the government guys, they confirmed it. There's a cover-up. The paper won't talk to me. The local police can't do anything in Mexico. I'm all alone. And I'm scared."

The tears came, and our spiritual guru went to work.

Singer stood from his chair and sat beside Patti on the sofa. In his calm, confident tone, he said, "It's okay to be afraid. We all experience fear in our lives, but yours is sharper right now, and that's why we're here. We're not going to let anything happen to you."

She shoved him away. "What can you do? Huh? What can you do against the government? They know what happened to Spencer, and they're going to cover it up, and there's nothing you can do, and you know it!"

Singer scooted away to give her a little room. If possible, his tone softened even more. "Those men weren't from the government, Ms. Baldwin. We'll find out who they were, and we'll make sure they don't bother you again, but most important, we'll find your brother and do our best to bring him home safely."

She wiped away the tears. "I'm sorry. I didn't mean to react like that."

Singer moved a little closer. "Don't be sorry. We're very good at what we do, and even if the government is involved in all of this, we're not afraid of them, and we have a track record of holding them accountable when they go too far. We're not easy to scare, and now you've got all of us standing between you and them."

She leaned toward our sniper and laid her head on his shoulder. "Thank you."

Singer said, "Don't thank us yet, ma'am. Let us do our job first, and then you and Spencer can thank us together."

She wiped her face with her palms, and our sniper handed her his handkerchief. That brought a smile to her face.

He asked, "Have you ever been to Georgia?"

She furrowed her brow. "Like Georgia in Eastern Europe?"

He chuckled. "No, ma'am. Like Georgia in America."

"Just to the airport. Everybody's been to the Atlanta airport."

He gave her a gentle nod. "Yes, ma'am, they sure have, but I'm not talking about Atlanta. There's a little town on the coast called St. Marys. It's where we all live. We've got a nice, comfortable place there with plenty of room. Maybe you'd like to stay there for a few days while we sort through this."

She kept scowling. "I told Chase that I don't have any money. I can't afford—"

Singer took her hand. "We're not asking for money. We're asking you to let us keep you safe while we find your brother. That's all. You'll never owe us a dime, Ms. Patti."

The tears returned, and her head fell back against the shoulder that held the butt of so many rifles with which he'd taken so many lives through the years. She'd never see that side of Singer. To her, he'd always be the gentlest man she'd ever meet. "Georgia sounds nice."

Chapter 10
Playing the Martyr

I ran down the mental checklist of everything that a normal American would have to do before going into hiding three thousand miles from home, and the list grew beyond my ability to comprehend what a normal American was.

I said, "I know this is all a bit overwhelming for you, but if we're going to protect you from whomever these people claiming to be government representatives are, we need to know who's going to miss you."

"What do you mean?" Patti asked.

"I mean friends, family, boyfriends, girlfriends, baristas, mail carriers, the old man who walks his dogs late at night in your neighborhood."

That caught her attention. "How do you know about Mr. Robinson?"

"As I told you, we're very good at what we do. Think about it and give us the list."

She stared into space for a long moment. "Obviously, I don't have a boyfriend. The only family I have left is Spencer. I have a couple of friends, but they have babies, and as you can see, I'm quite alone. I'll simply tell them I'm going away for a while. Their lives are too busy to worry about me."

I couldn't shake the uneasy feeling I got when she said, "Obviously, I don't have a boyfriend." Something about that statement didn't taste right. I wanted to explore the comment, but I tucked it away for later.

"What about an editor, publicist, or agent for your writing? Anybody like that?"

She shook her head. "Not yet. Hopefully, I'll get to that point, but for now, it's just me, all alone, writing my little story."

"My wife is a screenwriter. Perhaps she can share some tips and tricks about how to break into the scene."

Her eyes lit up. "That would be fantastic."

I made a mental note about her excitement. "The weather is really nice here, but it's a little different down in Georgia. You'll want to pack plenty of shorts, T-shirts, and flip-flops. The house is comfortable and spacious, so you'll have plenty of privacy, but it's hard to hide from the heat and humidity. How long will it take you to pack?"

"How long do I have?"

"I'm going to speak with your brother's editor down at the *Bee* and see if I can shake anything out of him. If anybody knows the truth about Spencer's original assignment, he'll be the guy."

Patti said, "He won't talk to you. He's a pompous ass, and his secretary is a perfect fit for him. Nobody gets past her without an appointment, and that man's not given anyone an appointment in ten years."

"He'll see me," I said. "I can be quite persuasive."

"I'm telling you, you're wasting your time, but I can be ready to go when you get back. Can you leave . . . what was his name? The big one?"

"His name is Marvin Malloy, but everybody he loves calls him Mongo, and yes, we'll leave him with you. You can consider him your own bulldog of a secretary. Nobody's getting past Mongo. I promise."

Hunter and I headed for the *Sacramento Bee* at 1601 Alhambra Boulevard while the rest of the team escorted Patti back to her place to prepare for her move across the country.

Hunter asked, "What makes you think this guy's gonna talk to us?"

I pulled my Secret Service credential pack from my pocket. "Oh, he's not going to talk to us. He's going to talk with Supervisory Special Agent Fulton and his trusty sidekick, the Sante Fe Kid."

"Sante Fe Kid? Where'd that come from?"

I laughed. "I don't know. It just sounded like a good name for a trusty sidekick."

He pulled his own cred-pack. "You can keep that sidekick crap in the bag. On paper, I'm still Special Agent Stone W. Hunter with Naval Criminal Investigative Service."

"That you are, my friend. Let's go have a little fun with Editor Boy."

Patti was right. The editor's secretary was, indeed, a first-class bulldog.

"I'm sorry, sir. You'll have to make an appointment. Mr. Wells doesn't see anyone without an appointment."

I turned and scanned the room before producing my credentials and a pair of stainless-steel handcuffs. "Oh, he'll see us, or you're going to jail for obstructing an official investigation. Your move . . . "—I leaned back and examined the nameplate on her desk—". . . Brenda."

She reached for the phone, but Hunter laid a thumb against the receiver. "No, no, no, Brenda. No warning. We'll show ourselves in."

Hunter pulled the cord from the telephone, and we pushed through Mr. Wells's door.

"What's the meaning of this?" the man roared as my partner pulled the door closed behind us. "Who are you people? Get out of my office."

He reached for his phone, but Hunter was even quicker than before. He snatched the cord from the base and nestled into an oversized wingback.

Wells rose to his feet with indignation dripping from his face.

I held up my badge and ID. "Have a seat, Wells. We've got a few questions."

He thrust a hand into his pocket, presumably to withdraw a cell phone. "I'm calling security and my attorney."

I took a seat beside my partner. "Good. They'll come in handy. We'll wait. I'm sure your security force would love to see you get marched off in handcuffs for not revealing your source, or whatever it is you newspaper people claim to do these days. The lawyer will be fun, too. He can explain to you why he can't do anything to keep you out of federal custody for withholding information about a Pulitzer-winning reporter missing in a foreign country."

He remained on his feet, with his face growing redder by the second. "What's the matter with you people? Don't you ever talk to each other? I already told the other guys I wouldn't release any information about Spencer Baldwin until they approved it."

I held up two fingers. "Two things, Wells. First, I'm getting tired of being called *you people*, so don't do it again. Second, what other guys are you talking about?"

He leaned across his desk. "The guys from the Congressional Security Bureau."

Hunter threw up his hands. "Oh, those guys. The CSB. Well, we're clearly out of our league on this one. Go ahead, Supervisory

Special Agent Fulton. Explain to Wells why those boys from CSB didn't leave a business card."

Just as I'd done in front of Brenda's desk, I inspected the much nicer nameplate in front of the editor. "Robert B. Wells, editor in chief. That sounds fancy. Tell me, Bobby . . . You don't mind if I call you Bobby, do you?" Without giving him time to respond, I continued. "Did the agents from the Congressional Security Bureau have a badge and ID like mine?"

I tossed my credentials onto his desk. "Go ahead, Robby B. Take a good long look. Feel free to take a picture or photocopy of it if you'd like. Tell me one thing, though. Did they have badges like mine? Did they have ID like mine? Did they have a business card they left with you so you could call them as soon as you heard from Mr. Spencer Baldwin, your man in the field? Did they do that, Rob?"

Robert B. Wells, editor in chief, took a seat and loosened his tie. "What's going on here?"

"What's going on, Mr. Wells, is that you've been duped. A well-educated, important newspaperman who's responsible for keeping the people of Sacramento, the capital city of California, informed on the news—the truth, the fair and honest information they need—has been played. Let me guess. These two so-called CSB agents . . . Did they come to your office like we did, or did they corner you somewhere outside the hallowed halls of this bastion of journalistic integrity? A gas station, perhaps?"

The wheels inside his skull were clearly spinning at maximum speed. "What are you saying?"

I crossed my legs. "I'm saying your reporter, Spencer Baldwin, is missing in Mexico, and two people claiming to represent a government agency that doesn't exist convinced you to keep a lid on it."

"What do you mean, it doesn't exist?"

Hunter shook his head. "Don't you have an internet connection on that computer? Look it up. See if you can find anything about the CSB."

Wells slapped his desk. "They warned me you'd try that trick. There is no public information available on the Congressional Security Bureau. It's a secret agency."

"A secret agency, huh? And that line worked on you?"

He said, "How do I know you two aren't here to test me to see if I'll break? Huh?"

I said, "You can know by calling the attorney general of the United States. You're the editor in chief of the *Sacramento Bee*, for God's sake. The AG will take your call. Call your congressmen—any of them, all of them. Do your homework, Wells. When all of this washes out, your name is going to be in the paper, but not under the headline you'd like. Tell us everything you know about the assignment Spencer Baldwin was on. Show us every email sent and received from him since he's been in Mexico. And tell us every detail of the assignment."

Wells closed his eyes and leaned back in his chair. After a long silence, he said, "I'm going to speak with legal counsel before answering any of your questions or giving you any information. If I'm advised by counsel that I should speak with you, I will do so. Until then, I cannot and will not risk divulging any sources of information or making any comments that could lead to harm befalling any of our journalists."

I pointed toward the cord lying on the floor. "Reconnect the phone."

Hunter did so, and I said, "Make the call."

Wells stared between me and the phone, and I said, "Make the call while we're here. Call your legal counsel, and get him in here."

"It's not that simple," Wells said. "You have to understand . . ."

I pulled out my shiny new handcuffs for the second time in one day. "No, Mr. Wells, *you* have to understand. You either make the call or make bail. And finding a federal judge to set bail this late in the day, on a Friday, no less, isn't going to be easy. Don't worry, though. The federal detention center is relatively clean and safe. You should be fine between now and Monday afternoon. The choice is yours."

He huffed and lifted the phone. "Get legal."

I could only assume the call went to Ms. Bulldog out front, so Hunter and I waited somewhat impatiently until the desk phone buzzed and Wells lifted the receiver.

"Yeah . . . You've got to be kidding me. Find them, and get them here today." He slammed the receiver back onto its cradle and sighed. "The legal department has gone home for the day."

I shrugged, stood, and dangled my cuffs. "Very well. Get on your feet, turn around, and place your hands on your head. You're under arrest for—"

He threw up his hands. "Wait, wait, wait. This isn't necessary. Look, I'll talk to you, but you have to know that I can't do it without legal counsel. Give me two hours. By then, I'll have had time to talk with legal, and I'll have an answer for you."

I turned to Hunter as if conferring. After a few seconds, I stowed my cuffs and held up two fingers. "Two hours, Wells. Two hours, and not a minute longer. If you don't take my call immediately, you'll get to play the martyr and go to jail protecting your source. That's what all you newspaper people dream of, right?"

Chapter 11
Family Ties

On our way back to the Sterling, Hunter laughed and couldn't stop. Finally, he said, "What would you have done if that guy said, 'Okay, go ahead and arrest me'?"

It was my turn to laugh. "I don't know. Something told me he wasn't willing to push it that far. Do you think he'll answer when I call?"

"No chance. That dude's going to hide behind his lawyers, but I don't really blame him. Would you want to be responsible for a journalist gone rogue and who's probably dead?"

I tapped the brakes. "Do you think Baldwin is dead?"

He shrugged. "I don't know, but probably. That's why I think it's not a great idea to get his sister's hopes up. If we go down there and can't find any sign of him, what are we going to tell her?"

"You're probably right. I shouldn't have been so cavalier about it. If he's there and alive, though, we're his best shot at getting back home."

"I agree," Hunter said. "Are you okay with Singer volunteering to take Patti to Bonaventure?"

"Yeah, he and I talked about it. If this thing runs as deep as I suspect, she's going to need some protection from whoever the Congressional Security Bureau is."

"Can you believe that? How did Wells not know he was getting jerked around?"

"Beats me," I said. "I just hope we get a little face-to-face with those guys before this is over. I'd like to know who they are. Wouldn't you?"

"I sure would. Are you certain the CSB doesn't exist?"

I said, "I know who to ask."

Skipper answered. "Hey, Chase. What's up?"

"Have you ever heard of something called the Congressional Security Bureau?"

"It doesn't ring any bells. Give me a minute, and I'll do a little digging."

Two minutes later, she said, "Nope, nothing. Either they don't exist, or they're some kind of super deep-cover agency. Clark might know."

"Is he still there?"

"Thank God, no. I finally convinced Tony and him to go shooting. They were killing me."

I changed the subject. "We're bringing a friend home."

"Oh yeah? Who?"

"Patti Baldwin. The more I sniff around this thing, the more it stinks. I'm going to tuck her away at Bonaventure while we figure it out."

"That sounds like a good plan, but are you covering all your bases?"

"I think so. She doesn't have any family except her brother, and she says the only friends she has are too busy to care that she's leaving town for a while."

"Just be careful," she said. "You know how those little details turn into big problems when we don't deal with them."

"I know. I'll dig a little deeper before we blow this popsicle stand. Oh, there's one more thing. I need you to keep an eye on a guy named Robert B. Wells. He's the editor in chief of the *Sacramento Bee*. Hunter and I paid him a visit to shake some truth out of him, and he lawyered up. I used my Secret Service creds to get in the door. He's a real back-office kind of guy. Just keep an eye on him. I'm scheduled for a call with him in ninety minutes."

"Will do," she said. "Anything else?"

"That's it. Just have somebody make up a bedroom for Patti."

"You got it. I'll see you in a few hours."

The call to Clark produced the same results. "No, I've never heard of anything like that. It sounds like they're yanking that guy's chain."

"That's what I thought," I said. "We'll see you sometime later tonight."

* * *

At Patti Baldwin's house, we ran down the list of every detail to be covered, and we checked every box.

I said, "We'll have your mail forwarded to a blind box in North Dakota. It's a service we use that opens your mail, scans it, and makes it available on a secure server. Our analyst will show you how it works."

"What about my car?" Patti asked.

"We'll leave it at the Sacramento Airport, so it'll look like you hopped a flight. Skipper—she's our analyst—will make it look like you flew to Bangkok or somewhere equally exotic."

Patti took a long breath and leaned against the edge of her sofa. "You guys are either really good at this, or you're kidnapping me and I'm helping you."

"Either way, you'll be safe with us," I said. "There is one thing we need to get out in the open, though."

Her expression turned solemn.

"As difficult as this is to hear, there is a chance that your brother has fallen victim to some pretty nasty guys who don't make a habit of leaving people alive. I know the thought is terrible, but the reality of the situation is this . . . We may get to Mexico and find out that Spencer didn't survive his encounter with the cartel. I need you to keep that possibility in the back of your mind. If he's alive, we'll find him, but it's always a good idea to expect the best but prepare for the worst. Understand?"

She forced a smile. "I know all of that, but Spencer is tough. He's been through a lot, and he always comes out the other side."

"I'm sure he is," I said. "I just want you to understand the potential reality. We're good, but we're not miracle workers."

"I understand. Did you get anything out of Wells?"

I shook my head. "He lawyered up, but I'm scheduled to call him in forty-five minutes. We'll see if he plays ball. I don't really expect him to."

I grabbed a legal pad and found a quiet corner to myself. No matter how many times I ran through the mental list of items not to forget, I could never shake the nagging feeling that I was forgetting something. Nothing about that mission was routine, and regardless of my reassurances to Patti, a lingering doubt dug its ugly claws deeper into my brain with every passing moment. With the first page of the legal pad almost completely covered with black ink and check marks, I could've gouged out my own eye for being so stupid.

"Hey, guys. We overlooked something none of us should've missed."

Everyone stopped their task and turned to hear what glaring oversight I was about to divulge.

I said, "We need to take a look at Spencer Baldwin's house. Maybe there's something there that'll at least get us started on the right trail."

Palms hit foreheads, and groans of disbelief escaped the lips of my team.

"Where's Patti?" I asked.

Hunter pointed up the stairs. "She went back up to grab one more thing. You know how that is. There's always one more thing."

She bounced down the stairs with two small bags in her hands, and I caught her on the bottom step.

"There's something else we need to do before we leave Sacramento."

She said, "Okay. What is it?"

"We need to take a look inside your brother's house. We suspect we might find something that'll help us locate him. We need somewhere to start our search, and we just might find that *somewhere* in Spencer's place."

She frowned in obvious confusion. "What are you talking about?"

"We need to search your brother's house or apartment before we leave town. I assume he had a place here in Sacramento, right?"

Her frown continued. "Uh, yeah. This is it."

"*What* is it?"

"This house," Patti said. "Spencer lives here."

"You and Spencer live here . . . together?"

"Yeah, that's right."

I suddenly felt like the most incompetent investigator on the planet.

Why didn't I know Spencer lived with Patti? What else am I missing?

"Would you mind if we took a look at your brother's room?"

She glanced back up the stairs. "Um, sure . . . I guess."

I didn't like her hesitance, if that's what it was. "Which room is his?"

She stepped aside. "It's the master on the right. Do you mind if I come with you?"

"That's fine." I turned to Mongo. "Come with us, and bring that big brain of yours. I don't want to miss anything."

The three of us ascended the stairs and turned right. Patti led us through the closed door and into a spacious master suite, beautifully decorated and clearly a bedroom for a couple.

"Does your brother have a girlfriend who stays here sometimes?"

Patti stared at the floor. "You might say that, but the truth is, she stays here all the time."

"Where is she now?" I asked.

It hit Mongo an instant before Patti said, "Spencer isn't really my brother."

"What?"

"Yeah, uh . . . he was adopted because my parents didn't think they could have children. They wanted a boy and a girl, but no matter how hard they tried, it never happened until . . ."

"Until what?" I asked.

"Well, they adopted Spencer in February. He was a newborn, and they found out they were pregnant with me in March."

"That means you're not genetically related, but you're still legally brother and sister, right?"

"We're a little more than that, actually. This is my bedroom, too."

There are few things I hate more than being the last person in a room to know a fact that's obvious to everyone else. I wasn't a good enough actor to hide my surprise, and I was caught entirely on my heels with nothing to say that could diminish my reaction.

"I'm sorry. I didn't realize . . ."

She wouldn't—or couldn't—look at me. "I'm sorry I didn't tell you up front. I guess I thought you knew since you already knew so much about Spencer and me. Now you understand why I don't have any real friends here. It's not exactly socially acceptable to be in love with your brother, even if he is your adopted brother."

I said, "We don't choose who we fall in love with, Patti. It's not my place to judge, and I wouldn't, even if it were my place, but information like this is important. Every detail we know might be the one piece of information that leads us to your . . . Spencer."

"It's not that I'm ashamed, you understand. It's just . . . like I said . . . I assumed you knew."

"No more assumptions, okay? If you must assume anything, assume we don't know, and tell us. Tell us even if you think it has nothing to do with finding Spencer."

She nodded and tried to smile. "So, you're not going to judge us for this?"

I didn't have to force my smile. "No, of course not. You're going through enough. You don't need anything adding more stress to your life. This doesn't change how we'll approach the mission. Spencer is still missing, and you still love him. The only difference is that you love him for entirely different reasons than we believed. We're still going to do everything in our power to bring him home to you, no matter what that home looks like."

Chapter 12
Georgia on My Mind

The search of Spencer's and Patti's bedroom proved fruitless, but his office on the third floor was a treasure trove of intelligence. Four massive file folders contained years of background information on the two cartels Spencer was researching. Copies of airline tickets, hotel reservations, and Mexican sources were neatly arranged and cataloged.

I held up the files. "May I take these? We'll make copies and return the originals."

Patti eyed the stack. "I guess so. I don't know if Spencer would want anyone having his files, especially if there are names of sources in there, but if you think it'll help you find him, I'm okay with you taking them."

She grew pensive and turned away.

I stepped beside her. "I understand how emotional all of this must be for you, but we truly are here to help. We have a lot of talent on this team, and I'd love for you to take advantage of all of it. Singer—the soft-spoken guy with the killer voice—is one of the most devout Christian men I've ever known. He's also an ordained minister and a wonderful counselor. You can talk with him anytime. He's always more than willing to listen, and sometimes just having an ear to hear and a shoulder to cry on is exactly what we need."

She rubbed a knuckle into the corner of her eye. "Thank you. That means a lot, but I'm not really the religious kind."

I said, "Compassion and religion aren't interchangeable. Singer won't preach to you. He'll listen and offer supportive counsel. He's my refuge when all of this becomes too much, and I'd be lost without him."

She nodded, still forcing back the tears. "That's sweet. It just hit me kind of hard when you asked for Spencer's files. He'd never show those to anyone, but if he's dead, I guess it doesn't matter who sees them."

I slid the bulging folders into a briefcase. "Let's get you to Bonaventure so we can go to work finding your . . . the man you love."

* * *

With Patti's car parked in the long-term garage at Sacramento International, we boarded the *Grey Ghost* for yet another cross-country flight. Our guest nestled into one of the leather captain's chairs and pulled her seat belt across her lap. "This is amazing. I guess you guys really are good at what you do."

I slid into the cockpit beside Disco and checked the time. "I almost forgot. I need to call our editor friend at the *Bee*. Are you okay doing preflight without me?"

He said, "Sure, I'll get by."

I climbed from the cockpit and made my way to the rear of the plane for some privacy, and so I wouldn't disrupt Disco's cockpit routine. Before I could pull my phone from my pocket to call Wells, it rang. I thumbed the answer key. "Chase."

Skipper said, "You're never going to believe this."

"What is it?"

"Robert Wells was just found dead in his office at the *Sacramento Bee*."

"Suicide?"

"I don't know yet, but that's not all. His secretary, Brenda Collier, is missing."

"What do you mean, missing?"

"Gone. Poof. No one can find her. The Sacramento PD put out an APB, but so far, nothing."

"Is that all you've got?"

She said, "For now, yes, but I'll call as soon as I hear anything more."

"Thanks, Skipper. We'll be airborne in fifteen minutes or less."

She sounded surprised. "You're not staying to look into what's going on at the newspaper?"

"No, I think it's more important to get Patti to Bonaventure. If Wells's death was a hit, we need to protect her, and there's no better place to do that than Bonaventure. We can always come back if necessary. Do you have any local sources?"

"I've got an analyst friend in the Bay Area, and I've already got him on it. He'll keep me updated, and I'll pass along anything he finds."

"Thanks, Skipper. I'll see you in four hours."

I took a long breath and tried unsuccessfully to cram this latest event into Spencer Baldwin's disappearance, but no matter how hard I shoved, it wouldn't fit. I leaned around the pallet of gear, caught Hunter's eye, and signaled for him to join me. He was standing in front of me in seconds.

"Wells is dead. They found him in his office at the *Bee* just a few minutes ago. Skipper doesn't know any details yet, but his secretary is MIA."

Hunter let out a whistle. "I didn't see that coming. Got any theories?"

"Maybe suicide out of guilt, but that doesn't fit his personality. He was too much of a narcissist to take his own life. At least that's how I had him pegged."

"What about the guys claiming to be from the Congressional Security Bureau? Do you think they may've gotten to him?"

"I don't know. Maybe. I just hope I didn't push him to suicide. I probably should've been less aggressive and offered to help instead of threatening him."

Hunter grimaced. "Ouch. I didn't think of that. Let's not take that leap just yet. I'm sure Skipper will have every detail as soon as it's available."

"I don't like this feeling, my friend. There's more to this thing than we know or understand. I just wonder how deep it's going to get before we hit bottom."

He shrugged. "That's why we make the big bucks."

"We're not making a dime on this one. It's all gratis."

He slugged me on the arm. "All gratis. That's potatoes with cheese, right? I love me some taters and cheese."

In spite of the weight of the moment, I chuckled. "Get up there and fly with Disco. We need to get you checked out in this thing so I don't have to fly all the time."

"Whatever you say, boss."

Hunter climbed into the copilot seat, and I buckled in beside Patti.

"How you doing?"

"I'm all right," she said.

"You're lying, but I'll let you get away with it this time. We're going to take good care of you. I promise."

"I believe you," she said. "It's just that I've never been involved in anything like this before. I don't know how to feel or what to do."

"I can't tell you how to feel, but all you need to do is tell us every detail you know, and don't hide anything. We'll take care of everything else."

"Is that a two-way street?"

"What do you mean?"

She said, "Are you going to tell me everything you learn along the way, or am I the only one operating under that rule?"

"No, we aren't going to tell you everything. You don't want to know what we'll see and do down there. It's not pretty, and it's never easy to explain. Ultimately, though, we'll either accomplish the mission to bring Spencer home, or we'll tell you exactly why we couldn't. We don't fail often."

"I understand."

I stilled myself and asked, "How well do you know Spencer's editor, Mr. Wells?"

"I've never met him, but I know who he is. Why?"

I practiced the speech in my head until I thought I could get it out. "I don't have any details yet, but I think you should know. Hunter and I visited him this afternoon, and we rattled his cage a little. There's no evidence to suggest we played a role in what happened after we left, but I just learned he was found dead in his office, and his secretary is missing."

Her jaw dropped. "Was it them? The same guys who threatened me?"

"We don't know yet, but when we find out, I'll make sure you know. I won't keep things like that from you."

She reached across the armrest and took my hand. "Thank you for doing this for me. I still don't understand why you're doing it, but I mean it. Thank you."

"You're welcome, and as scary as this may sound, I'm glad we got you out of Sacramento."

"Me, too."

"When we get home, we'll have our tech services officer configure your cell phone so it can't be traced."

She cocked her head. "You've got a tech services officer? Who are you guys?"

"We're the good guys."

* * *

The jet stream wasn't so kind to us for our time zone–busting flight. The massive tailwind had moved into Canada, leaving us to settle for 600 knots of ground speed with a decent wind pushing us eastward.

Clark met us at the airport with one of the Suburbans and parked near the foot of the airstairs. When I stepped from the plane, he said, "I figured you didn't want to drive our guest around in the Microbus."

"What's wrong with the Microbus?" I asked. "It's a classic."

"So is peanut butter and jelly, but I don't see you passing up filet mignon for a PB and J."

Skipper met us at the door back at Bonaventure, and I said, "Patti, meet Skipper. She's the analyst I told you about."

Patti stuck out her hand, but Skipper pushed it away. "We're huggers down here in the South. Come here."

I considered that to be the perfect welcome, but I'm not sure Patti agreed. By the time the case was closed, I had every faith she'd be a hugger, too.

Patti said, "Your name's not really Skipper, is it?"

"My parents named me Elizabeth, but it's been so long since anyone called me anything other than Skipper that I probably wouldn't answer to my real name. Are you hungry? Or would you like a drink? Or both?"

Patti sighed. "A drink would be really nice. It's been quite a day."

"I'm sure it has," Skipper said. "What would you like?"

The team and I carried Patti's bags to a second-story bedroom that wasn't as big as hers at home, but it would be more than sufficient. Back downstairs, I pulled Skipper aside and brought her up to speed on Patti's and Spencer's relationship.

Unlike me, she didn't seem surprised. "I thought something like that was going on. It was just a strange feeling I had."

"Women's intuition, I guess."

She said, "I just got some news on Robert Wells. Do you want it here, or should we go upstairs?"

"That depends on the news."

She said, "Let's get Clark and go upstairs. It's quieter up there."

We wrangled our handler from the kitchen, where he was involved in some sort of massive sandwich construction project, and made our way to the op center.

As a general rule, once the doors close and lock, we're all business inside that room, but Clark insisted on bringing his sandwich with him. He took an enormous bite, made a satisfied animal noise, and asked, "What's up?"

Skipper rolled her eyes. "Don't you ever stop eating?"

He made a show of swallowing. "Sure, I do. A guy's got to sleep sometime."

"Try to eat quietly like a normal human, please. This is serious."

"I'll do my best. What's going on?"

"My source in the Bay Area says the police have officially declared the two incidents completely unrelated. They say the missing secretary has no connection to the dead editor in chief."

Clark abandoned his sandwich. "What are they smoking out there?"

"I'm just telling you what my guy told me."

I said, "Let's focus on Wells first. Are they calling it suicide?"

"According to official reports, it's a suspicious death, and there will be an autopsy."

I asked, "Are they processing the office as a crime scene?"

"I don't know. All I know for sure is that they're not tying the two incidents together, and that's either a crazy decision, or it's an attempt to avoid casting suspicion on the secretary."

"Is that all you've got?" I asked.

"There's one more thing, and this may be the craziest of all. The FBI field office took control of the body, and he's in the morgue at RRM Sacramento."

I dug through the file cabinet in my head, but nothing came, so I asked, "What's RRM?"

She answered as if everybody should know. "It's the Residential Reentry Management facility in Sacramento."

Clark took another bite. "This thing just keeps getting weirder by the minute."

I said, "I agree. Run a full background check on both of them —the secretary and the editor. I want to know where their lives crossed outside of that office."

Chapter 13
Commitment

We secured the op center, and I found Patti sitting on the back gallery. "How are you doing?"

She looked up and raised her glass. "I'm doing okay. Thanks. This is a beautiful place. I can't wait to see it in the daylight tomorrow."

I touched the rim of my glass to hers. "Let's go for a short walk."

We descended the stairs and crossed the sloping backyard toward the North River until we landed in the gazebo. The soft lighting inside provided just enough illumination to bathe the cannon in an eerie glow.

Patti slid her hand across the pitted surface. "Is this from the Civil War? Or what is it some people call it? The War of Northern Aggression?"

I slid onto my favorite Adirondack. "By the time that particular war came along, this old girl had been in mud on the bottom of Cumberland Sound for nearly fifty years. She sank with a British man-o'-war just a few miles from here during the War of Eighteen Twelve."

"How did it end up here?"

"This place has been in my mother's family since the seventeen hundreds. It was originally a pecan and cotton plantation."

She cut in. "You mean with slaves?"

I took a sip. "Slavery is the worst thing this country ever did. It's a scar on our history and a terrible wound we inflicted on humanity, but not every Southern plantation participated in the atrocity. My ancestors, for example, purchased slaves from Charleston and Savannah and brought them here to work."

It was impossible for her to hide the disgust on her face.

"The untold story of that era in our history is this. My family, as well as many more, granted slaves not only freedom, but also a share of the profits from the plantation. The men and women who worked this plantation were freed the day they arrived here in St. Marys. Those who chose to stay were provided with education, healthcare, a comfortable place to live, and working conditions unlike what is portrayed in textbooks today. When the pecans and cotton were sold, everyone who worked the plantation was given a percentage of the income."

She said, "I doubt that was the norm for the day."

"You'd be right about that. Many, if not most, of the plantations were miserable places for slaves, and that's something we can never undo. I'm proud to be a descendant of men and women of moral character who viewed all life as sacred. I have the diaries and personal letters of most of my ancestors who lived and worked right here for hundreds of years. They're tucked away nice and safe in a vault at the bank, and they tell the story of a community of family, hard work, mutual respect, and prosperity. Based on the diaries, no one in history was ever forced to work on this ground except the children of ancestors. They were what we like to call 'indentured by bloodline.'"

"Do you have siblings?" she asked.

"I did, but she died as a child. It's just me and a cousin named Maebelle, who's married to Clark. You met him earlier."

She swirled the liquid in her glass. "I suppose there's no more cotton or pecans."

"No, those days are long gone. Although, we do have a couple hundred pecan trees still living on the property that produce tons of nuts every year. I'll teach you how to crack them with your hands if you're still here when they fall."

Something about my statement sent her deep inside her head, and I was intrigued, but I didn't probe. Instead, I waited and listened.

She finally asked, "How long?"

"To find Spencer?"

She nodded.

"I wish I could give you a good answer, but there's no way to predict what we'll find when we get down there. If everything goes smoothly, and it never does, it could be just a few days, but if it's the tangled mess I expect, it could be weeks."

"When are you leaving?"

"We'll have another meeting tomorrow morning, and Skipper will fill us in on the files we pulled from Spencer's office. She's spectacular when it comes to picking out what's important in enormous volumes of information. It would take me days to get through all those files, but she'll have them practically memorized by midnight."

"She sounds amazing."

I finished my drink. "She is, and you'll see that more by the day. She does a lot more work than anyone else on the team, and she's ir-replaceable. To get back to your question, if there's no reason for us to go back to California, we'll be in Cabo tomorrow afternoon."

She set her glass on the arm of the chair. "I know this sounds strange, but part of me doesn't want you to go."

"Why not?"

"I guess I'm afraid Spencer might be dead, and if you go and find him, I'll know. Sometimes, it's better not to know."

I slid to the edge of my seat. "There's something you have to understand. We're not doing this for you. We're doing it for Spencer and the other Americans who are likely missing down there. I don't know if they're related, but we'll find out. I don't mean this to sound cold, but you're not the mission. Keeping you safe is simply *part* of the mission."

"I get that. Who will be here with me while you and the team are gone?"

"Clark, Skipper, and Hunter are the three you've already met. You'll meet Tony and Dr. Mankiller tomorrow. You'll be in very good hands. It's likely that my wife, Penny, will be back from L.A. in a few days as well."

"Is Dr. Mankiller his real name?"

I chuckled. "He is a she, and yes. She's Native American and descended from the first female chief of the Cherokee tribe."

"That's pretty cool. What am I supposed to do here?"

"Do whatever you'd like." I motioned toward the boathouse. "We've got a sailboat and a couple of powerboats. If you don't know how to sail, and you want to learn, anybody here can teach you. If you're into horses, we've got four of the horrific beasts. I'm scared of them, and they live for only one purpose—to torment me."

"Come on. They can't be that bad," she said.

"With everyone else, they're well-mannered and respectful. With me, they're demons from a fiery pit."

She giggled. "They sound delightful."

"That's not the word I'd use, but feel free to experience them for yourself. I remember you saying you don't shoot."

"That's right. Guns are terrifying."

"Have you ever fired a gun?"

"No, and I never want to. We'd be far better off without them."

I gave her a smile. "If you decide you want to see what it's really like to fire a weapon in an extremely safe, controlled environment, with a competent instructor, we can make that happen. We have a range, and all of us are well-qualified to teach you to shoot. Who knows? You might enjoy it."

"I don't think so, but thanks."

I pushed myself to my feet. "I'm off to bed. I've got a busy day tomorrow. Make yourself at home, and if you need anything at all, just ask anyone. Skipper will get you set up with the Wi-Fi passwords and alarm codes for the house tomorrow."

She looked up but didn't stand. "Thank you, Chase. This is . . . it's just overwhelming."

I leaned against the cannon. "The people around you here at Bonaventure live this life every day. We understand adversity and human conflict. It's our status quo, and it's our job to keep it from becoming yours. Goodnight, Patti."

"Goodnight, Chase. If you don't mind, I think I'll sit here for a while. I'm still on West Coast time."

"Mi casa es tu casa."

Surprisingly, sleep took me quickly, and morning came as if only an instant had passed. Breakfast could wait, but Skipper's briefing could not.

With everyone in their places, our analyst glared from behind her glasses. "It's bad."

From the expressions on the faces around the table, it was obvious I wasn't the only one who felt the surge of ice through the room.

Skipper said, "It's the Los Toros cartel."

The ice became daggers of raging fire, and for the first time in my life, I felt the scalding sting of fear inside my chest.

Skipper's tone became the voice of someone I'd never heard when she asked, "Does anyone *not* know who and what the Los Toros cartel is?"

I cleared my throat. "I thought they were the enforcement arm of the Gulf Cartel."

Skipper brought up a color-coded map of Mexico, Texas, Arizona, and Southern California. "Los Toros was formed by a group of thirty-one Mexican Army special forces commandos who went to work for Cártel del Golfo—or the Gulf Cartel—as enforcers until they broke off earlier this year and formed their own syndicate because their tactics were too extreme for Cártel del Golfo. They're literally the worst of the worst. Nothing is out of bounds for them. Anything from beheadings to dismemberment of living victims is routine for these guys. They aren't human."

Singer asked, "How do you know it's Los Toros?"

Skipper tapped her pen on the stack of files we brought from Spencer Baldwin's office. "It's all in there. He's had contact with the man who is believed to be second-in-command—a former Mexican Army captain named Miguel Otero. Otero is particularly fond of his bloodstained machete. He likes to remove fingers, toes, ears, and small pieces of flesh while keeping his victims alive and conscious as long as possible."

Singer relented. "Just because Baldwin had contact with Otero and researched the group doesn't mean Los Toros has him."

Skipper said, "You remember my analyst friend in San Francisco? He mirrored Robert Wells's hard drive at the *Sacramento Bee* before the FBI seized the computer."

She typed a few keystrokes, and the map on the overhead monitor was replaced by a picture of a man hanging upside down from a chain with a camera lens shoved inside his mouth.

She said, "In case you don't recognize him, that is Spencer Baldwin, and the photograph was an attachment to an email Wells received from Miguel Otero yesterday afternoon."

"Is he alive?" Hunter asked.

Skipper said, "My friend believes he was still alive when the picture was taken. Look at the muscles in his arms. They appear to be slightly flexed. If he were already dead, it's likely those muscles, as well as the rest of his body, would be limp. Also, take a look at his eyes. The resolution isn't good enough to zoom in too close, but it looks like the pupils are slightly different sizes. That's another indication of brain activity. It's not possible to know if he's still alive, but when this picture was taken, I believe he was."

I leaned back in my chair and shivered.

Clark eyed me with a look I'd never seen from him. "Chase, we're not committed yet."

I groaned. "Walk downstairs, look into Patricia Baldwin's eyes, and tell her we're not committed yet."

For the first time, I saw the age in Clark's eyes as he gave the slightest indication of a somber nod.

I said, "Gentlemen, I'm going to Mexico to bring some Americans home. As always, there are no orders, and every mission is volunteer."

Without exception, every man stood in silent solidarity with the warrior inside each of them clawing at the door of the cage, hungry for the fight.

Chapter 14
The Last One

Seeing the collection of the bravest, most loyal men I would ever know standing in front of me, daring the most brutal drug cartel on Earth to step into the ring with us, was a moment I'll never forget. I love every one of them as if they were my own blood, but I couldn't—or wouldn't—take them all into the fight. If Tony or Hunter never came home from the mission, it would destroy a part of me no prosthetic could replace.

I savored the moment and said, "Have a seat, gentlemen. We have some decisions to make." Everyone sat, and I said, "First, do we tell Patti what we know, and do we show her that picture?"

A chorus of "No" resounded, and as badly as I wanted to be fully honest with her, I had to agree that no benefit would come from her seeing that image.

I said, "Let's keep the picture to ourselves, but what about letting her know Los Toros has him?"

Groans and grumbles came from the team, and Singer said, "What good is served by telling her?"

"I don't know," I admitted. "I can't explain it, but I feel a sense of obligation to her. I believe we—meaning I—should tell her we know who has her brother, but there's no reason to tell her it's Los Toros."

Shrugs came, and the consensus was reached that I'd tell her part of what we knew.

"Next," I continued. "We have to talk about personnel. This thing is going to get filthy, and there's no way around it. Los Toros deals in two commodities—narcotics and extreme violence. We are going to fight, and there will be bloodshed from both sides. We have to face that reality up front."

Singer said, "We live in that reality every day of our lives, Chase. We're prepared to do what has to be done. American lives are at stake, and it's obvious that nobody else is going to get them back. It's up to us, and I think I speak for everyone when I say we're ready, in spite of the danger."

Heads nodded, and mutual agreement rose from around the table.

I said, "I'm not going to lie. I'm nervous. I'm going to be a father in a few months, and the thought of that baby being born into a world without me terrifies me."

Singer leaned forward and spoke barely above a whisper. "Then don't go, Chase. We'll go without you. You say it before every mission. Everything we do is volunteer. There's no requirement for any of us to go on any mission we don't feel comfortable doing. The same is true for you."

"I can't do that. I can't let you go without me. I made a commitment to Patti, and I'm going to live up to that commitment. If I'm nothing else, I'm a man of my word. I'm going, but we need to talk about who's not."

Hunter slapped the table. "I know I said I'd go down with one good body blow, but this is too important for me to stay on the bench. I'm going."

Clark said, "I know you're thinking about leaving me behind, but I'm with Hunter. This thing is too big to sit out. Besides, you're going to need all the help you can get when we put boots on the ground."

Before I could protest, Tony said, "I'm up. If you guys think I won't be a handicap when the fighting starts, I want in."

Skipper squeezed her eyelids closed and grimaced, but she didn't argue. She didn't have to.

I said, "As we've discussed on many occasions, this is an all-volunteer force, but it is not a democracy. I have, and will continue to consult with you, sometimes as a team and sometimes individually, about how you think we should proceed. Ultimately, I'm responsible for our results, be they victorious or disastrous. With that in mind, here's the most reasonable way to proceed."

I paused long enough to have a drink of my quickly cooling coffee. "Getting two tons of firearms, explosives, knives, and ammunition into Mexico isn't particularly difficult when the right palms are greased. This is not how we will get it done. I don't want any record, official or otherwise, of us ever having been there. The only way I believe that can be done is aboard the *Lori Danielle*. Does anyone disagree or have a better option?"

Heads shook, so I said, "Get Captain Sprayberry on the phone."

Skipper checked her watch, and I knocked on the table. "I don't care what time it is on the West Coast."

She didn't delay another second. The phone line was on speaker, and it was ringing.

After a few seconds, Barry answered. "Yeah, what is it?"

"Captain Sprayberry. It's Chase. We need the ship."

"Huh?"

"I'm sorry to have disturbed you, but I need you to wake up, and we need the ship."

He said, "Sorry. We were conducting sea trials until zero-three-hundred this morning. We'll complete the trials and additional repairs in another couple of weeks. When do you need the ship?"

"Tonight," I said.

The line was silent for a moment, and then he said, "Tropical, subtropical, or arctic?"

"No ice this time, I promise. We're going to Cabo San Lucas."

"I don't have my full crew. Many of them have been on leave during the dry-dock and sea trials. It'll take twenty-four hours to recall them."

"Very well," I said. "Make it happen. We'll have three pallets of gear and ten personnel. Can you source three or four DPVs?"

The sleep was gone from his voice. "Sure. There are plenty of desert patrol vehicles floating around out here. I'll nab up as many as I can find. Those things are disposable."

"You're the best. I'm sorry I woke you, but duty calls."

"Such is life. Oh, before you go, I may have a line on at least a couple of those SEALs who overheard the kidnapping story. Do you want me to set you up with them?"

"Absolutely," I said. "I'll touch base when we head west. It could be as early as tonight, but no later than midday tomorrow."

He said, "We'll be dockside in San Diego awaiting your arrival. I'll have the inoperable equipment list for you by then as well."

"Thanks, Barry. We'll see you soon."

Skipper cut the line and cocked her head. "Ten personnel?"

I said, "It'll make sense soon. Now, where were we?"

Clark said, "You were about to tell Tony and Hunter they couldn't go."

"Thanks for the reminder, but you're wrong. Everybody's going. Tony, you're in the CIC with Skipper, and you're running the show when she's asleep. You good with that?"

"Absolutely," he said.

I turned to Hunter, and he threw up both hands as if he were bearing down on me with a rifle.

I said, "Cute, but probably not accurate. You're going as a gear manager and armorer. As much as I hate to say this out loud, you're an alternate in case one of us goes down. We can't afford to be a man down when we're facing an enemy like Los Toros."

His single nod spoke volumes, and I moved on to Clark. "And for you, old man, you're our link to the Board, should that become necessary, and you'll back up Hunter as an alternate gunner. I hope we don't need you on a trigger, but if we do, there's nobody I'd rather have."

"Whatever you need."

I said, "That leaves two more people. The first is Patti Baldwin. I don't feel good about leaving her here without a babysitter. How do you feel about putting her on the ship with us?"

The looks on the faces of my team said they didn't love that idea, but I wasn't asking for a vote. I merely wanted to hear their thoughts.

Hunter said, "How about bringing in Clay and a few of his guys to keep an eye on her?"

"That's not a bad idea, but I'll make that call after we discuss the final member of the entourage." I couldn't believe that name was about to come out of my mouth, but I couldn't find a better option. "This is going to get bloody, and it's going to get that way fast. We have to be ready, willing, and capable of taking this thing so deep into Hell where even Los Toros fears to tread."

It hit Clark and Skipper simultaneously, but their reactions were 180 degrees apart. Skipper's face screamed, *No! Don't do it, Chase!* But Clark knew, without a doubt, I was dead right.

I said, "I'm calling Anya."

The air drained out of the room for everyone except Kodiak. He said, "Is that the Russian chick?"

"It is," Hunter growled.

Kodiak said, "Yes, sir! This thing just keeps getting better by the minute."

Skipper rolled her eyes and pointed her pen straight at me. "If you do this, you're telling Penny."

I stood. "Any questions?" No one spoke up, so I said, "Get some breakfast, double-check the loadout, and supplement as necessary. Skipper, I need you to find every fact that's known about Los Toros and memorize it. You're briefing me on the plane."

"Wait. I'm going?"

"Yes, I said everybody. And you're part of everybody."

The op center emptied of everyone except Skipper and me.

I said, "Tell me about that look when you realized I was talking about Anya."

She stuck her pen into her ponytail and spun to face me. "It's the worst idea you've ever had as far as your life goes. You've got a pregnant wife who believes you're retiring, and you're about to tell her you're taking your ex-girlfriend to Mexico for a little vacation."

"That's not entirely accurate."

"It will be precisely accurate to Penny. Trust me. I'm the only one on this team with estrogen, so I'm the subject matter expert."

"I agree it isn't ideal, but—"

She said, "You don't have to justify it. I understand, and I agree there's nobody on Earth better for this mission than Anya, but that ain't how Penny's gonna see it. You better hope and pray that Anya's grown a big black wart on her nose, gone brunette, and gained fifty pounds 'cause that perfect little body your wife had six months ago doesn't fit in the same size pants anymore."

"Penny will always be gorgeous to me."

Skipper cackled. "You're in for quite a ride, hotshot. Go ahead. Call her and wake her up with this news. You'll see."

I took the stairs down to my bedroom and perched on one of the chairs by the fireplace.

Penny answered as if she'd been holding the phone in her hand. "Good morning."

"Hey, sweetheart. You're up early."

She said, "Yeah, I've been up for an hour or so. I'm working on a major rewrite. Is something wrong? You never call this early."

"Not wrong, but there are a couple of things we need to discuss."

"This doesn't sound good."

I took a deep breath and silently prayed I wouldn't screw this up. "Two things. First, we know who has the American hostages. At least one of them."

"That's great. Does that mean you can get them back?"

"It's a start, but the cartel who's holding them is particularly nasty, and they don't play by the same rules we do."

"That sounds dangerous. Are you sure you shouldn't let somebody else handle this one?"

"There is nobody else. We're their best hope, and we're going. I just didn't want to go before telling you."

"This is the last one, though, right?"

I sighed. "It is, and it's a good one to go out on. There's one more thing, though."

"What is it?"

"This cartel, like I said, is particularly nasty, and they've got a real love affair with brutality. It's likely we're going to go head-to-head with them, and if that's going to happen, I want to have someone with us who can take things like that further than we're willing to go."

I was dreading saying her name, but Penny let me off the hook. She said, "You're taking Anya, aren't you?"

"I think she's the best choice, but I wasn't going to call her before you and I had this talk."

"I appreciate that. Go ahead and call her. Get one good long last look at her, and remember which one of us is carrying your baby."

"Do you want to come?" The words fell out of my mouth before I realized I was thinking them.

"What? You've never asked me to come on a mission with you. Do you really think it's a good idea for me to be in the middle of a fight like you're describing with a baby in my belly?"

"I didn't mean you'd be in the fight. We're taking the *Lori Danielle*. You can stay on the ship. It's not luxurious by any means, but at least you'd be there instead of worrying about me and Anya."

"Oh, I'm not worried about her."

"You're not?"

"No, you're smart enough to know she's not worth losing half your stuff for, and child support is killer for a guy who makes the kind of money you make."

"I wish I thought you were kidding."

"You know I'm not. Call me before you leave. And Chase, this is the last one. I want to hear you say it."

"This is the last one."

Chapter 15

I Need You

"How'd she take it?" Skipper asked the second I walked into the op center.

"She threatened to take half my stuff and get a huge judgment for child support."

"That's about what I expected," she said. "Is Anya still coming?"

"I don't know, but if you'll get her on the phone, I'll ask her."

She rolled her eyes. "I'm not sure I want to be any part of this, but I'll do it just so I can tell Penny I played referee."

The speakerphone came to life, and that unforgettable Russian accent filled the room. "*Da*, is Anya."

"Anya, it's Chase. How are you?"

"Chase? Really? Is not true. You would not call me."

"Yes, it's really me, and I'm really calling. I need you."

The comment drew Skipper's ire, and she glared at me as if burning holes through my skull.

Anya had a different reaction. She said, "Chasechka, I knew one day you would come to senses and realize you needed me. I need also you. Tell to me where you are, and I will come to you now."

"No, wait. That's not what I meant."

"Of course is what you meant," Anya said. "This is what came from your mouth, and is now perfect day. Tell to me where you are so I can come now."

"No, Anya. Listen to me. I need you for a mission. We have a mission in Mexico against Los Toros. They're a—"

"Drug cartel. Yes, of course I know this, but why are you having with them fight?"

"They have at least one American hostage and probably more. We're going to get them back."

"This is strange mission. This is not mission from Board, no?"

"No, not exactly. We're sort of freelancing on this one."

"And you need me to come with you because I am only person you know who is more dangerous than Los Toros, yes?"

"Something like that. Where are you?"

"Where I am is not important. I will come to you, but first, you must tell to me where."

I said, "We're flying from Georgia to San Diego, either tonight or tomorrow morning. We'll work from the *Lori Danielle*. She just came out of dry dock."

"What is this *Lori Danielle*?"

"It's our ship."

"You have a ship? Chasechka, you are becoming most powerful man in all of world, yes?"

I laughed. "No, not hardly. It's just a ship. Are you coming or not?"

"This is ridiculous question. Of course I am coming. You must only tell to me where."

"How long will it take you to get to San Diego?"

"Less than twelve hours. This is fast enough, yes? If no, you can pick me up."

"Make it twenty-four hours, and I'll see you in California."

She said, "I am so excited. Is wonderful to be back on team that is yours. This means for short time, maybe I am also yours again."

"Let's not go that far," I said, but she had already ended the call.

Skipper said, "I'd like to go on the record as being the first to say that bringing Anya in is the best tactical decision and worst personal decision you've ever made all rolled into one."

"Think about what's in my head right now. I'm having a baby that I never thought was possible, and I'm facing one of the deadliest enemies I'll likely ever fight. Do you think there's room in there for me to think about what might have been with Anya? The answer is no. I've got enough on my plate without being tempted to stray. You're worrying about something that's never going to happen."

She sighed. "Whatever you say."

I asked, "Is Patti up yet?"

Skipper brought up the interior cameras and pointed toward the square with the kitchen in the frame. "She's having breakfast with the rest of the guys. If you're going down there, would you tell Tony to bring something up for me? I'm starving."

"Sure, but first, I want your opinion on whether to take Patti on the ship with us."

"I don't know. I could argue it both ways. What do you think?"

"I feel the same. Bringing in Clay and a few of his guys is a good idea, but if we liberate Spencer, I'm sure Patti would love to be there when we put him on the ship."

Skipper said, "How do you think she'd feel about being there if you recover his *body* and bring him aboard?"

"I don't know."

Skipper clicked her tongue against her teeth. "Why not talk to her and see what she wants? It's not like she's incapable of making a decision."

"That may be the best option. I'll send up some breakfast. Do you want anything in particular?"

"Whatever," she said. "I need some calories and coffee."

I made my way to the kitchen and built a plate for my favorite analyst. As I turned to head back up to the op center, Tony said, "Is that for Skipper?"

I nodded, and he jumped up from the table. "I'll take it."

"No, that's okay. Enjoy your breakfast. I'll be right back."

"Are you sure?"

"Sit down. I've got this."

Skipper never looked up when I slid the plate onto the console beside her. She simply said, "Thank you, sweetie. Love you."

I tried not to chuckle. "Love you, too, snookums."

She shot a look over her shoulder and laughed out loud. "I thought you were Tony, and if you ever call me snookums again, I'll have Anya gut you like pig."

Back in the kitchen, I said, "I spoke with Anya, and she's in. She'll meet us in San Diego tomorrow."

Patti looked up from her breakfast. "Who's Anya?"

Hunter swallowed quickly and said, "She's another operator. We bring her in sometimes. She's got a skill set we need from time to time."

"Then why isn't she on the team?" Patti asked.

Hunter had done all he was willing to do to protect me, so he looked up and asked, "Yeah, Chase? Why isn't she on the team?"

"She used to be," I said. "But she got an opportunity with another team and moved on."

Hunter raised a finger. "Do you have a pen? I need to write down that answer so I won't forget next time."

I held up a biscuit. "I'm going to feed you this through your ear if you don't behave."

I ate with the team, and it would've been easy to believe it was just another day at Bonaventure with the gang all together, but I could see a look behind their eyes—a look that gave even seasoned warriors pause. The enemy on the horizon was no common army. They were ruthless, fearless, and bloodthirsty.

When every plate was empty, I said, "Patti, let's have a talk."

She rose from the table and placed her plate beside the sink. "Sure, let me get another cup of coffee, and we can go to that gazebo if you want."

"I'll meet you there."

Minutes later, she stepped onto the deck of the gazebo and stood by the cannon, taking in the scenery of the North River and miles of endless marshland. "It really is beautiful here."

"Yes, it is," I said. "I'm glad you like it here. That's one of the things I want to talk about."

She took the same seat she'd occupied the night before and sipped her coffee. "I noticed something different about the guys this morning. I can't put my finger on it, but something's going on."

I said, "You're right. We're getting into our mission mindset, and that affects everyone differently. Most of us get quieter. It makes Kodiak laugh, and as for me, I get laser-focused to the point I ignore everything around me except the mission. That's probably what you're picking up on."

"Maybe, but it felt more like the guys weren't comfortable talking to me. Is it my relationship with Spencer that has them standing off?"

"No, not at all. We've learned a great many things about what's happening in Mexico overnight, and that knowledge has us planning for what's to come. That's all."

She grimaced. "I don't know about that. It felt more personal to me."

"The truth is, we know who has Spencer."

Her eyes lit up. "Is he okay? Where is he? When are you going to get him?"

"It's not that simple. Just because we know who has him doesn't mean we know where they are. There's still a lot of work to be done. We'll either leave this afternoon, or tomorrow morning, depending on what else we learn and how well the preparations go today."

"Is Spencer okay?"

I couldn't get the picture of him hanging upside down with the camera lens in his mouth out of my head. "I'm sorry, but we don't know his condition. We just picked up some intel from a few sources that indicated he was with one of the cartels from his files. That's good news. It gives us an excellent starting point."

"I didn't mean to sound so demanding. I'm just . . ."

"It's okay," I said. "Your anxiety is perfectly understandable. We need to talk about another issue, though."

"Okay, what is it?"

"We'll run the operation from a ship that's docked in San Diego. We'll park that ship off the coast of Cabo and use it as a base of operations. The ship is a working vessel, not a cruise ship. There are no luxuries aboard, but there are cabins and an excellent galley."

"Why are you telling me all of this?"

"I'm telling you because we've changed our mission parameters. We're taking the full team, including Skipper, and maybe even Dr. Mankiller."

"Who will be here with me?"

I said, "We have a couple of options. Number one is to call in another team to stay with you here at Bonaventure while we run the mission in Mexico. The other option is for you to come with us. You'd be safe aboard the ship, but there isn't much to do. You'd be far more comfortable here."

"I want to go. I want to be there when you find Spencer."

It was my turn to burn a little time with a sip of coffee. "There's something you have to consider if you decide to go with us. As we discussed last night, there is the ever-present possibility that we may find Spencer dead or not at all. If you come with us, you have to prepare yourself for both of those possibilities."

"What do you mean, you might not find him at all? Would you just stop searching at some point?"

I hadn't considered that I'd create such a pitfall simply by explaining the possibilities, but it was done, and I had to climb out. "We don't quit easily, but there has to be a limit. We can't spend the rest of our lives searching the Mexican desert. I can't put a hard time limit on the search, but it can't go on indefinitely."

She stared into her coffee cup. "When do I have to decide?"

"Before we leave. And the sooner, the better, especially if you want to stay here. It'll take some time to get the other team headed this way."

She nodded and turned quiet. "Is there such a thing as proof of life?"

"What?"

"You know, on television and in movies when someone is kidnapped, the negotiator or the people who are going to pay the ransom demand proof of life, like a picture of the victim with a current newspaper or hearing his voice."

I said, "What we do is nothing like the movies. It's not like we can get the cartel on the phone and demand to hear Spencer's voice. It just doesn't work that way."

She seemed to drift off into a world of her own, and I said, "I've got a lot of work to do before we leave, so I'm going give you some time to think about whether you want to stay or go."

She didn't look at me, but instead just nodded and gazed into the marsh.

I stood and headed for the house. To my surprise, Skipper was standing at the back door, waving for me to hurry.

I trotted up the stairs and through the door. "What's up?"

"Robert Wells's body has disappeared."

Chapter 16
Wheels Up, Feet Wet

I suppose it was my instinctual need to protect that spun me in my tracks and sent me running back to the gazebo. "Patti, you're coming with us. Let's move inside."

She slowly rose from her chair. "What's going on?"

I moved beside her and took her by the arm. "We'll talk about it inside."

Gradually increasing our pace as we moved toward the house, I let my right hand drift toward the pistol concealed beneath my shirt. By the time we reached the steps, we were moving slightly faster than a brisk walk, and Patti took the stairs two at a time. My sense of urgency was clearly contagious.

Inside the kitchen door, I handed Patti off to Skipper. "Take her to the op center. I'll be up in two minutes."

Skipper motioned toward the elevator, and I slipped back outside. The armory doors were wide open, and the team was hard at work inside.

I skipped down the stairs and said, "Listen up. We've got a situation. Robert Wells, the editor in chief at the *Sacramento Bee*, is missing."

Clark perked up. "Missing? I thought he was dead."

"Sorry. He is dead. His body is missing from the federal morgue at the Residential Reentry Management facility."

Clark laid the rifle he'd been holding back into the rack. "Is Patti inside?"

"That was my first move," I said. "Should we brief the Board?"

Clark said, "Double-time, guys. We can inspect and repair anything we find on the flight. I'll be back."

He and I sprinted from the armory to the op center and pulled the door closed behind us. Skipper was working furiously at her computer when we slid onto our chairs.

Clark said, "What aren't we seeing?"

Skipper didn't slow her pace on the keys and never looked up, but she said, "I'm working on it. Something big is going on, and I'm not putting it together."

"I feel exactly the same," I said as I caught a glimpse of Patti for the first time.

She was staring in wide-eyed wonder. "What is this place?"

I said, "It's the brain of our operation and the safest place in the house."

She asked, "What happened?"

"Robert Wells's body disappeared from the morgue. That means something is going on well above our heads, and we need to know what it is."

"Can I help?" she asked.

"No, just let us work. Are you still packed?"

"No, I unpacked everything last night."

I said, "Seal the house, Skipper, and activate the cameras."

Skipper reached for a second panel beside her station.

A second later, segmented squares showing every entry of the house filled a screen, and I said, "Go pack everything. The house is safe. When you're finished, just stay in your room, and I'll come get you."

Without a word, she stood and pushed through the door.

Clark leaned toward Skipper's console. "Are you getting anything?"

She groaned. "Nothing, and my friend is freaked out. He doesn't like being attached to anything this closely tied to the federal government."

"What makes him think this is a fed thing?" Clark asked.

Skipper shot a look across her shoulder. "Come on, Clark. Dead bodies don't get up and walk out of a federal morgue. This is a cover-up, and we need to know what they're afraid of."

He leaned back in his chair and studied the ceiling.

I watched him for a moment and asked, "Are you trying to decide if we should call the Board?"

"Yeah. If we do, we could get an official stand-down order."

I considered the ramifications. "But we could also get an official sanction for the mission."

"It's a coin toss," he said. "I don't know the best course of action."

"If my vote counts, I say we leave them out of this until we know what's really going on."

"Thanks, College Boy, but like you say, this ain't a democracy. You've got me to run interference between you and the Board, but I have to answer directly to those guys. I'm getting the feeling that no matter how this thing shakes out, there's going to be some heavy fallout."

I laid a hand on Skipper's shoulder. "Have you pulled up the recent pieces Spencer Baldwin wrote? He may have upset somebody's applecart, and that might give us a hint about who we're messing with."

She said, "I pulled them, but I haven't had time to read them yet. On the surface, everything looked benign, but I can send them to your tablet if you want."

"Do it," I said. "Maybe we'll get lucky."

She opened another screen, and two dozen articles penned by Spencer landed on my tablet. I rolled back to the table and opened the most recent article. It was about corruption at the FDA, but there was nothing in the story big enough to justify killing a newspaper editor.

There was a short piece about feuds inside the Bureau of Indian Affairs and a couple of fraud, waste, and abuse pieces in the post office, but still, nothing rose to the level of concern.

I waved my tablet. "There's nothing here. It's all small-time stuff, and whatever we're dealing with doesn't fall into that category."

Skipper growled and pounded on her keyboard.

I said, "Hey. Easy there. What's going on?"

"We need to know who else is missing. We need those SEALs."

I said, "Captain Sprayberry is setting up a face-to-face with a couple of them. That'll happen tomorrow morning, I hope."

"It can't come soon enough as far as I'm concerned. We're looking at this thing as if Spencer Baldwin is the centerpiece, but I've got a feeling this isn't about a journalist. This has to be something that started on Pennsylvania Avenue, or at least somewhere in that neighborhood."

Skipper's frustration was palpable, but I couldn't let that diminish our efficiency.

I said, "Pack it up. It's time to go wheels up and feet wet."

With everybody working together, the *Grey Ghost* was loaded almost to her maximum capacity, and I took a trip across the airport to have a chat with our resident mad scientist.

"Good morning, Dr. Mankiller."

She looked up from her workbench. "Good morning, Chase. You have to stop calling me doctor. It's just Celeste."

"Whatever you say, Doc. Are you up for a field trip?"

"Always," she said. "Where are we going?"

"I'll get to that. But first, let me tell you about the mission. There are some missing Americans who've likely been abducted by a particularly nasty drug cartel called Los Toros."

"Ooh, I've heard of them. Those guys don't mess around."

"We're planning to dance with them and get our countrymen back. I need you to pack up every gadget you have and get on the plane with us in an hour. Can you do it?"

She checked the clock above her bench. "No problem. It won't take that long. I'll be ready in thirty."

"I'll send over a truck to get you and your bag of tricks."

"So, I suspect it's Mexico."

"Oh, yeah, sorry. We're starting in Cabo San Lucas, but who knows where this will end."

"How long is the flight?" she asked.

"We'll fly to the West Coast and run the mission from the *Lori Danielle*."

She said, "Sounds good. I'll see you in half an hour."

By the time I made it back across the airport, my team had the *Ghost* loaded and the cargo door closed. I pulled into the hangar and ducked into the office to call Captain Sprayberry.

"Hey, Chase. Are you wheels up?"

I said, "Hey, Captain. We'll be airborne within an hour and headed your way. Did you have any luck getting anything lined up with the SEALs?"

"I did, but we're in a short window. I know you'll find this hard to believe, but all four of those guys came down on short-notice deployment orders. They're being sequestered tomorrow at noon. Will you be able to meet with them before then?"

"Absolutely," I said. "Set it up for six hours from right now. Can we do it aboard the ship?"

"I'll get on it, and the ship is yours. I recommend the hangar bay or CIC. Those are the two quietest spots on board."

"Sounds good. How's the crew recall going?"

"We'll be fully staffed by midnight and ready to shove off on your orders."

"Thanks, Barry. I know I'm asking you to jump through a bunch of hoops, but this one came together a lot faster than I expected."

"We're all on the same team, Chase. We knew what we were getting into when we signed up. Besides, you pay us far better than any shipping company, so you're not going to hear very many complaints on this boat."

"I appreciate that, my friend. We'll see you in a few hours. Oh, there's one more thing. Is the armory stocked?"

"It is," he said. "We didn't empty it for dry-dock since we'd still have security crews aboard."

"Great. Thanks."

Clark came through the door as I was hanging up.

"Was that the captain?"

I said, "It was, and he's got the SEALs scheduled for a face-to-face in exactly six hours."

He took a seat in front of the small desk. "I've got some news."

"This doesn't sound good."

"I just got off the phone with another handler, and we're going to have some company."

"What? I'm not okay with that."

He said, "Take it easy. They're not going to Mexico, but the missing bodies caught more attention than I expected."

"Bodies?"

"Yeah, they suspect the secretary is dead, too. There's been no activity on her cell phone or credit and debit cards since Wells's death."

"What does this mean for us?" I asked.

"It means we can focus entirely on Mexico and forget about the mess in California."

"Come on," I said. "You know as well as I do that the two are inextricably linked. It might as well be the same event."

"I don't know what *inextricably* means, but I came in here to talk to you about how much information we should provide for the other team."

I thought about his question for a long moment. "You mean the picture, don't you?"

"Exactly."

I said, "The FBI has Wells's computer, so there's no chance of them giving that up. If the other team's analyst has a link to Skipper's friend in San Fran, they may get the hard drive data from him, unless we head that off."

"Let's get her in here."

I dialed Skipper's number, and she said, "Yes?"

"Clark and I are in the hangar office. Can you come in here, please?"

"On my way."

She came through the door a minute later. "What's up?"

Clark briefed her on the other team's newly assigned tasking of investigating the missing bodies in Sacramento and then asked, "Is your friend, the analyst, assigned to one of our teams?"

She bowed her head. "No, he's not, but he's also gone black."

"Gone black?" I asked.

"Yeah, I can't get him to answer his phone, texts, emails, nothing. It's not like him."

"Do you know where he lives?" Clark asked.

"Yes. I've been to his place a couple of times. It's nothing like our op center, but he's got a pretty good setup."

"What about security?" I asked.

"He doesn't have any physical security other than alarms and cameras, but all of his data is locked down like Fort Knox. I'm not saying it's impossible to hack, but I don't know anybody who could pull it off."

"How about communications with you?" Clark asked.

"There's a call history, but his email is secure."

I turned to Clark. "Do we have anybody in the Bay Area who can do a wellness check on him?"

Skipper covered her mouth. "You don't think somebody got to him, do you?"

I said, "I'm not saying that. You said he was a little freaked out about dealing with something tied to the feds. It's likely he's just hiding and not taking your calls, but I think we should at least have someone knock on his door."

"Oh, my gosh. I can't believe I didn't think of that. Do we have anybody out there?"

Clark said, "I don't know anyone. Maybe we should go en route to San Diego."

I said, "That's a no go. We have to be at the meeting with the SEALs in five and a half hours."

Skipper said, "We can drop you and the rest of the team in San Diego, and I can go to Frisco. If he's there, he'll answer the door if it's me."

I eyed Clark, and he said, "Fine, but you're not going alone. We'll send Hunter and Mongo with you."

"I'm good with that," she said.

I stood. "I'm going to send a truck over for Celeste and her gear. We'll be ready to go as soon as they're back."

"You're bringing her?" Skipper asked.

"Yes, I thought it would be better to have her with us."

Clark slid his chair against the wall and pushed himself up. "This thing is getting bigger by the minute. I'm afraid it's going to become like beating our heads against a dead horse."

Chapter 17
Penalty Box

I spent the next three hours of my life sitting only inches from Skipper and absorbing every morsel of information she identified as potentially valuable on the Los Toros drug cartel.

"They're a terrorist organization," she said. "The narcotics are simply the source of income to fund their insanity when it comes to terrorizing rival cartels, as well as anybody they choose for any reason. There seems to be no logic behind their barbaric rampages. They kill indiscriminately, slaughter whole families, and seem to commit torture simply for their own amusement."

After our marathon session, my head was spinning, and I knew far more than anyone should know about one of the most vile collections of subhumans on the planet. My desire morphed from recovering Spencer Baldwin and any other Americans in their custody to wiping the entire Los Toros network off the face of the Earth.

Disco emerged from the cockpit and took a knee by my seat. "We'll be on the ground in half an hour, and Captain Sprayberry dispatched two trucks to haul gear and people. Is there anything else you need when we land?"

"That should do it," I said. "We'll refuel while they're offloading the gear, if we can. That way, you can make the quick turn for San Francisco."

He said, "That's what I was thinking. Are we shoving off tonight?"

"I'll have to talk with Captain Sprayberry, but I'd like to be underway as soon as possible."

"How long will the San Fran stop take?"

"There's no way to know. It depends on what Skipper finds when she gets up there. It could be a pop-and-go, or it could drag on if she sees something she doesn't like."

He said, "All right. We'll keep it flexible."

We touched down and taxied to the cargo ramp, where two flatbed trucks and a massive forklift waited for us to roll to a stop. Almost before the engines spun down, the fuel truck was alongside. As we headed down the airstairs, a crew van pulled up with Ronda No-H at the wheel. We tossed personal gear onto the van, and I grabbed Skipper.

"Don't get bogged down up there. He's either there or he isn't. It's not a search and rescue mission. It's a door knock and go. I know he's your friend, but we don't have time to commit to a search."

She said, "I know. I'm just worried about him. He's really shy, and he never really goes anywhere. I'm feeling pretty bad about dragging him into this thing."

"You didn't drag him. You asked, and he said yes. It's that simple. Do you know if he had a bug-out plan?"

"If he did, he never told me," she said.

"Do you know anything about the team or teams he works with?"

"I don't. I would never tell him about you, so I never ask him about his operators."

I gave her a hug. "Be careful. Don't get sucked in. And get back down here as soon as possible. We can't do this without you. Are you okay with Disco, Mongo, and Hunter?"

She stepped back. "Yeah, that's a pretty hard-hitting team if it gets weird up there, so I'm happy. See you soon."

I grabbed Hunter's collar. "Don't let her get sucked into anything up there. Knock on the door. If he's not there, get back on the plane. We don't have time to screw around."

"Got it," he said. "I'll keep the ball rolling."

By the time I climbed onto the front seat of the crew van, the pallets were strapped down and tarped on the flatbeds, and the *Grey Ghost* was full of jet fuel.

Ronda watched the door of the airplane close, and she pointed out the window. "Uh, what's going on here? Where's my man going?"

"Don't worry," I said. "He's just making a short hop to San Fran, and he'll be back."

"He better be," she said. "You yanked him away too fast last time he was here, and that wasn't cool."

I laughed. "I'll try to be cooler this time."

We arrived at the dock, and the *Lori Danielle*'s deck cranes were deployed and ready to hoist our gear aboard. If everything on the mission fell into place the way our arrival in San Diego had, we'd be home in time for dinner.

Captain Sprayberry met us at the top of the gangway. "Welcome aboard. But aren't you short a few crewmen?"

I shook his hand. "We're down four, but they'll be back in a couple of hours. They had an errand to run up in the Bay Area."

"An errand, huh? That sounds ridiculous. Your SEALs are up in the hangar bay. Is that good with you?"

"It is," I said. "How many are there?"

"Three."

"Let's split them up," I said. "I'll take one in the hangar bay. Send one with Singer to the CIC. And can we borrow a cabin for the third?"

Barry said, "Sure. You can use my cabin."

"Perfect. Kodiak will take the third man. Just let them talk. Don't ask a lot of questions. When you're done, we'll send them back to Coronado, and we'll compile the data and see how close their stories match up." I motioned for Patti to come up. "Captain Sprayberry, this is Patricia Baldwin. She's our guest."

The two shook hands, and I asked, "Could you have the quartermaster get Patti settled in?"

He said, "Of course. It's nice to meet you, Ms. Baldwin. Come with me, and we'll get you set up."

Kodiak, Singer, and I double-timed up to the hangar bay and introduced ourselves to the three SEALs. Naval special warfare operators in the movies are always 6'5" with perfect physiques and surfer tans, but no stereotype could be further from the truth. The SEALs were in great shape, but they looked more like high school track stars than pro wrestlers.

I said, "You guys know all about interrogations, so I don't want you to think that's what this is. We just want to hear your stories. We may ask a few questions, but not many. All of us have TS clearances, and after today, we've never heard of you guys, we've never met you, and we've certainly never had a conversation with you. Are you good with that?"

The frogmen nodded, and we broke into pairs and headed off to hear their stories.

I pulled up a chair and said, "It's Griff, right?"

He took his seat. "Yes, sir."

"Don't call me sir. I'm just a dude. Call me Chase. I don't represent any branch of the U.S. government. Think of me as what you probably want to become when you leave the Navy. We're taking applications, by the way."

Griff chuckled. "I figured you guys were something high-speed when we saw this boat. Is it yours?"

"It's a team asset, and she's got a few surprises tucked under her skirt. If you'd like a tour when we finish, I think we can make that happen."

"That'd be cool, sir. Thank you."

I held up a hand. "Seriously, enough with the sir. I'm just Chase. How long have you been with the teams?"

"I graduated BUD/S six years ago, sir . . . I mean, Chase. I've got a dozen deployments under my belt and a few scars to show for it."

"Thank you for what you do. Men like you are the reason we get to live in the greatest country on Earth."

He nodded. "From what I see, it looks like maybe we're doing the same kind of work but in different tax brackets."

It was my turn to nod. "Like I said, you'll get out of the Navy at some point. Look us up when you do."

"I'll do that. What do you want to know?"

I relaxed my posture and tried to appear conversational. "I'd like to know what you heard in Cabo about missing Americans."

He started talking, and the ire in his face grew with every mention of American hostages. Finally, he said, "But that's not the worst part, sir."

I ignored the *sir* and kept listening.

"When we reported it to our command, at first, they were interested, but a day later, it got weird. They shut us down hard. Now, they're throwing us in the penalty box."

"What does that mean?"

"You know, it's like punishment for something you did wrong. We're getting sequestered tomorrow at noon for a deployment nobody knows anything about. I think they don't want us telling the story about what we heard down there, so they're sending us someplace terrible to get our minds right. If they find out we talked to you, God only knows what'll happen to us."

I owed him enough respect to be honest with him, so I said, "It's like this, Griff. We're going down there, and we're going to find those Americans and bring them home. We're not getting paid, and God forbid we end up on the news. We do what we do in the shadows, and nobody needs to know anything about us."

"That sounds familiar, sir. And if you don't mind me saying so, I wish I could go with you. I don't know what all of this is about, but I've smelled enough stink in my career to know when it's regular and when it's hard-core. Somebody who's got some power wants this stink to go away, and they're doing their best to cover it up so nobody will ever dig it out."

"Is there anything else you think I should know?"

He stared at the ceiling of the hangar bay. "I can't think of anything, but if you were serious about looking you up when I get out, I'd appreciate a phone number or something."

"Have you got a pen?"

He smiled. "I don't need a pen, sir. Just give me the number. I won't forget it."

"One condition . . ."

He looked up. "Name it."

"You don't tell anybody what you saw and heard today."

He huffed. "Not a chance. I'm in enough trouble as it is. There's no chance of me running my mouth about this."

I gave him my number and the number to the op center. "When do you get out?"

He shrugged. "With this debacle, I'm thinking sooner rather than later."

"Still want to see the boat?"

He grinned. "Yes, sir."

I rounded up the other two SEALs and gave the trio a behind-the-scenes tour of the *Lori Danielle*. "On the surface, she's a nice, polite research vessel, but if you piss her off, she's got a nasty bite."

Adequately impressed, the three warriors thanked us for listening, and Griff said, "It's too bad we never met and you guys don't exist. I think we could've had some fun together. You know, reading poetry and singing folk songs around a campfire."

"That's us," I said. "We're real kumbaya kind of guys."

Griff stepped toward me, shook my hand, and looked into my eyes with a steely stare. "If you find them, sir, stick a knife in one of them for me."

"You got it."

Singer, Kodiak, and I huddled in the CIC and discussed what we learned. The three SEALs were either telling the truth, or they'd rehearsed their story until all three agreed down to the letter.

"What's your take?" I asked Kodiak.

He played with the hair of his beard. "I believe 'em, and if Los Toros is as serious as they say, I can't imagine anybody else taking hostages in the area. The way I figure it, that's Toro turf, and nobody's gonna mess around on that piece of dirt."

Singer said, "I agree. Everything about their story rings true, and I think Kodiak hit the nail on the head. That city belongs to the Toros."

I leaned toward my teammates. "Now's your last chance to back out. Once we toss off the lines, we're committed to the fight."

Kodiak pulled his knife. "Point me toward those lines, and I'll turn them into confetti."

Singer shot a thumb toward Kodiak and grinned. "I'm really starting to like the new guy."

Kodiak sheathed his blade. "And I'm loving being the new guy."

Chapter 18
Burning Down the House

I found Patti on the aft deck, leaning against the stern rail and peering up at the superstructure of the ship.

I said, "Did you meet the quartermaster?"

"You mean Christine. Yes, she's fantastic. She gave me a really nice room, and she took me on a tour of the ship. This thing is amazing. The more I learn about you, the more curious I am. I've never met anyone who owns a ship before."

"I don't really own it," I said. "I'm just responsible for what we do with it."

"According to Christine, you're the man."

"I don't know about that. We're a team, and when we have a job to do, we work together better than any team I've ever seen. I'm a fortunate guy who's been blessed far beyond what I deserve."

"What do you research?"

"What?"

Patti pointed toward the deck. "Christine said this is a research vessel. What do you research?"

"Oh, that. I don't really get involved with that portion of the operation. We lease the ship out to organizations conducting oceanographic and marine biological research. We use the vessel for other things."

"Like finding Spencer," she said.

"Exactly like that. And that's something I need to talk with you about. You're going to see, hear, and experience things that you can never talk about. Once the actual mission begins, the team and I will do some training and preparation that will look and sound like nothing you've ever seen. For our safety, it's important that you never discuss any of what you see and hear with anyone outside the ship. Can you do that?"

She stared into the sky. "I'm a writer. What if I fictionalize what I see and hear?"

I considered her question. "I need you to sign an NDA. Do you know what that is?"

She nodded. "Sure, a nondisclosure agreement. But can we include a clause about putting what I see in fiction?"

"I think we can work that out, but we'll need editorial review prior to publication."

She said, "I can agree to that."

I stilled myself for my next comment and struggled with whether to begin the statement with *if* or *when*. I finally settled and said, "If we find Spencer alive and repatriate him, we'll insist on an NDA from him as well."

"I can't speak for him," she said, "but I would think he'd be so grateful that he'd agree to most anything."

"Your NDA will include talking to him about what you saw and heard. Can you live with that?"

She sighed. "I don't know. I can try, but when he asks questions, and he will ask thousands of them, I can't lie to him."

"We can deal with that when it comes up. For now, just know that you've been given access no one else has ever had, and if you share details about us, our tactics, or capabilities, you'll put our lives and the success of future missions in jeopardy. That's why we must insist on confidentiality."

"I understand," she said. "It's all so fascinating, though."

"I'm sure it appears fascinating, but our lives are pretty dull when we're not working. We're just regular people."

She closed her eyes. "No, Chase. Regular people don't risk their lives to save someone they've never met. There's a name for people like that. It's hero."

"Don't put us on a pedestal yet. We've still got a lot of work to do."

She spoke softly. "I don't know how to thank you for what you're doing."

"Thanks aren't necessary. Just let us do our job, and we'll do our best to get Spencer out of Mexico as safely as possible."

* * *

Dinner aboard the *Lori Danielle* was nothing like a meal at Bonaventure. Even though the ship was over 500 feet long, interior space was at a premium, and the galley was no exception. It was a little cramped, especially with the stacks of stores lining the walls.

I said, "We don't have a lot of storage space on board, so the crew has to stack nonperishable provisions wherever they can find room. You'll notice the stacks diminishing as the days play on. Such is shipboard life."

Patti said, "You don't have to apologize. This is all so fascinating to me."

Our dinner arrived on metal plates with common stainless-steel utensils. The food was excellent, but the presentation left something to be desired.

Patti said, "I didn't know what I expected, but this is really good."

"They serve four meals a day on board—morning, noon, and evening chow, plus mid-rats. That's short for midnight rations. The crew works around the clock, and they have to eat. Feel free to come down here anytime you'd like. There are a few parts of the ship, like the engine room, bridge, and hangar bay, that'll be off limits because they're dangerous, but I'm sure the quartermaster told you all about that."

"She did," Patti said. "And I understand, but maybe you could show me those parts of the ship sometime."

"We'll see. We've got a lot of work to do. Speaking of work, we have one more team member who'll join us before we shove off tomorrow morning. She's hard to explain, but she's crucial for this mission. Her name is Anya, and she's a former Russian intelligence officer."

"Russian?"

"Former Russian. She's an American now. I'm telling you about her because she's a bit of a powerful force. You'll understand when she comes aboard. She's hard to miss. She may become your best friend, or it's more likely she'll never say a word to you, but don't let that bother you either way. She's an excellent operator with a unique skill set."

"I guess I can't talk about her either, huh?"

"Definitely not."

Skipper, Mongo, Disco, and Hunter slithered into the galley before evening chow was over, and I said, "Patti, would you mind excusing us for a few minutes? We need to discuss a situation that's developing elsewhere."

She lifted her plate from the table. "Sure. I've got a lot of writing to do anyway. I'll be in my room if you need me."

The rest of my team took seats, and I said, "Let's have it."

Skipper checked the room. "Somebody burned his house down."

"Somebody?" I asked.

She said, "It could've been him. He may have torched it before he ran, but that doesn't sound like him. He's not that tactically minded. It's more likely somebody ransacked the house looking for anything they could find pertaining to this mission and then burned the place to the ground to cover their tracks."

"Forgive me for asking," I said, "but his body wasn't recovered from the fire, was it?"

"No. We talked to the captain of the fire department closest to his house, and he told us no one was home when the fire broke out, but that it was definitely arson."

"That's a good sign."

She groaned. "Yeah, I guess . . . Unless they took him."

Hunter said, "Is Anya here yet?"

"No, I told her to get here within twenty-four hours, but I haven't heard from her yet." I turned to Skipper. "Have you?"

She said, "No, but that's no surprise. She's not great about reporting in."

I said, "You're right about that. The captain says he's ready to shove off, so we'll toss off the lines as soon as she gets here." Almost before I finished my sentence, my cell phone chirped. "Go for Chase."

"Chase, it's Barry. There's a woman at the gangway claiming to be part of your team, and she appears to be Russian. What would you like me to do?"

"I'm sorry, Captain. I should've briefed you. She's with us. Please let her aboard and have somebody bring her down to the galley."

"As you wish," he said.

Minutes later, the quartermaster pushed open the galley door, and Anya Burinkova slid past her. "Is beautiful ship, Chasechka, but person on deck would not let me come on board. Did you keep secret that I was coming?"

I motioned toward an open seat at the opposite side of the table. "Not on purpose. Have a seat, and we'll bring you up to speed." The quartermaster stood in the doorway, and I said, "I'm sorry. I should've warned you. This is Anya Burinkova, and she'll be with us for the whole mission."

"It's nice to meet you, Anya. I'm Christine Billings, the quartermaster. I'll have a cabin prepared for you. Let me know if you need anything."

Anya said, "My cabin will be beside Chase, yes?"

Christine eyed me as if begging for help, so I said, "Both cabins beside mine are occupied. Just put her somewhere near the rest of us."

Skipper said, "There's an empty cabin beside mine. Put her there. That way I can keep an eye on her."

Anya gave our analyst a look I couldn't decipher, but it wasn't pleasant.

Kodiak stood and stuck out his hand. "I've heard a lot about you. I'm Kodiak."

Anya eyed him and finally shook his hand. "I have heard nothing about you."

"That's the way I like it," he said. "That makes me a clean slate."

It was impossible to tell if Anya was ignoring Kodiak or playing hard to get for her own amusement, but there was no question about what was happening behind those eyes when she set them on me. "Why am I here, Chasechka?"

Asking her to stop calling me the pet name was a waste of time. "You're here because we're about to start a fight with people who are master knife fighters and love nothing more than slicing opponents apart and watching them bleed to death. No one understands edged weapons like you, and I need you to teach my men how to survive against an opponent like you."

She said, "I cannot teach you to survive knife fight with me. Fighting with me ends in only one way, but I can teach you to maybe stay alive against opponent who is not me."

"We'll take it," I said.

She examined the faces at my table. "This does not mean I will only teach. I will also fight beside you. If these people are what you say, Chasechka, it is better if I am with you."

The hum of the deck cranes being stowed caught my attention, and I asked, "Is your gear aboard?"

"I have only two bags, and both are inside ship with quartermaster."

"Do you have body armor and guns?"

She shook her head. "I have neither because I knew you would have these for me. I will have pistol and rifle. You have these for me, yes?"

"Of course."

"What is thing you say? Never bring knife to gunfight? This is maybe true, but knife is silent."

Kodiak rejoined the conversation. "But people aren't silent when you stick them with a knife."

Anya stood, lifted a butter knife from the table, and slipped behind Kodiak. She wrapped her left arm around his head, grabbed his forehead, and exposed his neck. Then she pressed the tip of the knife against the side of his neck, just below his right ear. "If I press blade through neck beginning here, and inside one movement insert blade just in front of spine and drive forward, this will slice trachea below vocal cords. If air from lungs cannot move past vocal cords, only sound victim will make is body hitting floor." She slid the knife into Kodiak's shirt pocket and said, "I am ready to teach whenever you are ready to learn."

Chapter 19
Bullet or Blade

I stood at the hatch to the navigation bridge and peered inside. "Permission to come aboard?"

Captain Sprayberry turned from the console. "Absolutely. Come aboard, Chase."

I stepped onto the bridge. "How's your crew recall coming?"

"We're at full strength and ready to cast off on your order."

"Now that our Russian is aboard, we're ready to go. What's our time en route?"

"That's up to you," he said. "It's nine hundred nautical miles. If we cruise at fifty knots, we'll make the passage in eighteen hours. At that speed, though, we'll burn a lot of fuel."

"What's our peak efficiency speed?"

"Seventeen to twenty-four knots."

I ran the numbers in my head. "Plot a course and speed that will put us off the coast of Cabo after dark, day after tomorrow. We have a bunch of training to do and gear to set up."

"You got it. Is there anything else?" he asked.

"Just for my peace of mind," I said. "We are at full strength in defensive weaponry, right?"

He gave a satisfied smile. "Offensive *and* defensive weapons systems are all up and operational."

"Thanks, Captain. I'm going to get back to my team. We've got a lot of work to do."

I found the team in a semicircle around Anya on the stern deck. Patti was still leaning against the rail and watching with devoted attention.

I slid beside her. "What are they doing?"

"So far, they're just talking. Well, that's not accurate . . . The woman, Anya, is talking, and the others are listening. You mentioned something about her having a skill set you needed on the team. What exactly can she do that you guys cannot?"

"It's not a matter of can," I said. "We have the skill. It's a matter of what applying that skill would do to our heads. Anya's trained and experienced in extremely brutal edged weapons application. There probably aren't ten other people in the world who can do the things she's capable of doing with a knife. Being able to do it physically is only half of the equation, though. Being able to live with yourself after slicing another human into bite-sized pieces is the other side of the coin."

She furrowed her brow. "Oh, I hadn't thought of that."

"Anya was trained by the KGB before the wall came down. She's fearless, brutal, and unstoppable."

Patti sighed. "And beautiful."

"Yes, but she was trained to use that as a weapon, too. It worked on me a dozen years ago."

"Oh, really? Now that sounds like an interesting story."

"That's a story you'll never hear."

She looked up at me. "From the look in your eye, it's a story that isn't over."

"You're wrong about that. It's most definitely over and done. If you'll excuse me, I think I'll join the class."

I slipped behind my team, determined to avoid interrupting the class, but I should've known that couldn't happen.

Anya said, "You are late, and there is punishment for this. Come to front."

I stepped around my team and stood beside the teacher. She pulled an orange knife from her bag and tossed it toward me. Rather than catching a flying knife, I sidestepped the approaching weapon and let it clatter to the deck.

Anya giggled. "I would never throw real knife at you, Chasechka. Is dull on blade and only training knife. It cannot hurt you."

I lifted the knife from the deck and found a blunt, rounded tip and flat, dull surface where the cutting edge should've been. "I've been on the receiving end of your knife work," I said. "You'll have to forgive me if I don't always trust you."

She covered her heart with both hands. "Aww, this makes me sad, but also small amount happy. You just made for me first and most important rule of fighting with knife. Rule is simple. Do not be there to get cut. When I threw harmless training blade at Chase, he moved away. In Krav Maga, this is called clearing centerline. In Russian knife fighting, is called *ostat'sya v zhivykh* . . . staying alive."

I held up the orange knife. "Is that the only point you wanted to make, or am I supposed to do something with this?"

She said, "Now is time for second most important rule of fighting with knife. There is nothing worse than knife fight. Everyone who goes into knife fight will bleed. If you fight person with knife, you must be willing to be cut and probably cut badly. Never forget this. If there is any other option, do not have fight with knife. This is understood, yes?"

Anya's captive audience nodded and instinctively reached for their sheathed blades.

She took my wrist and moved my arm over my head. "If being attacked by person with knife in position like this, you know he is not well-trained fighter. I will demonstrate why this is true." She stepped forward until her body was pressed against mine. "Now cut me."

I tried to lower the blade and make contact, but her shoulder pressed against the triceps of my right arm prevented me from employing the weapon.

She whispered, "Thank you for dancing with me, Chasechka," and then took a step back. She lifted her bag with her foot and dumped the contents onto the deck. "Everyone take training knife and put real knife inside bag. You will have instinct to draw real knife, and I do not want this."

Everyone followed her instructions and traded their razor-sharp blades for harmless training knives.

She said, "One by one, I want to show you how this feels because is important to know how to get close to opponent without being cut. If knife is high, this is almost perfect defense. What is perfect defense?"

Kodiak said, "Don't be there."

Anya flashed him a brilliant smile. "You are now favorite student. I will give to you gold star."

The next several minutes were spent with Anya pressing her body against each of the team and demonstrating the effectiveness of the technique.

She said, "Now, practice this with each other until you can do it perfectly. I will make corrections when you do wrong."

She watched and made minor adjustments to everyone's technique until she was confident everyone could perform the move well. "Now, do one more time, but also think about position of your right hand. With this hand, you are free to deliver many stabs very quickly. I want always for your mind to think attack, attack, attack. Your attack must be violent, fast, and continuous. Stop only when opponent is dead. Knife fight is fight always until death."

All of us had been through basic and advanced knife fighting training, but never under the tutelage of a Russian assassin.

She put us through several more drills designed to increase our effectiveness in blocking and disarming. Most of the techniques were new to us, and we mastered them quickly.

Finally, she took a knee and spoke softly. "Everything we have done so far is reaction to attack. Tomorrow, I will teach to you attacking properly. Knife is also offensive weapon, even though you have been taught it is only for defense. This is terrible error in American training. You will see."

She paused long enough to let the idea of using a knife offensively sink in. "Before we are finished for tonight, I want to put inside head one more important thing. Many people, especially Americans, believe slashing wildly in knife fight will eventually cause opponent to lose enough blood to stop fight. This may be true sometimes but is terrible belief. I want to put for you thought inside head of always making deliberate cuts and stabs."

She stood and demonstrated an underhand strike. "Think now which muscles I am using to make my body move like this."

Her star pupil said, "Bicep, pecs, and delt."

"Is good answer, but is not all of answer. Remember, I said what muscles I am using to make *body* move, not just knife."

Mongo said, "Back leg, and core for balance and power."

"Very good, Marvin. You are now favorite student. Take from Kodiak gold star. Is now yours." That got a chuckle, and Anya kept teaching. "Underhand strike is deadly, but is also attack that exposes many weaknesses. Bear Boy, come to me. I will give to you chance to have again star."

No one moved, and I tried to figure out who she was calling Bear Boy.

Finally, she threw up her hands. "It was joke. Kodiak is kind of bear, yes?" Bear Boy moved in front her, and she said, "Show to me underhand attack."

Kodiak stepped forward and started the attack. Anya sidestepped the approaching knife, parried the attacking hand with a powerful left, and planted her right knee on the deck, just in front of Kodiak's boot. She shot her blade between his legs, planted it just beneath his glute, and drew through his crotch and upward toward his appendix. "Now tell to me how long he can continue fight."

Kodiak said, "I'm done. You just fileted my femoral artery, and I never saw it coming."

The Russian stood. "This is what I mean when I say make deliberate strikes. I could have sliced wrist, elbow, or bicep and stopped immediate attack, but by using killing strike, fighter is never again threat, and I can now focus on others who are threat. This makes sense, yes?"

Everyone nodded, and she said, "This is very advanced technique and takes many times practice, but there is simpler, safer defensive attack. I will show to you." She motioned for Kodiak. "Come with underhand again, but this time, do at full speed."

"Full speed?"

"Yes, this is how fight happens. No one slows down to make fight easier for opponent."

Kodiak shuffled forward and brought his knife upward at blinding speed, but Anya cleared to the right, sent a crushing outside block with her left hand to deflect the coming attack, and landed the pommel of her knife directly on Kodiak's throat.

Both fighters froze in place, and Anya said, "Less movement, almost instant kill, and most of all, I am still on feet instead of kneeling. Is much better, but lesson is to always strike to end fight immediately. Every attack must be deliberate and without hesitation. You understand, yes?" The fascination of Anya's students piqued, and she said, "One more thing before finishing for tonight. Someone has plate carrier, yes?"

"I've got mine," Kodiak said.

"Give to person who is fastest drawing pistol."

Kodiak grabbed his vest. "I don't know who's the fastest, but I'm not slow."

Anya scanned the team. "Give to Chase. He is very good with hands."

Kodiak tossed the plate carrier to me, and I pulled it over my head.

I said, "It's a little snug, but it'll do."

Anya held out her hand. "Give to me pistol."

"Are you going to shoot me?"

She chuckled. "No, of course not. I am going to do something much worse to you."

I drew my Glock and placed it in her hand.

She dropped the magazine, racked the slide, and caught the ejected round before handing the pistol back to me. "Look closely to see gun is safe and clear."

I racked the slide several times and inspected the chamber and mag. "It's clear."

"Good. Put back inside holster. I want everyone to think about how much faster pistol and bullet are than knife fighter. If you have opportunity to end knife fight before it begins by using pistol or rifle, always do this. Bullet is supersonic, so knife is very slow compared to bullet, yes?"

Everyone agreed, and Anya took six steps backward. "To prove theory about bullets being faster, I want for Chase to now draw and shoot me because I am threat."

"Seriously?" I asked.

"Yes, go ahead. Do it."

I shot my hand toward my holster, gripped the Glock high on the weapon, and thumbed the retention release. Before the muzzle of my pistol cleared the top of the holster, Anya's favorite fighting knife stuck with a thud in an M4 magazine on the front of my borrowed plate carrier.

I left my pistol in its holster, plucked the knife from my chest, and waved it in the air. "And what are we supposed to learn from this?"

She said, "You are supposed to learn knife is also bullet in skilled hands. Do not think knife is only dangerous when close to opponent. This is all of lesson for tonight. Think of these things, and we will practice tomorrow. Chasechka, you are okay with this, yes?"

"Yes, I'm good with it, but don't ever throw another knife at me."

She smiled and took her blade from my hand. "Okay, I will never throw another knife at you. I will always use only this one to throw at you."

Chapter 20
Boat Sleep

There's no sleep like boat sleep. I'll never understand it, but sleeping while the boat gently rocks me is one of the best feelings I've ever known. A five-hundred-footer like the *Lori Danielle* didn't rock and sway like *Aegis*, my fifty-footer, but it was still slumber like none other.

Breakfast was served at six thirty, and the whole team was right on time.

Hunter was first, but he wasn't the last to take a shot. "Oh, look. It's Chasechka with a knife stuck in his chest-echka."

"Cute," I said. "You try to beat her and see how it works out. She's not human."

Kodiak listened and laughed while the rest of the team had their fun with me.

He said, "I'll tell you one thing. I'm pretty sure I've never seen anything sexier than that woman with a knife in her hand."

Several of us echoed, "Don't!"

I said, "She's sucking you in. It's what she does. Don't fall for it."

"She's welcome to throw anything she wants at me anytime she wants."

Mongo piped up. "You'll be sorry."

Kodiak rolled his eyes. "You too, big man? What did she do to you?"

"It's a long story, but trust us. Just don't."

Clark tapped on the table. "We're having a good time, but seriously, did you guys think about what she showed us last night?"

Singer said, "I certainly did. I haven't been through the knife training the rest of you guys have, but I was impressed and terrified."

Disco said, "Me, too. She's crazy good."

It was my turn. "We all need to be that good. These Los Toros guys are in love with anything with a sharp edge . . . especially their machetes. It's crucial that we listen and learn from Anya instead of drooling over her, Bear Boy." That got a laugh, but I said, "I'm serious. This is one of the reasons she's here—to prepare us for facing a bunch of fearless, superior knife fighters. Don't make the mistake of taking any of this lightly."

We ate, and thoughts of surviving two dozen knife fights in the coming days wouldn't leave my head. I wondered if I was the only one having those thoughts.

Clark finished his last sip of coffee and planted the cup on the stainless-steel table. "What's on the agenda for today, College Boy?"

"More knife training with Anya, but first, I want to test-fire everything and make sure each piece of gear is ready to go. We can't make any assumptions about our capabilities. We're in for a bloody fight, and I'm not ashamed to admit I'd love to have a platoon of Rangers with us."

Clark made a show of counting heads—Mongo, Kodiak, Singer, and himself. "Here's your Ranger platoon."

"I wouldn't trade the four of you for an entire brigade. Let's get to work."

Of the forty-eight rifles we test-fired, only two failed, and Hunter soon had them repaired and back in service. None of the pistols failed. Every damaged piece of gear was repaired or replaced, and my team was armed to the teeth and ready for war . . . or so we thought.

Our Russian adjunct professor gave us an entirely new perspective. She passed out blunt-edged training knives and red felt tip markers. "Color edge of blades with marker until all of cutting side is red."

We followed her instructions while she colored her blade in orange.

When everyone's blade was painted, she said, "I will not hurt you, but I will mark you. You may be as brutal as you wish, but do not stab with force. Even tips of training knives can puncture with enough force. You will need me in fight with you when we meet our enemy, so do not injure me badly enough to put me on sideline. I will begin with Marvin because I have trained him with knife in past."

Mongo stepped away from the team and faced off with Anya. She lunged toward him with an outstretched hand gripping her blade. The big man expertly stepped inside the thrust and sent his blade sliding up her arm and across the inside of her elbow and bicep. She landed a foot behind his left knee as he spun, sending him to the deck face-down.

She stepped away and held out her arm, revealing a long red line across the inside of it. "Is very good cut. If knife was real, I would be out of fight and bleeding terribly."

Hunter helped our giant to his feet and said, "Nice work, Mongo!"

Anya said, "Yes, very nice work, but look at left side of neck."

Mongo raised his head and exposed an orange line from just beneath his chin, across the front of his throat, and around the side of his neck.

She performed a series of similar encounters with each of us, quickly killing everyone while receiving mostly minor wounds to herself. Nothing could've proven how poorly prepared we were to face skilled knife fighters better than that demonstration.

The remainder of the day was spent sparring with each other under Anya's critical eye. She corrected minor positioning errors and demonstrated how we could make our attacks and defenses more efficient and deadly. By the end of the day, we were covered with ink, sweat, and exhaustion, but we were dramatically better knife fighters than we'd been only hours before.

Anya passed her bag around, and we deposited our training knives inside.

She zipped the bag and took a seat on the deck. "Listen closely. If you wish to stay alive, do not allow yourself to be pulled into a knife fight. You are shooters. I am knife fighter. In gunfight, you will always win against me, but inside fight with knife, I will win."

She held out her arms and showed the multiple red lines across her skin. "Even I will be cut in knife fight. Everyone will be cut, and that is terrible. You must decide if you are willing to kill these people to recover hostages. If answer is yes, you must not be afraid to use rifle at distance too far to throw knife effectively."

We sat in mesmerized disbelief at the wisdom pouring out of a woman who'd once been our enemy and may have saved our lives in the previous twenty-four hours.

Kodiak stuck his hand in the air. "I've got a question. How long did it take you to get this good with knives?"

She said, "Thirty-eight years, and tomorrow, I will be better because I have learned from all of you. If learning ends, we are near our death. This means always seek knowledge and new skill."

Graduation from the Russian academy of bladework wasn't a formal affair, but I had no doubt each of us was replaying everything we learned inside our heads and reliving every mark and bruise we earned.

As we parted ways and headed for the showers, Anya caught me by my arm. "We must talk privately."

We stepped to the starboard rail, and I said, "Thank you for doing this."

"I will always do for you anything you ask, Chasechka. You have strong team, but they will not survive contact with Los Toros if fighting with knives. They are not ready."

"That's why I asked you to come. I need you with us every step of the way."

She cocked her head. "I do not think this is real reason I am here."

"Anya, if you think this is some sort of stroll down memory lane or a chance to see you—"

She laid a hand on my chest. "No, this is not what I think. I think I am here because I will do things your team will not. I believe you wish to have me do terrible things because you think I do not have conscience after killing up close."

"No, that's not what I . . ."

Perhaps she was right. Perhaps I didn't want my men to have to fight like wild animals and live with the consequences of wearing the blood of our enemy on our hands.

"Is okay, Chasechka. This is something I can do, but please do not ever ask this of me again. I have *prizrak* inside my mind for every person I have killed."

"Forgive me," I said. "I don't know the word *prizrak*."

She thought for a moment. "In English, is *phantom* or maybe *ghost*."

Suddenly, I was no better than her Russian masters who dispatched an innocent girl to kill because they lacked the stomach for it. I was the same as the men in high castles turning her into a whore and killing machine with no thought of what such a life would do to the orphan girl from north of Moscow.

My shame rose like bile from my stomach, and I gagged on the sickening bitterness of what I'd asked of a woman I once loved. "Anya, I'm sorry. I should've never called you. It was wrong of me to ask such a thing of you."

"Is okay, my Chasechka. There are things you cannot know that make me yours for a thousand years and then a thousand more. These people you are going to fight are not human. I know of them, and even I am afraid of them. I am glad you asked from me this thing. I will do it because you may probably die without me, and I would never be able to live with myself if this happened."

For the first time, I saw the tiny lines around her eyes and the weariness in her gaze. "How much longer can we do this?"

She tried to smile. "Perhaps this is what we are, and we will do it until it destroys us, even if it does this one piece at a time. Your leg, your hand, your ears. My foot, my shoulder . . . my heart."

"I hope you're wrong."

Anya looked past me as we sliced through the Pacific at twenty knots. "So many beautiful things are in all of world, and you and I seek terrible places and terrible people and terrible situations. Is impossible to keep terrible outside of us. Every time we touch what is evil, little bit of it gets inside us, and we must carry it forever. What will happen to us when all of those little bits of evil are bigger than the bits of good inside us? Is that when we will be empty and have nothing left to give? Is that what finally ends us and people like us?"

I'd never heard her say anything like that before that moment at sea. It was a new side of her I didn't know existed. She was feeling it, too. The years and fights and lives had begun to burden her, just as they were doing to me, and in that moment, I wondered if she and I were really as different as I believed us to be. What my country asked of me wasn't so different from what hers had once demanded of her.

I reached for her hand but stopped myself before taking it in mine. "There's something I have to tell you."

She didn't stop herself from taking my hand in hers. "I have something also to tell to you, but now is not time for either of these things. Perhaps there will be time for both when this is over."

Skipper's voice cut through the evening air like one of Anya's blades. "I don't know what's going on out here, but it needs to stop right now!"

"Nothing's going on," I said. "We were just discussing how dangerous this mission is going to be."

"That's not what it looked like from here. It's time for dinner and sleep . . . alone."

Chapter 21
That Time in Moscow

Day two at sea began unlike anything I could've imagined. Breakfast was the cook's attempt at Southern biscuits and gravy, and the attempt was monumentally successful. We ate like ravenous dogs until the hatch to the galley burst open and Anya exploded through the door, yelling at the top of her lungs and wielding a section of plastic pipe only slightly smaller than a baseball bat. Of the eleven people in the galley, she managed to thump nine of us before we were able to identify the episode as a test of some sort.

With her rampage complete, she lowered her weapon. "Raise your hand if you have pistol." Most hands went up, and she said, "Keep hands up if you thought about using pistol to stop me." Every hand went down, and she huffed. "Why not?"

"Because you weren't a real threat," Kodiak said. "We all knew it was you, and other than a whelp or two, you weren't going to hurt us with a piece of PVC pipe."

She shook her head. "You and I will have private session, and I will show to you how to kill everyone inside room with this piece of pipe."

Kodiak shook his head. "I'm not sure I want that information anywhere in my skull."

I finally refocused the group. "Okay, we get it. You ambushed us and managed to land blows to most of us, but what are we supposed to learn from whatever that was?"

She took a seat near the end of our table. "Imagine pipe is machete, and I am Los Toros. No one even thought of drawing pistol. I would have stopped immediately if someone did draw. This did not happen, though. Everyone sat and stared and did not try to stop me. Perhaps *you* should tell to me what you should learn from this." From the looks on our faces, we all got the message in the same instant, and Anya said, "Breakfast is finished. Now we learn how to fight against man with machete."

I didn't want to spend another day on the stern deck being bludgeoned and embarrassed, but in the interest of staying alive, I had no choice. To my surprise, though, the lesson was short.

Anya stepped in front of the team with her trusty plastic pipe. "Do you remember first thing I taught to you about fighting with knife?"

Hunter said, "Everybody gets cut."

Anya shook her head. "No, that was second thing. First thing was how to stop overhand attack with knife. I showed you how to step close to attacker and pin arm while keeping your right hand free to stab, cut, and punch. You remember this, yes?" Everyone nodded, and she tossed her pipe to Singer. "Attack me, and pretend you have machete."

Singer raised the pipe and burst toward her.

She demonstrated the identical defense as the first technique she taught us and then stepped back. "Good. Now, attack me in different way with machete."

Singer lowered the pipe and swung it parallel to the deck from right to left.

Again, Anya stepped inside and blocked the swing using a slightly modified body position. She pushed Singer away and said,

"Is same, but directed toward inside of arm instead of underside. You see this, yes?"

Turning her attention back to Singer, she said, "Now, attack underhand like we learned yesterday."

Singer fidgeted and turned the simulated machete to several different angles while we watched. Finally, he said, "There's no way to attack underhanded with a machete."

"There is," Anya said, "but is different. Strike from side, but you must lean body to lower machete near ground and swing upward. Is very dangerous strike. Between legs and under arms is most deadly. This attack is almost impossible to defend from fighting distance, but if you stay very close to opponent, this attack is unusable."

Singer asked, "Are you saying we should get as close as possible when they're swinging machetes?"

"No. I am saying to not get within twenty feet of man with machete. Kill him from that distance with rifle, but if you must fight hand to hand with man who has machete, you will lose if you are not locked up with opponent. That is terrible place to be, but not as terrible as three feet away."

She paired us up and had us practice the attacks and defenses for an hour. After she'd corrected our mistakes and we felt like we'd mastered the basic techniques, she said, "This is all I have to teach you. Anything else is only practice, but you do not have time for this. You already know about fighting from instinct and muscle memory. Your muscles have not done these things long enough to have memory, so you must fight intentionally with your mind. I have only one thing left to say. Do not have knife fight. Make Los Toros bring knife to *your* gunfight."

We took a break, hydrated, and practiced for two more hours.

Just before lunch, we piled into the CIC for our briefing, and Skipper took charge of the assembly. "You guys smell like goats, so

I'll keep this as short as possible. We'll be on-site in just under ten hours. I've been digging through DEA reports and cross-checking reported locations against satellite imagery. There are two camps Los Toros seems to use more than any others."

She brought up a map of the desert north of Cabo San Lucas. "The first is here, near El Anelo. This is the only camp with activity within the past forty-eight hours. We'll talk more about that activity in a minute, but for now, I need to tell you about an ingress point. There just happens to be a dry riverbed leading right to the camp. We can insert the desert patrol vehicles north of the airport and the toll road. That'll give us maximum concealment so the locals don't start asking questions about a helicopter carrying dune buggies underneath it. We have to make some decisions, though. We can't insert the team and the DPVs simultaneously. It'll take at least three flights—one to deploy the team, and one for each of the DPVs. They weigh too much to carry two at a time."

I turned to Disco. "That's your end of the stick. What are you thinking?"

He said, "I think we need Gun Bunny. She weighs at least fifty pounds less than me, and she's a better NOE pilot. With her in the cockpit instead of me, we'll be able to carry more and stay closer to the ground."

"Get her in here," I said.

Skipper made the call, and while we were waiting for her to arrive, Clark said, "Did you say something about sling-loading the DPVs under the Little Bird?"

Our resident chopper pilot squeezed into the CIC minutes later and pulled off her hat. "Hey, guys. Sorry I'm late."

Barbie wasn't the typical combat helicopter pilot. After a relatively brief career flying AH-64 Apache helicopters in the Army and receiving a cockpit full of enemy fire, she found her way into the civilian market, where she was promptly scarfed up by Captain Wayne Stinnett, the skipper of the *Lori Danielle*'s predecessor. At the controls of a light chopper, Barbie "Gun Bunny" Brewer had no equal, and I couldn't have been happier to have her as a member of our crew.

She said, "I'll take the sling-load question, if you don't mind. Our Little Bird hasn't qualified as a normal category aircraft for some time, but she's now even further from the FAA-certified bird she was when we bought her. I designed, installed, and tested a sling-load system to allow her to carry almost sixteen hundred pounds. Of course, we can jettison the load from within the cockpit if it gets hairy. The temperatures in Mexico create a density altitude problem, but I'll easily be able to handle the weight of one DPV at a time."

Skipper eyed Clark. "Does that answer your question?"

"It does," he said. "And I can't wait to see it. I've ridden a lot of Little Birds into and out of shooting matches, but I've never seen one with a sling-load."

Gun Bunny gave Clark a wink. "I look forward to showing it to you."

Kodiak threw up his hands. "Really? You're flirting with him now?"

The pilot yanked Kodiak's hat from his head and tossed it onto the table. "Have some respect. You know you're my Flirty Gurdy."

Kodiak shook his head. "From Bear Boy to Flirty Gurdy . . . What's a guy gotta do to keep the one name he's had for twenty years?"

"Enough!" Skipper demanded. "We've got a lot to talk about, so save whatever this is for later. Way later."

Kodiak reclaimed his hat, and Gun Bunny took a seat.

Skipper continued. "Of course, it's up to Chase, but I think the best option is to insert one desert patrol vehicle and our two lightest guys. They can guard the DPV while Barbie comes back for another load."

I said, "I like that idea, but one of our two lightest guys isn't a guy. Anya, are you okay inserting with Kodiak?"

That brought a glare from Barbie, and Anya said, "Do not worry. I have only eyes for one man, and he is not Bear Boy."

Barbie frowned. "Bear Boy?"

"It's a long story," Kodiak said. "But we'll be fine unchaperoned."

Anya nodded. "Yes, we will be fine."

Barbie asked, "Do we have a total weight for the payload?"

Hunter said, "I'm still working on it, but it's safe to say we can do it all in four lifts."

I asked, "Is there any way we can make it work in three? If we have to wait for four cycles, we're going to spend a lot of time standing still out there."

Hunter said, "We can cut gear or personnel and make it work in three, but our current loadout is heavy."

Gun Bunny said, "I'll get with Hunter after the meeting and see what we can do. With the new modifications to the Little Bird, I might be able to make it work."

I said, "You two work it out and let me know. For now, the plan will be Anya and Kodiak with one DPV on lift number one, the second DPV and Mongo on lift two, and the rest of us and as much gear as we can haul on lift three. If a fourth lift is required for gear, we'll have to do it, but getting in and out three times undetected is going to be hard enough. I'm afraid a fourth run is almost guaranteed to be noticed."

Gun Bunny said, "If you've got some good satellite shots, I can plan three or four routes through those low mountains."

"I'm sending the aerials to your tablet now," Skipper said.

I said, "The op will be a run up the dry riverbed, as close to the camp as we can get. And where's Dr. Mankiller?"

Skipper said, "She's probably down in the moonpool. Why?"

"Get her up here."

Celeste came through the hatch minutes later and stepped into a hornet's nest.

I got her first. "Did you bring those mini UAVs?"

She shuddered. "Woah, there's a lot of people in here."

I snapped my fingers. "Me, Doc. Look at me. The mini drones. Did you bring them?"

"Uh, yeah, I brought a few, but they haven't been tested to the point where I would feel comfortable—"

I cut her off. "I'm not concerned about comfort. Get them ready to fly tonight. Do any of them have night-vision capability?"

"Yeah, all of them."

"Good. Skipper will give you the grid coordinates to the target. We're planning a reconnaissance run tonight, and I want those drones in the air over the target."

"Okay, sure, whatever you say. But I'll need to fly them."

Skipper said, "Fine. Plan to be here in the CIC with me tonight. We'll work together."

Celeste said, "Okay, that'll work. And there's something else you may not know."

"Let's hear it," I said.

She squirmed where she stood. "Uh, I've been working on arming some of the small drones, and I've learned I can carry six ounces of C-Four and have enough battery to fly thirty minutes and still have sufficient charge to set off the blasting cap. I know six ounces isn't much, but it's enough to turn somebody's good day into one he'll never remember."

Kodiak giggled like a schoolgirl. "Six ounces of C-Four is more than enough to make this old breacher very happy. I can think of a few thousand uses for that right off the bat."

I said, "We need a comprehensive list of everything you're hold-ing in your arsenal, testing, working on, designing, thinking about, or even dreaming of. You've changed this mission dramati-cally with just six ounces of flying C-Four. Don't hold out on us."

"That's going to be quite a list," she said.

"Look around this room, Doc. This is quite a team. Just think what we'll be able to accomplish when this team and your brain get on the same page."

She almost blushed. "I hadn't really thought about it like that, but now that you mention it, maybe I'll let my imagination run wild."

I said, "And we'll do our best to keep up."

Skipper cleared her throat. "We're getting off task again."

"Sorry," I said. "Let's talk about the exfil."

Skipper wrinkled her nose. "What about the part between the infiltration and the exfil?"

"Until we put eyes on that camp, we have to play it by ear. Let's assume the ground game goes smoothly . . ."

That brought a roar of laughter through the room.

"It could happen," I said.

Clark looked at me across his glasses. "Name one time when the ground game went smoothly."

"There was that time in Moscow."

He slapped his knee and laughed. "You mean that time you fell in the half-frozen Moscow River and almost froze to death?"

"Well, there was that," I admitted, "but let's move on. Assume the mission has been a success and we get out of there with one or more American hostage. Let's talk about how we're getting back to the boat."

Clark was finally breathing normally after his laughing fit, so I continued. "If we can get out on the helo, that'll be our exfil plan A. I'm okay abandoning gear and the DPVs, but no explosives, ammo, or weapons. If we have to leave any of that behind, we're blowing it sky-high before we go."

Gun Bunny asked, "How many hostages are you expecting? I'm not afraid to cheat on the max gross weight of the Little Bird, but there's only so much physical space in that thing. If I shove six of you guys, including Mongo, into the cabin, there's no room for anybody else. We'll have to come out in lifts."

Skipper got that mischievous look. "Not if we can borrow a chopper from the Mexican Army. I just happen to know where there are three of them, and at least one has flown in the last two days."

I said, "You're talking about stealing a multi-million-dollar piece of hardware from the Mexican government."

"I prefer to think of it as requisitioning it for humanitarian purposes."

I said, "Okay, then. Let's add requisitioning a chopper to the to-do list."

Chapter 22
Little Ol' Me?

We broke for lunch and headed to the cargo hold to weigh and pre-position gear. Hunter was right. There was no possibility of flying two desert patrol vehicles, six personnel, and every piece of gear we could possibly need on just three trips into the desert.

For the first load, we weighed a DPV, Anya and Kodiak in full gear, and Gun Bunny. The load was three hundred pounds too heavy. The only choices were to leave off one person or cut the amount of gear they'd carry into the desert.

I said, "Let's strip their gear to minimal necessity."

Anya and Kodiak pulled off pieces of gear until the total load was within 100 pounds of the maximum gross weight for the chopper. I gave Gun Bunny a look, and she said, "No problem."

With lift number one set, we repeated the task with the second DPV and Mongo. It turned out that he weighed almost exactly the same as Anya and Kodiak combined, and the second load was ready.

Lift number three required some creativity. Disco, Singer, and I would be the only passengers, so that gave us a little extra room for the gear our first three operators had to shuck. We made the weight, but there was still a hundred fifty pounds of water and two hundred pounds of ammunition on deck.

"We can't go without bottles and bullets," I said.

Gun Bunny sat on deck with her back against the superstructure and her fingers running wild across the keys of her calculator. While I was building the fourth lift in my head, she said, "Chase, I can make it work. Look."

She held out her calculator. "If we split the ammo between the two DPVs and take them on the first two runs, that'll only leave the water to put us over on flight number three. I can leave off enough fuel to offset the difference, but that means I'd have to refuel between flights two and three."

Disco said, "That's doable. The crew can turn hot gas without you shutting down, so it wouldn't add more than a few minutes to the operation."

Gun Bunny pocketed her calculator. "I like it. If everything goes well, we should be able to have all the gear and personnel on the ground in less than an hour."

"That's optimistic," I said, "but if anybody can pull it off, you're the one."

"I appreciate your confidence in me."

I said, "It's not confidence. It's demonstrated ability. I don't know how much we're paying you, but if you pull this off, it's safe to say you'll change tax brackets."

"I don't do it for the money, Chase. I've been an adrenaline junkie since I was a little girl, and working with this crew gives me the fix I need every time."

"I think we all fall into that category. Let's get a little rest before we ride your pony to war."

Calories and naps consumed the remainder of our afternoon and evening until Skipper knocked on my cabin door and declared, "We're one hour out."

I showered, dressed, and headed to the CIC. Within minutes, the team was assembled, and Captain Sprayberry's face appeared on the overhead monitor.

He said, "We'll be at anchor in fifteen minutes, and flight ops are approved. The temperature is eighty-four degrees, and the wind is from two-three-zero at twelve knots."

That old familiar feeling came rushing back as six pairs of boots hit the deck and six warriors rose to take the fight to our adversary and bring Hell with us.

In our desert camouflage, ballistic helmets, and night vision, we could pass for SEALs or Delta anywhere in the world, with one exception. No one who looked like Anya Burinkova ever wore a SEAL Trident or an SF green beret.

I grabbed the Russian by her plate carrier and yelled over the roaring wind of the Little Bird. "Don't you get dead out there!"

She yelled back, "If I do, you need to know . . ."

Whatever she said next never made it through my hearing aids and bone conduction device, but the look on her face said it was something deeply important to her. I didn't have time to explore that, and even if I did, Hunter's command eliminated the opportunity.

"Load up!"

I grabbed the top of Kodiak's ruck and yanked him to within inches of my face. "She's a warrior, just like us. Don't look at her any differently than you look at me out there. Got it?"

He shoved a palm into my shoulder, spun me around, and yelled, "Nope. Your butt's a lot cuter than hers, boss. I'll see you in the sand."

An instant later, Gun Bunny pulled pitch, and the Little Bird strained under the weight of two operators and the desert patrol vehicle slung beneath. I watched the chopper that was never designed for such a mission climb away into the night, and my unauthorized operation was officially underway. I sent up a silent prayer that I'd bring everyone home with their hearts still beating and leave no Americans behind in the hands of barbaric butchers.

Hunter double-checked the rigging for the second DPV and positioned Mongo precisely where he should've been for the pickup. Seventeen minutes after flying away, the hum of the Little Bird wafted across the Pacific, and Gun Bunny hit the switch, bringing the navigation lights to life.

Hunter keyed his radio. "Bridge, deck boss, helipad is clear, and stern deck is standing by for pax pickup and sling-load."

Although I couldn't hear the radio calls between the bridge and the Little Bird, I had confidence they were coordinating the complex dance that would be Gun Bunny's arrival, pickup, and rigging of the second DPV.

I stepped beside our giant. "Hey, big man. When you get out there, do me a favor and don't let Anya hurt Bear Boy."

He grinned down at me. "He's gotta learn."

I gave his shoulder a slug and backed away as Gun Bunny descended toward the deck. She brought the Little Bird to a hover a foot above the deck and froze the chopper in the air as if it were resting on a pedestal.

Hunter yelled, "Load up," and Mongo placed a massive foot on the helo's portside skid. Even under Mongo's heft, the seasoned pilot never let the aircraft move. Mongo took his seat, and by the time he was strapped in, Hunter had the sling attached to the cargo hook.

Hunter backed away, checked the wind, and gave the signal to go. The chopper strained against the load, but just as before, Gun Bunny coaxed the massive load into the night. A hundred feet away from the ship, she doused the navigation lights, and the machine disappeared into the darkness.

Singer, Disco, and I pulled on the remainder of our gear and moved to the helipad. I press-checked my rifle and pistol to ensure a round was seated in each chamber, and my tools were as ready as I was.

Gun Bunny shaved sixty seconds off her previous time of seventeen minutes and descended toward the pad. Three crewmen in blue jumpsuits, gloves, and helmets crouched low at the edge of the pad until the Little Bird's skids touched down and the blades were flat.

Hunter yelled, "Fighters go," and the three of us ducked our heads and mounted the chopper.

I watched over my shoulder as the fuel team connected the nozzle to feed the thirsty machine. Minutes later, Hunter gave the all-clear signal, and we lifted off without anything hanging beneath the chopper.

Once clear of the superstructure, the lights went out, and I asked, "How'd the first two lifts go?"

Gun Bunny kept her eyes trained outside the windshield with her night-vision goggles in place. "I caught a crosswind in the riverbed and laid the second DPV on its side, but Mongo managed to muscle it back upright. Other than that, everything was smooth. We caught the eye of a few donkeys, but I didn't spot any humans looking up."

"Excellent," I said. "Stay on the ready when you get back to the ship. I don't expect to need an exfil tonight, but I don't want to wait if it gets hairy."

She said, "Don't worry. I won't leave you stranded. And if you get pinned down, we've always got Ronda on the Minigun, if we need her."

"You two make quite a pair."

She said, "That girl sure is good on that gun."

"And you're not bad up here in the driver's seat."

"Aw, shucks. Little ol' me?"

The riverbed came into sight seven minutes later, and we turned into the wind and headed for the deck.

Gun Bunny asked, "Do you want me to touch down or remain in a hover?"

I said, "Put it down so we can verify the condition of the gear before you fly away."

She nodded and continued her approach. As we neared the ground, sand filled the air around us, and Gun Bunny leaned through the door and looked straight down through the torrent of sand and debris.

Gun Bunny nestled the skids onto the ground and flattened the pitch of the blades, but she kept the turbine running. We dismounted and ran clear of the blades to find the other half of our team securing the site.

I found Kodiak and asked, "What's the status of the second DPV?"

He gave me the thumbs-up. "Undamaged and operational."

I spun and signaled Gun Bunny to depart, and she was gone in seconds, leaving another dust storm in her wake.

We conducted an inventory of gear, commo check, and then mounted the DPVs.

"Let's go to live coms," I said. Out of habit, I reached for my throat mic but quickly remembered Dr. Mankiller's device affixed to my jawbone. "CIC, Alpha One, all personnel and equipment are on deck and operational. We're moving toward the objective."

"Roger, Alpha One. Alpha Seven and Eight are geared up and standing by. The Little Bird will be on deck in sixty seconds."

Knowing Clark and Hunter were ready to join us if things got out of hand was reassuring, but I didn't want to risk putting Hunter in the fight.

Singer stuck his tablet to the Velcro on the panel and brought up the navigation software Skipper programmed.

I glanced at the second DPV with Kodiak at the wheel, Anya in the right front, and Disco in the back. "Are you ready to roll?" I asked, and Kodiak said, "Let's move!"

Kodiak positioned his DPV behind and left of ours to stay out of the dust cloud we'd create, and we accelerated northward through the dry riverbed.

The terrain looked eerie and foreboding through my NODs. Compared to the subtropical rainforests we'd worked so many times, the landscape could've been that of the moon. Other than some low scrub brush and tumbleweeds, there was nothing for miles in every direction. The one exception was the sprawling resort town of Cabo San Lucas to the south. The lights of the city brightened the southern sky like a modern-day oasis. We wouldn't spend any leisure time in the party town, but with a little luck and a lot of determination, we'd do something a few Americans and the team would never forget. What lay ahead was as much a mystery as what brought humans to that godforsaken stretch of desert thousands of years ago.

Chapter 23
Movement to Contact

The U.S. Army *Field Manual 3-90-1* defines movement to contact as an offensive task designed to develop the situation and establish or regain contact to create favorable conditions for subsequent tactical actions. Although I never served in uniform, I studied every document I could get my hands on to learn small-unit tactics, and in Master Sergeant Clark Johnson, I had one of the best instructors a civilian like me could ever hope to know. On that night, our movement to contact was slightly outside the normal procedure. I had no interest in making physical contact with our adversary. Instead, I only wanted to put eyes on their camp and launch a dozen or so miniature drones Dr. Mankiller added to our arsenal.

The satellite imagery Skipper scored for us was excellent, but the shots were taken from directly overhead, so they didn't give us a great depiction of the profiles of the fences and structures. My goal was to find a position from which we could observe and photograph the camp and hopefully get a glimpse of an American.

We made short work of the four miles between our drop-off point and the fork in the riverbed that led to the camp, without encountering another human. We pulled to a stop just upstream of the right fork, and Kodiak pulled beside us.

With our DPVs idling and our coms working exactly as designed, I said, "We've got another thousand yards before we should be able to put eyes on the target. Let's stash the vehicles here and move in the rest of the way on foot."

Without a word, he drove his vehicle into a clump of bushes, climbed out, and pulled the camouflage netting across the top. I did the same on the opposite bank of the riverbed. Without night-vision devices or thermal imaging, no one would see our DPVs, and we'd hopefully be able to approach the camp silently without anyone detecting our presence.

Singer pulled his .338 Lapua Magnum from its case and slung it across his back. I led the movement, and we made our way up the slight incline until a rock wall rose out of the landscape ahead. We paused, listened, and waited for alarms, dogs, or spotters picking us up.

I whispered, "We're still black. Singer, I want you to post up to the east and get a good line of sight into the camp. Let me know when you're in position."

His one-word answer came. "Moving."

The rest of us held position while our sniper moved into his observation point. I expected ten to fifteen minutes, but to my surprise, he reported less than five minutes later. "Alpha Six is in position with a clear line of sight and three men smoking outside the small structure on the northern edge of the camp. No other activity."

His report of "no other activity" could've meant one of two things. Either he could see the entire camp and he was certain there was no other activity, or he couldn't see the full picture, but he didn't detect any further activity. I needed to know which it was.

I said, "Verify you have eyes on the entire compound."

He quickly came back with, "Negative. I have eyes on the northern half, but the slope behind the wall blocks my view to the south. I recommend launching the drones."

I motioned for Disco to break out our tiny flying friends and set them free. He opened the case, pulled out six drones, and activated them.

I said, "CIC, Alpha One, six drones are active. Report when you have coms with all six."

"Roger," Skipper said. "Stand by." One by one, tiny shielded propellers spun on each of the miniature drones, and Skipper said, "Link acquired. Launch all six."

Disco threw them into the air, and they came to a hover a few feet over our heads. They slowly moved closer to each other until there were less than six inches between any two of them. They moved off to the southwest as if connected to each other by some invisible force.

I said, "Are you going to fly them into the compound in formation?"

Dr. Mankiller's voice sounded in my head. "Negative. I'll fly them to the camp as one unit, then break them off into singles to eliminate their sound signatures."

I said, "Roger. Feed the video to my tablet."

I pulled the blinders around the edges of my screen, and soon, the image of the camp appeared on my device in six blocks. "Are you recording the video?"

Celeste said, "Affirmative."

I flipped between squares, carefully watching the videos each drone was recording, until something caught my eye. I said, "Freeze drone four, and move in as close as you can to the window at the bottom left of the screen."

Skipper said, "Singer, do you still have eyes on the smokers?"

"Affirmative. They haven't moved, and they obviously don't see or hear the drones."

Celeste's voice returned. "How close?"

I said, "Take it to within six feet above the window, and give me a shot inside the building if you can."

I double-clicked the box for drone number four and watched as the screen filled with footage from the single camera. The image was dark and a little grainy, but my suspicion from the farther distance was confirmed. "Those are handcuffs."

Celeste said, "You're right. Do you think those are Spencer Baldwin's hands?"

"I don't know, but I know how to find out. Keep that drone in place, and fly one back to me that can carry the six-ounce payload you mentioned earlier."

She asked, "Are you sending in C-Four?"

"Negative," I said. "I'm sending in something far more dangerous."

A drone appeared in a hover about two feet from my face, and I snatched it from the air. From my notepad, I pulled a single sheet of paper and wrote: "Number? Name? American?" After rolling the paper around the pencil and binding it with a rubber band, I pulled my handcuff key from my plate carrier and slid it behind the band. I used a second elastic to connect the payload to the miniature drone and said, "Okay. See if it'll fly."

I tossed the drone into the air, and it wavered for a few seconds before finding its balance.

Celeste said, "It's heavy on one side. Try to center the load."

I grabbed the tiny machine from the air and situated the load closer to the center. On the second attempt, it flew without listing, and I said, "Put it in those hands in the window."

She flew the drone away, and I turned back to the video feed. An edge of the rolled paper was visible on the screen, but there was still plenty of usable camera angle. Celeste flew the device back across the wall and to the window. The hands were still there, and she practically landed the drone on the man's knuckles.

The hands flinched and pulled away as if startled, but our drone pilot didn't give up. She flew the gadget toward the window and came to a hover over the sill, then she eased the small machine ever closer until it came to rest with the camera still capturing dark video of the interior of the room.

Finally, the cuffed hands lifted the tiny drone and slid the paper from the rubber band. The hands disappeared, and I silently hoped he was answering my questions.

As I impatiently waited for the hands to return, Singer said, "Movement."

I closed the blinders over my screen and raised my head. It took a minute for my eyes to adjust from the screen back to my NODs, then I scanned the scene. "I don't see any movement. Where is he?"

Singer said, "They split directions. Two men with rifles that look a lot like M-Fours."

"M-Fours?" I asked.

He said, "Affirmative. The mover coming toward us is definitely carrying an AR platform. I only got a glimpse of the second guy before he turned away, but it looked like the same rifle."

"What are they doing?"

"It appears to be a roving patrol. Man one is scanning, but his rifle is slung. I don't think they know we're here."

Speaking as quietly as possible, I said. "Get the drones out of there. Send them high, and pan the perimeter for a roving sentry."

Celeste said, "Drone four is still in the dark, but I'm bringing the others out."

I was tempted to watch my screen, but I didn't want to give the sentry anything to see in the vast darkness of the desert—especially not the light of a tablet.

Skipper said, "I just got a good look at both sentries and their rifles. They're definitely built on the AR platform. Those are American guns, Chase."

A thousand questions poured through my head, but none of the answers mattered in that moment. Remaining still, quiet, and undetected were the only things any of us needed to worry about.

I peered toward the compound and could easily see the sentry walking the perimeter from left to right, but I was too far away to see his weapon. American weaponry in the hands of Mexican cartel members wasn't rare, but if they were full-auto rifles, a hand-to-hand knife fight was no longer the deadliest event we were likely to face on the mission. With six of us, and possibly as many as thirty of them, I didn't like the odds if we were using the same rifles, and I especially didn't like playing against those odds on someone else's home field.

Singer said, "They're crossing. Man two is carrying the same rifle as the first guy. Skipper's right. They're ARs."

I played out the coming minutes in my mind and said, "Singer, let us know when the rovers are back inside the walls. I want to move to the north side and complete my picture of this place."

Singer said, "Roger. How many are you taking?"

"Pick a spotter, and I'll take the other three."

He said, "Send Mongo."

"Roger. Report sentries clear."

"Roger."

I watched the second man pass from right to left, retracing the previous man's steps in reverse. My watch said it was eight minutes past midnight. That was close enough to the top of the hour for me to believe the roving patrol came out every hour on the hour, but that would be sloppy security, and based on what Skipper told me, there was nothing sloppy about Los Toros.

The sentry walked out of sight, and I waited for Singer's call. Finally, he said, "Both sentries are back inside the wall."

"Roger. Alpha Two is moving to your location."

Mongo rose to a crouch and moved away to the east, staying as low as possible, trying not to give the cartel anything to shoot.

Singer talked him into his hide, then said, "Alpha Two is on station. Move at will."

I said, "Kodiak, you're with me. We're going west. I want Anya and Disco to move northeast. Report movement or anything suspicious."

We broke into two teams and parted ways. Our movement was slow and methodical. At least one of us was always looking at the compound, even when the other was checking terrain and navigating. We paused on a small rise to the northwest and studied the new angle. After drinking water and watching for several minutes, we continued our circumnavigation.

I said, "Alpha Four, Alpha One. Sitrep."

A situation report would help complete my mental picture.

Disco said, "We're on slight high ground with relatively good visibility into the camp. No unusual activity. We're moving north."

I said, "Roger. We'll rendezvous northeast of the compound and wait for another patrol."

"Roger."

I called for Skipper. "Is there any movement from drone four?"

"Negative," she said. "We're still waiting. If the guy in cuffs can't read English, God only knows what'll happen."

I began to question my decision to send in the note. If the cartel found the drone or the note, our operation could be blown, but somewhere inside my head, I still believed the risk was well worth the potential reward. If we could get a head count and establish a means of two-way communication with the hostages, everything about our mission would become clearer.

As we moved to the northeast, Kodiak said, "Friendly contact."

I glanced away from the camp long enough to see Disco and Anya slowly making their way toward us, so we stopped behind the concealment of a row of brush and waited.

They joined us, and Anya said, "Is simple compound and easy to penetrate. We need only now to know how many of them are inside."

I said, "I agree. All we can do for now is watch, wait, and count."

We made our way back to the small rise, where Kodiak and I paused on the way around.

I said, "Let's hold position here and wait for another roving patrol."

We lay on the hot desert sand, never taking our eyes off the compound as the minutes passed like hours. At three minutes before 1:00 a.m., Celeste said, "Drone four is active."

Chapter 24
Seven Come Eleven

I hadn't forgotten about the note-passing endeavor I hoped I'd started with the handcuffed man behind the barred window, but the roving patrol and the burning of a flawless image into my mind of exactly how the camp looked had become more important in the previous moments. With the report of drone number four being alive, my anticipation was again piqued to see the handwriting on the tiny slip of paper . . . if the paper was on its way back out of the camp.

"Fly it to me," I ordered as all thoughts of the next roving patrol vanished from inside my head.

"Thirty seconds," came Dr. Celeste Mankiller's excited response.

Right on time, drone number four came to a hover a foot in front of me, and I collected it from the air. The rubber band was in place. The pencil was still on board. The handcuff key was missing. And to my delight, the paper was rolled neatly and double-banded to the narrow body of the drone barely the size of a matchbox.

There are three events in a young man's life he never forgets, regardless of how many decades have passed: his first puppy, his first bicycle, and the first time the girl he thinks he loves melts into his arms. The small, seemingly innocuous slip of paper between my fingers eclipsed all three of those events. I no longer owned a bicycle. There was no puppy in my life. And the woman I knew I loved without question was a thousand miles away, sleeping soundly, while my child grew inside her belly. I wouldn't trade that piece of paper for a thousand first times with Wendy Berkshire, the chestnut-haired, blue-eyed girl who had a fondness for baseball players— especially one pretty good sixteen-year-old catcher.

I passed the drone off to Disco and unrolled the miniature scroll. Beneath the word "Number," in shaky writing, was the number 7, but that wasn't the only number. In even smaller writing, beneath the 7, was the number 11.

What is he trying to tell me? Seven Americans and eleven total captives? Seven still alive of eleven original prisoners? Seven in his building and eleven someplace else?

The mystery prevailed.

Beneath the word "Name," he scribbled "Simms, Douglass," and something that might've been the beginning of the name "Dean," but I couldn't be sure.

Why only three names if there are seven prisoners? Are only three still alive? Why isn't Spencer Baldwin's name one of the three?

Beside the word "American" was the one-word answer that chilled me to the bone. "Yes!"

I passed the answers to Skipper back aboard the ship, and her questions echoed my own. "What does seven and eleven mean?"

"I was hoping you could decipher it. I've got some ideas, but they're based on nothing. What's the first thing that came to your mind?"

She said, "I don't like where my head went, but maybe it means seven hostages still alive out of eleven originally taken."

I sighed. "That's one of the possibilities, but not the only one."

I tried to think back to my agonizing days in SERE school, where I learned the physical and psychological necessities of survival, evasion, resistance, and escape. I tried to apply the mindset from that training to the head of the man who'd scribbled on my paper. If I could put my brain in his body for the past several days, how would I answer my three questions? No matter how hard I tried, I couldn't do it. For the moment, we were left with 7 and 11, and regardless of the meaning of those two mysterious numbers, our mission had suddenly become clearer. There were Americans behind that wall. Some of them were still alive, and we were going to get them out.

While I was celebrating the success of establishing limited two-way communication with at least one prisoner, Singer's voice rang in my head. "Movement."

I looked up to see a pair of men, possibly the same two as before, splitting up at the main gate to the compound. Just as before, one man worked clockwise while the other worked in the opposite direction. My watch reported two minutes past 1:00 a.m., confirming my suspicion of a perimeter check at the top of every hour, but something about the regularity of the patrol still bothered me.

Why would an organization of former military special forces soldiers operate on such a predictable schedule?

Anya slid close to me. "I can eliminate both guards silently if you wish."

"Not yet," I said. "There will be time for that once we get a better picture of the whole situation. For now, let them believe the coast is clear."

She whispered, "You have become patient and strong leader. Is very good improvement, and I am impressed, Chasechka. There was time when you were reckless and always moving. This is much better."

"Thank you," I said. "But this isn't really the time for praise. We've got work to do."

She smiled. "See? New Chase is better Chase."

We held our position and waited for both guards to complete their rounds. It took twenty minutes for each of them to make it back to the gate, and I concentrated on the scene, when half of the gate swung open. Two more armed men were positioned directly inside the gate, and I assumed there was at least one more who opened and closed the swinging gate.

Two roving guards, two stationary guards, a gate operator, and three men smoking cigarettes. That's eight well-armed men, at least. The picture was coming together, but a few pieces were still missing.

I said, "CIC, I want to send the drone back in. Does it have sufficient charge for another circuit?"

Celeste said, "Affirmative. It has thirty minutes of battery life remaining. Keep in mind, though, it's dark in that room, and I'm sure the prisoners don't have night-vision goggles."

"That would explain the handwriting. We'll try again just before the sun comes up. Do we have a drone capable of loitering a few thousand feet over the compound with a decent camera?"

"We have three of those. The best one is configured for eleven thousand feet and has an excellent camera. It has a twelve-hour endurance."

"Night vision?" I asked.

"Negative."

I said, "Put it in the air thirty minutes before sunrise, and film everything that happens in that camp. The primary goal is to count bad guys. We're in for a fight, and I want to understand the odds."

"You got it. Do you want the video feed to your tablet?"

"Negative, but make it quickly available if I change my mind."

She said, "Roger."

Before I could finish my conversation with Celeste, Singer said, "Movement! I count six this time. They're moving east, directly toward my position."

I trained my eyes back through my NODs and saw the squad of men rounding the edge of the gate with rifles at the ready.

"I've got 'em," I said.

Singer asked, "How close do we let them come before putting them down?"

No one else was going to answer his question, so I said, "Can you escape unseen?"

"Probably not. Four of them have night vision."

The confident, patient leader Anya saw half an hour before sank in an ocean of indecision, but I managed to say, "When you're certain they're closing on you, put them down."

I watched them continue to the east and played through the consequences of gunning down six cartel members within two hours of hitting the ground.

Before I let myself fall hopelessly into the pit of my own creation, a wave of lights passed overhead. I turned my attention back to the compound gate to see a van accelerating through the opening and turning east.

I tried to refocus on the gunmen on foot, but the light from the van's headlights made it challenging to focus through my night vision. I said, "There's a van on the move."

Singer said, "I've got him, but the shooters are still coming."

What's happening? What are they doing?

Singer's calm baritone resounded in my head. "I'm giving them fifty more yards, then I'll have to engage."

I said, "Engage at will when contact is imminent."

"Roger."

Although I couldn't see Singer and Mongo, I had no doubt they were both in prone position with rifles ready. The Lapua would be of no real value in the engagement, but at the close range, neither of the former Green Berets would have any difficulty eliminating the gunmen with their M4s.

The van made a hard left turn onto a sand-covered road leading northeast and picked up speed. As I watched the taillights grow dimmer in the distance, I expected to hear rifle fire from the east, but it didn't come.

Singer said, "The gunmen are breaking north along the road. It looks like they're setting up a perimeter of some kind."

The more the scene in front of me developed, the less sense it made, and the next sound I heard stirred the pot of confusion even more. I rolled onto my side and stared into the sky to the northwest. The sound was unmistakable. Anyone who's ever lain in the mud, sand, or muck, with blood pouring from their body, longed for the sound I heard so clearly in the desert night.

The approaching *whop* of a Huey helicopter's rotor blades beating the air into submission was the sweetest sound a wounded warrior could ever hear, but for me, on that night so far from home, with confusion rattling around in my head, the sound of that approaching helicopter spelled nothing less than coming chaos and worsening odds for the good guys in the rapidly approaching battle.

I announced, "Chopper approaching from the northwest."

Singer said, "I hear it, but I don't have eyes on it yet. The shooters have established positions along each side of the road with about a hundred yards between them. It looks like they're planning to either protect the van when it comes back or kill the next vehicle coming down the road."

The navigation lights of the Huey came into sight barely above the low hills to the west, and I watched it continue toward the camp.

I said, "Can anybody guess what's going on?"

"I've got one, College Boy."

Clark's combat mind operated a fraction of a second faster than everyone else's, so I was happy to hear his voice.

"Let's hear it," I said.

"My bet would be that your pen pal in that camp got busted, and they're hauling their highest-value prisoner out of there before you come bursting in with guns blazing. They're going to fly somebody out on that chopper. At least that's my guess."

Singer said, "If Clark is right, we have to stop that van. I can still kill it, but only for a few more seconds."

The clock was ticking, and my brain was melting.

What if Clark is wrong? What if we engage the van, deal with the six shooters, and still have to fight whoever's left in the camp? What if the Huey has nothing to do with Los Toros?

Singer said, "Three seconds, Chase."

A decision had to be made, and for reasons I'll never understand, I didn't want to sound indecisive with Anya watching and listening to my every move.

Firing on the van would start a chain reaction that could only be stopped by the annihilation of the cartel or my team. Either way, the fight would be long, bloody, and impossible to endure without losing at least some of my team, my brothers-in-arms, my family.

I gave the order, "Hold your fire."

Chapter 25
New Kid in Town

I could almost see Clark's face back on the ship. He handed me a gift-wrapped decision with a big red bow on it, and I kicked it back under the Christmas tree, unopened.

Anya leaned toward me again and whispered, "Clark is wrong."

Other than glancing at her, I didn't respond, and she didn't seem to expect me to.

The chopper drew ever closer until it overflew the northern end of the compound, and its searchlight illuminated the desert floor like the sun. The beam of light exploded through my NODs, and I closed my eyes against the onslaught and flipped the device up and away from my face.

The scorching light seemed to burn a swath across the sand and scrub brush as the Huey descended toward the earth.

I said, "Singer, can you see where the chopper is landing?"

"It's just across a rise, so I'm blind to the touchdown point."

I called Celeste. "Are you still linked to the drones?"

"Affirmative."

"Great. Send at least one to the northeast of the compound, about two thousand meters, and spot a landing helicopter. I need eyes on that operation."

Drone number four, that had been my carrier pigeon, came to life and leapt from Disco's hand. It was gone in an instant, buzzing its way northward.

Celeste asked, "Do you want it on your tablet?"

"Affirmative."

Almost before I finished the word, my screen came alive with a well-lit image of a Huey in the middle of a roiling sandstorm. When the dust settled and the image cleared, I watched in awe as a man with a bag over his head and his hands cuffed behind his back was led from the chopper toward the van. The two men forcing the captive along were anything but gentle. The man ended up on his knees twice and completely face-down once before they shoved him into the back of the van.

Anya, Disco, and Kodiak peered across my shoulders at the small screen.

Disco said, "They're not flying anybody out. They're making a delivery."

"It certainly looks that way," I said. "Could it be Baldwin?"

"It's impossible to know with that bag over his head, but whoever he is, he's important enough to garner a private flight."

Part of me wanted to take out the road guards and assault the van, but that would put the remaining hostages still inside the compound in danger, and I didn't need that on my conscience.

To my surprise, the Huey's rotor blades slowed to a stop, and the pilot slid from the cockpit and headed for the van. His saunter made him appear relaxed and at ease with the situation. He took a glance back at his chopper and continued toward the van. When he approached one of the armed men, he seemed to have a conversation that ended with the gunman pointing the pilot toward another man near the driver's door. He strolled around the hood of the van and approached the other man. A few seconds after the two men began conversing, the man by the door drew a pistol, stuck it to the pilot's forehead, and pulled the trigger.

I stared in utter disbelief as the pilot's body melted to the sand. The gunman put two more rounds into the corpse and climbed into the driver's seat of the van.

"That didn't look like a knife fight to me," Kodiak said.

I had to agree. "It looks like they've stepped up their game and graduated from machetes to handguns. I think I would've preferred it if they kept the blades."

Clark said, "Why would they kill the pilot?"

I thought about every reason I could come up with, and one kept floating to the top. "Maybe they want to make sure nobody knows where they brought the new kid on the block. Maybe he wasn't Los Toros and they considered him expendable."

Clark said, "Chopper pilots aren't exactly a dime a dozen down here, but they must have another one. Otherwise, they've got a five-thousand-pound hunk of aluminum in the middle of the desert and nobody to make it move."

The two men who'd muscled the prisoner from the chopper and into the van grabbed the pilot's feet and dragged him away from the Huey and at least two hundred yards into the desert. One of them doused the man with a liquid, and the other tossed a match onto the body. Flames leapt into the air as the flesh from the man's body melted from his frame and turned to smoke.

I'd seen a lot of horrifying sights, but I'd never watched a man's corpse burn in the middle of the night. Something told me I'd never get that vision out of my head, but little did I know that by the time the mission was over, that would be one of the least terrifying memories of the experience.

With the pilot's dead body still engulfed in flames, the men mounted the van, and the driver pulled back onto the road. As the van passed southward, each of the roadside guards stood and ran to join the others. The driver pulled around the compound and through the gate that swung open only seconds before his arrival. The six gunmen followed the van into the compound on foot, and someone closed the gate behind them.

I called Singer. "Do you have eyes on the van?"

"Affirmative."

"I expect them to put him in the same building with our friend in handcuffs, but keep an eye on them."

"Wilco."

I said, "Celeste, put a drone in that compound. We need the best video we can get when they pull the new prisoner out of that van."

"I'm on it."

Disco asked, "Are you using number four again, or do you want a fresh one?"

She said, "Launch all of them, and I'll fly the ones with the most charge left."

He opened his satchel and released the drones. Three of them flew away under Celeste's command, and the remainder landed back on the desert floor in front of Disco.

Singer came over the radio. "He's coming out."

From our vantage point, we couldn't see much of the compound, but we had a clear view of the gate.

"Is he still bagged?" I asked.

"Negative. They just yanked the bag from his head, and you were right about the building. They're shoving him toward the same building as the other prisoners."

"Are you getting drone footage yet?" I asked.

Celeste replied, "Affirmative, but I can't tell if that's Baldwin."

Skipper said, "The video isn't good enough for facial recognition either."

I closed my eyes and tried to take myself a million miles away. I needed the solitude and the slightest moment of silence to make the decision that could determine the fate of the imprisoned Americans so close to my fingertips, yet so distant behind gates, walls, weapons, and barbarians. In that silent moment, clarity came, and on its shoulders rode the decision only I could make.

I opened my eyes and gave the orders. "Launch the Little Bird with Gun Bunny, Ronda No-H, and Clark. Put Clark on the ground beside the abandoned Huey, and stand off with the Minigun to provide air support. We're hitting the compound as soon as you're in position."

It wasn't rare for Skipper to second-guess my suggestions when we were gathered around the conference table inside the op center, but in the field, when lives balanced on the razor's edge, she never wavered, and that night in the Mexican desert was no exception. She said, "Roger. Airborne in sixty seconds."

Every sports psychologist I've ever met insisted on envisioning the desired outcome. When I stepped to the plate with my bat in hand, I watched that little white ball soar across the right-field fence. Every time a runner rounded third and set his sights on home plate, I watched the collision end in a cloud of dust, with me gripping the ball deep inside my mitt and the runner slinking back to the dugout, wishing he'd stayed on third.

The coming battle should've been no different. I should've watched my team pour through the gates and over the walls and fences to liberate the Americans, regardless of the number. I should've watched our foe fall beneath our boots, no matter how great their number. I should've watched Ronda pour death from above with the belching barrels of the Minigun.

The picture of every American safely flying away inside the stolen Huey and hanging from the Little Bird should've filled my head, but instead of the fairytale ending I dreamed of experiencing, the reality of the battle lay somewhere short of that perfect outcome. Warriors would fall, and some of them could be mine.

Blood would soak the ground, and some of it could be mine. Lives would be forever changed, and the responsibility for that change would be eternally mine.

I said, "Singer, can you provide overwatch from your position?"

He answered instantly. "Affirmative. I'm dispatching Mongo back to your position."

I would never consider assaulting the camp without Singer's practiced eye peering through his scope across the barrel of the rifle that was practically an extension of his own body and mind. Having Mongo rejoin the assault team was a forgone conclusion. Although the big man did very few things covertly, his brute, his wisdom, and his drive more than made up for the noise and destruction he left in his wake, but that wasn't the entirety of the reason I wanted the giant by my side. For reasons I'll never understand, Mongo had long before become my gargantuan guardian angel. No one would get to me without going through Mongo, and that shield brought with it a confidence unlike any other. As powerful as that consideration was, it didn't encompass the whole of Mongo's necessity in the battle. Should I fall, he would immediately become the operational commander and assume the responsibility that had been mine.

The buzz of the Little Bird approaching from the south pulled me from my dream and back onto the battlefield. I said, "Singer, report any reaction to the chopper inside the camp."

"Roger. The wind is picking up from the west, and Gun Bunny is hugging the terrain. They may never hear her."

I raised my head and caught a glimpse of the Little Bird as it flew well wide of the camp and downwind.

"Let's move to the gate. Mongo, you're with me on the north side. Kodiak, Disco, and Anya, take the south side."

We advanced on the compound, staying as low as possible and taking advantage of rises in the terrain to camouflage our approach. A hundred feet from the gate, I gave the order to hold position and rig the kamikaze drones.

Disco opened his pack and tossed slabs of C-4 to each of us. We pulled off hunks of the sticky explosive in sizes we believed to be six ounces or less. The adhesive property of the putty held it securely to the top side of each drone. We plugged the two-wire lead from the blasting caps into the power outlets Celeste built into each tiny flying machine. Whether she knew the ports would one day provide the power to demolish the devices in sacrificial application of something I'd never know, I was more pleased with the decision to bring her on board than almost any other choice we'd made in recent years. She would change how we operated and save more lives than we could count while doing so.

I called the CIC. "Give the drones a short test flight."

Celeste activated the mosquitoes and brought them to a hover a few feet away. Most held position well, but a couple required the removal of a few pinches of C-4 to stabilize.

I asked Kodiak, "You saved enough C-4 to blow the gate, right?"

"You know it. Just tell me when."

From our position near the gate, we were blind to the east, so I said, "Alpha Seven, Alpha One. Sitrep."

Clark said, "I'll be airborne in the Huey in twenty seconds, and the Little Bird is moving to the southwest."

"Roger. Little Bird, Alpha One."

"Go for Little Bird," Gun Bunny said.

"How long until you're in position?"

"Thirty seconds, and Ronda is on the gun."

I said, "Kill anybody or anything that comes through the gate without announcing it's one of us. Got it?"

"Roger, Alpha One. Nothing and nobody get through that gate alive."

I checked my teammates. "Everybody ready?"

"Let's do it," Kodiak said.

Anya caught my arm before we continued. "Tell to me rules of engagement."

"Don't get dead, and kill everybody who's not American."

Chapter 26
Breacher Up!

We moved into position without being seen, and the explosive drones hummed near the top of the wall above our heads.

Clark reported, "Huey is airborne."

Skipper reported. "CIC is go."

Singer said, "Alpha Six is go."

Gun Bunny said, "Little Bird is go. We'll press as soon as you blow the gate."

I took a long, deep breath. "Come out of here alive, no matter what it takes. If I go down, Mongo is Alpha One. Let's do what we do best."

I touched the side of my helmet with my fist, the signal for Kodiak to go to work, and ordered, "Breacher up!"

He didn't hesitate. In seconds, enough C-4 was pressed into the gate hinges to blow the heavy metal barriers to Cuba.

I said, "Everybody on me. Keep your team in sight, and move as one. This is it. Blow the gate!"

We ducked, turned away from the gates, and Kodiak said, "Fire in the hole."

All four charges belched as one, sending dust, sand, and debris in every direction. The massive gates twisted and danced like barn doors in a tornado, and the force of the explosions hurled them inward. We followed like a pair of centipedes, Mongo and me on the left, and Kodiak's team on the right.

As we pushed through the smoke and dust, a pair of armed cartel fighters appeared like apparitions in front of us. I put two rounds in the first man's chest, and one through his left eye, just as I'd practiced thousands of times. Mongo executed the second man with the same lethal precision, and the rifle reports from the right side of our force said they'd done the same.

I took advantage of the instant of silence. "Little Bird, move up!"

"Moving," Gun Bunny said.

Our peaceful moment ended as an army of cartel fighters formed before our eyes. They ran in every direction, taking cover and concealment behind anything they could find, but our moment of hesitation left us in no-man's-land with no cover. I glanced to my right to see Kodiak's team moving south toward a stone building that would provide them with precious cover, but our side offered nothing.

The cartel opened up, and the report of their rifles sounded exactly like ours. We were firing the same ammunition through the same weapons with the same killing intent.

Firing into a volley of what sounded like friendly fire felt wrong in every imaginable scenario, but it wasn't the sound that would keep us alive; it was our will to overcome the evil behind the rifles that would make us victorious, if that was possible.

Kodiak said, "We'll keep 'em pinned down while you find cover."

Mongo and I raced northward and found a low pile of rocks that was far from ideal but better than anything else in the area. We dived for the cover and rolled into position to join the firefight.

The chaos, fear, and truth of battle, from the days when blades and spears ruled the field, have changed little in the hearts of those who wage the war. The hiss and snap of full-metal-jacketed projectiles racing by ahead was a terrifying reminder of the murderous intent in my enemy's heart, just as the muzzle flashes from my rifle reminded my foe of my yearning to survive and my need to destroy him. Whether the ominous whistle of a modern bullet or the wind from a Roman sword, the truth remains: We will fight for what we believe is worthy of defending, be it seemingly endless riches or the lives of those we love. We will fight, and we will die, and the world will turn tomorrow, just as it did yesterday, with new victors, and new vanquished and ancient evils, and older good.

"Singer, we could use a little help down here."

I don't know whose voice it was, but it was neither mine nor Anya's, and no truer words had ever been spoken on the battlefield or off.

Our sniper's massive .338 Lapua roared from the east, and with it, one living soul departed its earthly body, time after time, until the fighters finally determined the direction of the deadly fire and retreated. They moved behind vehicles, buildings, and barricades of every kind in a desperate scramble to preserve their lives. The retreat gave my team the time and break in fire we needed to reposition and establish a crossfire.

Celeste's drones hovered overhead, capturing every movement on the surface, but I couldn't open up my tablet and allow its glow to illuminate my face. Doing so would've been the equivalent of pressing my own weapon to my head. Instead of my eyes, I relied on my ears to draw the scene of the fight in front of me.

Skipper painted the picture. "Five down at the east end of their line. At least a dozen moved behind the structure holding the prisoners. Six or possibly seven are taking cover behind the truck and the van at your ten o'clock."

I leapt from behind the low pile of rocks and sprinted to a small stone structure twenty yards away. Once in position, I poured rifle fire onto the van and truck to cover Mongo's movement. Despite his size, he moved with the agility of an athlete and landed beside me on the sand.

I called team two. "Kodiak, report."

He said, "No wounded, no killed. We're in position to push ten or twelve men around the prison house and expose them to you."

"Do it!" I ordered, and we waited for the firefight to come alive again.

Kodiak, Disco, and Anya unleashed hell, careful to avoid sending rounds into the prison house. The tactic worked. As the dozen men retreated from the cascading fire from the east, they showed themselves to Mongo and me, and we made them pay.

Caught in the deadly crossfire, they shot wildly into the darkness as confusion consumed them and we continued to mow them down.

Skipper continued her play-by-play. "Chase, the men behind the van are flanking to your left."

"How many are left by the prison house?"

"Four or maybe five."

I laid a hand on Mongo's shoulder. "Keep putting fire on them as they retreat from the house. I'll cover the flank."

He didn't have to answer. The steady stream of fire from his rifle told me he was determined to eliminate the threat in front of him. I turned and lay in the prone position with my left boot draped across his calf. The weight of my leg against his would keep both of us aware of the other's position.

Again, Singer's rifle roared twice, and Skipper called, "Two more down to the east. And Chase, they're still flanking you. You need to—"

I didn't hear what she said next. The report of my rifle drowned her out. I put two men down and strained to see the third.

"Where'd he go, Skipper?"

She said, "He's behind what looks like four or five stacked barrels, and he's not alone. Two or three more men just joined up on him."

I found the barrels and put thirty rounds into them before changing magazines. "Are they still back there, Skipper?"

"Affirmative. The barrels must be full of something."

There's only one thing that comes in barrels in the Mexican desert.

I said, "Singer, put an incendiary on my laser."

My infrared laser designator shone like a beacon in the night through our NODs.

Singer said, "Roger." He sent the round designed for only one purpose, and in the middle of that dark night, his round fulfilled its lethal purpose.

I closed my eyes and flipped up my NODs to avoid the flash as the incendiary round met the fumes of the fuel from the barrels I'd turned into Swiss cheese. A massive orange flame thundered into the sky, illuminating the camp as if it were noon.

"Nice shooting, Singer."

I took in the battlefield in front of me and devoted it to memory while the fire illuminated everything within a hundred yards.

Kodiak said, "We're advancing. We've finally got them outnumbered."

"You're almost right," Skipper said. "I count nine still moving."

"I've got four," I said.

Anya said, "I see only three."

The seven we had in sight suddenly felt like seven hundred. In what must have been desperation, they opened up on us full auto, spilling rounds as fast as their American M4s could cycle.

"Hold your cover," I ordered. "They have to run out of ammo sometime."

We made ourselves small and listened as round after round whistled past, ricocheting off every surface they struck. The storm of fire through my hearing aids sounded far away and other-worldly. I wondered how it sounded to Mongo and the rest of the team.

One by one, their rifles fell temporarily silent as empty magazines were replaced by loaded ones and the rain of lead continued to fall.

"They're advancing," Skipper announced. "There's eleven now. Chase, there's five advancing on your left. And Kodiak, you've got six coming straight on."

I growled. "Singer, put some rounds down here. We're being overrun."

"I don't have a line of sight," he yelled. "But I'm moving. Expect fire in fifteen seconds."

"We'll be bleeding out in fifteen seconds," I almost screamed. "Little Bird! Get in here! We need some lead in the air."

I felt, more than heard, the buzz of the approaching MH6 Little Bird as Gun Bunny raced across the fence to the southeast, and the thunder of the M134 Minigun in Ronda's hands belching 6,000 7.62mm rounds per minute could've been the sound of a legion of warring angels descending from the heavens. The desert in front of us exploded with a thousand geysers spewing sand and stone into the air as if the Earth were throwing up her hands in surrender.

As the fire kept falling, I yelled, "Don't hit the prison house!"

Gun Bunny didn't answer, but the angle of fire changed, the stream of lead sweeping to the north, away from the prisoners.

"Hold your fire," I ordered, and the Minigun fell silent as the Little Bird angled back to set up for another gun run if necessary.

I said, "Skipper, any survivors?"

"I've got heat signatures in the prison house, but no movement in the open."

I said, "Send Disco to me."

Kodiak dispatched him and provided cover while our chief pilot moved to join Mongo and me.

When he made the crossing, I said, "Disco, you and Mongo sweep for living from the left, and Kodiak, I want you and Anya to sweep right."

"Roger," came Disco's one-word reply, and I stepped toward the prison house.

I moved slowly with my night-vision goggles in place, scanning every inch of ground in front of me for a surviving cartel member. Falling victim to a drug runner playing possum wasn't on my to-do list. When I made it to the small house, I positioned myself by the window where my note had been passed and said, "We're here to get you out. How many are in there?"

"Were you the one who sent the drone?" a voice asked.

"Affirmative. How many?"

"There are seven . . . no, eight of us now."

"Do you know if the door is rigged with explosives or any other booby traps?"

"How would I know?"

I said, "When the guards came and went, did they spend longer than necessary opening or closing the door?"

"Maybe. I wasn't really looking for that. Just get us out of here."

"We will, but we have to make sure we keep everyone alive. Just hold tight. I'm going to have our bomb tech take a look at the door."

"Just get us out of here, man!"

"Stay calm. You're going to be safe. We just have to make sure we don't get anyone hurt or killed while we're pulling you out."

I called Kodiak. "Sitrep."

He said, "Camp is clear. We count twenty-nine dead, no survivors. We're setting perimeter security now."

"Very well. I need you on this door at the prison house. It may be rigged."

"On my way," he said.

The voices from inside the house rose with excited emotion. Some were crying. Some were yelling for us to get them out. Others sounded as if they were praying.

I said, "Listen up. I need you to move away from the door and to the sides of the room. Press yourselves against the walls, and stay there until we know the door isn't rigged to blow. Got it?"

The voices quieted, and they were replaced by the rattling of chains.

I said, "I sent in a handcuff key. Are you still locked up?"

The man said, "We're chained together at the waist and ankles, and the key you sent is no good on these locks."

"Don't worry about that. We'll get you out. Just stay away from the door until you hear me say differently."

It grew quiet enough to hear the crackle of the fuel fire still burning strong on the other side of the camp.

Kodiak showed up. "Give me some light."

I activated my infrared light and shone it on the perimeter of the door. Through Kodiak's NODs, it would've looked like daylight. He ran his hand carefully around the edges of the door, then pulled a tool from his kit. It looked like a butter knife, but the blade was as thin as foil. He probed the crack between the door and the jamb with the tool until he'd completed a full circuit of the opening.

"What do you think?" I asked.

"It's clear," he said. "But that's a serious lock. If you want to get inside, we'll either have to scrounge through a bunch of dead bodies looking for a key, or I can blow the door."

I moved back to the window and said, "The door isn't rigged, but in order to get you out, we have to set off a small explosive charge to blow the door open. It's going to be loud, but it's not dangerous. Just keep yourselves pressed to the walls, and look away from the door."

Kodiak rigged the shaped charge and pressed it to the hinge side of the door.

It was time to call a cab, so I said, "Alpha Eight, Alpha One, get that bus in here double-quick. We're blowing the prison door, and we'll have eight civilians."

Clark said, "I thought you'd never ask. I'm on my way, College Boy. Oh, there's something you should know. This bus belongs to the DEA. It's covered in placards in English with U.S. Government written all over them."

DEA?, I thought. *Why would the cartel have a DEA helicopter?*

The sight of the burning body of the Huey pilot flashed through my head, and I choked on the thought. Trying to force the horrific sight out of my mind, I said, "Blow the door."

Kodiak banged on the door of the prison house, and for the second time that night, he called out, "Fire in the hole!"

The explosion was small, well-controlled, and perfectly efficient. The door separated from its hinges and fell inward as it pulled the locking mechanism from the jamb. The eight prisoners rushed us as if fleeing a fire, and we stepped aside to avoid being trampled.

"Easy!" I said. "It's okay. You're safe now. We're going to fly you out of here and onto our ship."

A woman asked, "You're SEALs, aren't you?"

I said, "We're just here to take you home. That's all. Is anyone badly hurt?"

"No, we're hungry, thirsty, and happy to see you."

Kodiak and I passed out bottles of water as the *whop* of the Huey's rotors sounded from the south.

"That's your ride," I said. "I need to know if one of you is Spencer Baldwin."

Before anyone could answer, the Huey's searchlight illuminated the ground around us, and Clark began his descent into the compound. I glanced up to see where he was planning to touch down just as a streak of white smoke from the northwest scorched its way toward the helicopter. The rocket-propelled grenade struck the Huey just behind the engines and severed the tail boom. Clark's magic bus had just become a five-thousand-pound, falling, burning coffin.

Chapter 27
The Fallen

The world stopped turning, and I stared in utter disbelief as what remained of the Huey helicopter spun beneath its still-beating rotors. The eight former prisoners of Los Toros stared skyward alongside me, but the scene they saw unfolding before their eyes was the destruction of their chariot out of captivity. What I saw was the end of a life of selfless service, devotion, and endless sacrifice for the preservation of freedom. What I saw was death's relentless claw reaching from the pits of Earth and into the sky, raking, pawing, and grasping for the life of my friend, my teacher, my brother.

I bellowed, "Where's my security to the west? Who fired that RPG?"

Whoever was coming had just struck a blow for which they would pay with their lives. Perhaps it was my fury, or the benevolence of God, but I never heard the Huey collide with the earth. Looking back now, I don't remember hearing anything except the pounding of my heart, like the sound of a drum of war charging me onward, fueling my very existence to avenge the death of the best man I'd ever known; the man who'd held me in his arms, stopping my blood from staining the ground; the man I'd carried from the Khyber Pass when his mortal body refused to give up his spirit; the man who'd turned me from little more than a boy, into a warrior.

Rage fired me, revenge drove me, and endless loss transformed my measured, calculated command of the battlefield into a torrent of unstoppable madness.

I turned to the first man I saw and grabbed his shoulders. "Can you shoot?"

"What?"

"I said, can you shoot a rifle?"

He shook his head violently, and I shoved him aside.

The next man answered before I could ask. "Yes, yes. I can shoot."

I shoved my rifle into his hands and forced him back through the opening where the door to the prison house had been only minutes before. "Get back in there, and kill anybody who comes through the door."

He staggered backward, dragging his fellow prisoners, still shackled at the waist and ankle, back into their temporary purgatory. Mongo stuck his rifle into a second man's arms who'd reached out when I asked for a shooter.

As if joined by an unseen force, Mongo and I moved as one. We yanked rifles identical to our own from the dead hands of the fallen cartel fighters, and then we bounded over the tailgate of the truck the shooters had used for cover and onto its roof. The perch gave us the elevation we needed to see—for the first time—the oncoming band of fighters apparently responding from the second Los Toros camp. The sweat and hatred in my eyes made estimating the size of the force more difficult than it should've been.

I said, "Somebody tell me how many of them there are."

Skipper asked, "What's happening, Chase?"

I yelled, "Tell me how many people are coming for me!"

It was Singer's steady, determined voice that cut through the emotion. "I count twelve to fourteen in three trucks, and they've got a technical. It looks like a fifty-cal on the lead vehicle. Are we sure they're Los Toros?"

Clarity called to me, but chaos reigned, and I bowed before her. "Singer, kill the technical! Little Bird, stop the first two trucks, but the third one is mine."

I leapt from the top of the truck and ran for the gaping wound where the gate had once been. I never looked back to see him, but the pounding of boots told me Mongo was only one step behind. I pressed the magazine release on my stolen rifle and shoved a full mag into the well at the same instant Singer and the Little Bird opened up on the aggressors. The man on the fifty-cal took Singer's first round and flew from the truck as if yanked by the hand of God. Singer's second shot tore the gun from its mount, and his third pierced the windshield directly in front of the driver. The death of the driver, coupled with the rugged terrain, sent the truck tumbling and rolling down a slope to the left.

Ronda's deadly skill behind the Minigun halted the second truck with a five-second burst of hundreds of rounds. Smoke and steam boiled from the wreckage, but no one emerged from inside.

I raised the rifle to my shoulder and flipped the selector to full auto. With the trigger crushed beneath my finger, I willed every round into the bodies of the men inside the third truck. When it bounced to a stop, a solitary fighter stepped from the passenger side door, and I met him with my shoulder, sending his body crashing into the frame of the cab. He exhaled a mighty breath like a blowing whale, and I yanked the rifle from his hands. I stuck the muzzle into the cab and slammed the trigger, emptying the weapon into any living creature still inside. With his weapon empty and out of his hands, the man drew his machete and shoved me off of him.

I watched him come, and just as Anya had driven into our heads, I sidestepped the blow, letting the blade whistle harmlessly through the air. Looking down at my rifle, I threw it into the sand, shucked off my helmet, and drew my knife.

He recovered from the missed attack and spun to face me once again. The gleaming blade of my fighting knife shone in the glow of the truck's headlights and glistened in stark contrast to the blood-soaked blade of his machete. He extended his arm with the blade wide and long. The blow would be upward and aimed at my crotch or my armpit. In his mind, he would end the fight with one mighty upward swing, but he had no idea what sort of animal stood before him.

I welcomed the attack. I yearned for his arrogant advance. Instead of waiting for him to make his move, I stepped toward him, and the swing came. He groaned as the muscles of his chest and arm propelled the razor-sharp weapon through the air. I threw myself from my feet, landing on my side with the blade missing by only inches. Grabbing his booted foot, I yanked the man from his stance, sending him sprawling to the ground. The clang of his blade striking rock and sand echoed through the night. Springing from my position, I buried my knife between the middle knuckles of his weapon hand, rendering the appendage little more than useless as blood poured from the wound.

He dropped his machete and cupped his fileted hand into his left palm.

I yanked him to his feet, recovered his machete, and shoved it against his chest. "Fight me, you coward! Take your blade and fight me!"

The whites of his eyes grew as my rage bloomed before him. He gripped the machete with his weak hand and stepped back.

I threw up a hand and yelled, "Wait!"

My outburst startled him, and he flinched, giving me just enough time to shuck my body armor. The thirty pounds of steel plates and rifle magazines thudded to the desert floor as I faced my foe, the man who, in my mind, killed Clark Johnson.

He thrust himself toward me, ignoring my knife and wildly swinging his massive blade. I studied the rhythm, matched the swings to his strides, and let him come. When he was at arm's length and filled with a fool's confidence, I parried his downward strike and sliced him from shoulder to hip, opening his chest to the same dirt and rot-filled air in which my brother lay. He pawed at his chest and gasped for air as I stared into his terror-filled eyes, begging him to attack again.

To my delight, the fear left the man as he accepted the inevitable outcome of his lifetime of choosing the wrong path, the wrong life, the wrong existence. He raised the machete over his head and yelled like a man possessed as he threw himself forward, desperately yearning to take part of me with him when he left the world of his own making.

As he came with his blade high, I stepped into him, burying my shoulder beneath his arm, trapping the blade forever skyward. I thrust my knife between his legs and drew with all my strength, all my anger, all my fury, and felt the blade sink through his flesh from his crotch to his chin.

His blade fell first, then came his lifeless body, dissolving into my arms. There was no remorse, no sorrow, no pity. There was only bloodlust to see another man stand and fight where his brother had fallen. What humanity had been within me left my soul the instant Clark plummeted to the ground and to his death. I was less than any man should be, and somehow, more than any wild creature could dream of becoming. In that moment, I was a mindless machine driven by every emotion and every evil no man should taste.

When Mongo grabbed the corpse and tossed it off of me, I felt the man's blood scorching my skin, and I tasted the desperation in his final breath. The man who'd become my self-appointed protector hefted me from the ground and shoved me against the truck that was riddled with my bullet holes.

Death lay everywhere around me in a silent world of darkness pierced in diverse angles by beams of light exploding from fires, dying vehicles, and weapon-mounted lights in the sand.

In an instant, I was everything I had fought so hard to prevent my team from becoming. I was a mindless killing animal with no capacity for compassion and no ability to contain the beast within. I was everything I feared Anya was, and somehow, in that moment, I was exactly what I had chosen to become.

Is it possible to un-ring the bell? Can the line be uncrossed? Had I finally reached the end of my sanity?

As if the heavens had opened up before me, I saw the face of my unborn child, the tears of the woman I loved, and the void where I had once belonged—where my home had once lain and where I may never again be able to stand.

Mongo shook me with the violence of a man trying desperately to pierce the veil of insanity and pull me back through that ethereal boundary through which man should never pass. Although there were no sounds, I read Mongo's words as if they were scribed upon my soul.

"Clark is alive!"

Chapter 28
The Risen

One of the marks of a competent assault team is its adaptability when the chain of command crumbles from the top. I had not only crumbled, but I had succumbed to the primal calling of a madman. Mongo recognized the fall and rose to the demand.

He said, "All stations . . . all stations. Alpha Two is now Alpha One."

Those were words I never thought I'd hear, but as I shoved my one remaining hearing aid back into my ear, I couldn't call Mongo's assumption of command anything short of the perfect battlefield call.

Skipper's voice came. "Is Chase . . ."

Mongo said, "Chase is alive and mobile, but he's out of the fight. He's with me."

He motioned toward my plate carrier and rifle lying in the sand. "Pick up your gear."

I followed his order and fell in step behind our new commander. His calm, confident tone served to bring the adrenaline down to a manageable level and restore the organization I'd destroyed.

He said, "Say status of Alpha Eight."

Skipper said, "He's alive, aboard, and headed to sick bay. I'll report his condition when we know more."

He said, "All elements, stand fast on security. Disco, move the six healthiest Americans from the house and put them on the Little Bird. She'll be on deck in less than five minutes."

Disco said, "Roger."

Mongo called our sniper. "Alpha Six, I need you inside the compound on the highest structure for overwatch."

Singer said, "Roger, Alpha One. Six is coming in."

His next call was back to the ship. "CIC, I need perimeter security in all directions. Put those drones in position to avoid any more surprises."

Skipper said, "They're in position now, and the feed is live on your tablet. We're also monitoring all sectors from the CIC, and we'll report any movement."

He finished with one more network-wide order. "This thing isn't over. We've got a lot of clean-up to do. Everyone except Alpha Six and Alpha Four, I want you to police up the rifles. They're going back to the ship with us."

Things were falling into place without me. The team operated like clockwork with Mongo in command. In that moment, the thought of hanging up my boots came easily and without the bitterness it had left in my mouth every previous time I'd said this was my final mission. I could leave the team in more-than-capable hands, and nothing about our efficiency and lethality would change. I was but a single cog in the machine that was Operation Team 21, and I was replaceable.

The Little Bird landed just inside the gate, and Disco situated the first six former prisoners onto the chopper. Seconds after touching down, Gun Bunny was gone, leaving nothing but dust in her wake.

I felt like I'd left the world of the living, and everything was still happening while I watched from seclusion behind a glass through which life cannot pass.

By the time the Little Bird was back on the ground, Disco had the remaining prisoners and a massive pile of American rifles aboard the chopper. The third shipbound flight of the post-battle night was gone, and all that remained was the team of six operators and nearly fifty dead bodies, including one burnt corpse that had likely once been the earthly presence of an American DEA pilot.

With the roar of battle and the pounding blades of the chopper long gone, Mongo turned off his satellite coms and grabbed my arm. "How you doing, Chase?"

I nodded. "I'm good."

"Are you sure? What you did back there isn't what we do. We're not judge, jury, and executioner. We accomplish the mission with emotion aside because it's the right thing to do. We saved the prisoners, and we probably eliminated the Los Toros cartel, but you took it too far."

I looked away. "I know. It was . . ."

He shook me. "It doesn't matter what it was. You're in charge. You're the standard, and these men won't follow you into the fires of Hell if they can't trust you to keep it together."

I couldn't look him in the eye. "I know. When I saw Clark go down, I went with him."

"Listen to me, Chase. Dealing with fallen brothers is one of the things that makes us capable of keeping freedom alive and out of the hands of barbarians like the people we put down tonight." He released my arm and planted his massive palm on my chest. "You're in charge. You're the heart of us. Don't show us how to become the enemy. Teach us to do it right every time . . . Every time, Chase."

Finally, I looked into his face and saw his faith in me. I saw earnest devotion and endless sacrifice staring back at me. I let his confidence lift me from the abyss into which I'd fallen and said, "I have the helm."

The big man turned his radio back on and announced, "I am now Alpha Two. Chase has command."

Having lost one hearing aid while fighting with the final cartel soldier, my hearing was a little distorted but not gone. The Little Bird announced her presence with the typical buzz of her rotors, and Gun Bunny touched down like a hummingbird.

I grabbed Disco and Mongo. "Go pick up the remains of the Huey pilot they killed and burned. Whoever he is, he deserves to lay at rest at home, not down here in this godforsaken desert."

They flew off to the northeast, and I asked Kodiak, "How much C-4 do you have left?"

"Maybe half a pound. Why?"

"I want to torch this place."

He said, "I'm on it."

The Little Bird took off, I assumed with the burnt remains of the pilot on board, and I called, "Little Bird, Alpha One. Give Ronda No-H a little gunnery practice on our desert patrol vehicles."

"Roger, Alpha One. Demo the buggies."

I couldn't hear the Minigun, but the orange fire erupting from the muzzles of the M134 gave me confidence that no one would recognize the lumps of demolished aluminum in the desert as having once been DPVs used by American commandos to liberate eight hostages and annihilate Los Toros.

The world around me seemed to be consumed by that orange fire. From the still-burning barrels of fuel to the four infernos Kodiak initiated within the camp, what had once been a den of demons was being reduced to barren, scorched desert.

I called the team together when the sound of the Little Bird wafted in from the west, and the look of exhaustion dripped from their faces. "Quite a night, huh?"

Weary nods of agreement were all I got in return.

The chopper touched down, and the clunky landing said we weren't the only tired operators that night. Gun Bunny had flown more than her share of sorties on that endless night, and as much as she craved the action, there was no question she was ready to fall into the sack and put the night behind her.

I slid onto the left seat and gave her a nod. "Nice work tonight. I'll take us home. You've earned a break."

She sighed and leaned back in her seat. "You have the controls."

"I have the controls."

One last glance over the mayhem we poured out gave me the peace to know justice had been served, Americans had been liberated from captivity, and a true evil had been erased from the planet. My team and I did that, and I couldn't think of a better way to end my career as a covert operative and transition into the world of fatherhood and retirement.

I pulled the chopper off the ground and turned to the west. As the coastline of the peninsula passed beneath our skids, I cast a glance toward the city of Cabo San Lucas, still alive and throbbing, fueled by American dollars and appetites for debauchery. I wondered if the huddled masses bouncing and gyrating in time with the overamped music had any idea what the last three hours looked like only twenty miles from the heart of the city. Would anyone other than my team and the recovered hostages ever know the full horror of what unfolded on that scalding desert night? Would we remember it in its entire truth, or would our minds soften it to make it more palatable and easier to forget? How many more teams like mine, and nights like that one, would it take to rid the world of the evil the violent drug trade pours out on the innocent and the willfully ignorant?

As I scanned between the vast sea of darkness through the windshield and the pulsing city, a pair of objects caught my eye, and I peered into the unfocused area between the nightlife and the darkened sea. Pointing out the door, I said, "Look at that. What are those?"

Gun Bunny leaned forward and peered across me. "Those are bad news. They are, quite possibly, the worst news of our night."

I flipped the radio frequency and hit the button. "Bridge, Alpha One."

"Go for Bridge," Captain Sprayberry said.

"We've got a pair of Mexican Navy patrol boats steaming your way out of Cabo. I estimate their speed at twenty-five to thirty knots."

"Roger, Alpha One. We're tracking them on radar. Say your ETA."

I glanced at Gun Bunny, and she held up five fingers.

"Five minutes."

"Stand by and continue inbound," he said.

There was little doubt the navigation officer was plotting and calculating time to intercept.

Captain Sprayberry said, "Alpha One, say fuel remaining in time."

I glanced at the gauges and then at the pilot.

She said, "Less than thirty minutes."

"How much less?" he asked.

Gun Bunny keyed up. "What's the math, Captain?"

He said, "We don't want an international incident with the Mexican Navy. Our only hope of avoiding that is to run or blow them out of the water. We can do either, but I prefer option number one."

She ran the numbers in her head. "In this wind, we can make forty miles west or fifty-five miles north. Your call, Captain."

He said, "Let's split the difference. We're off station now and bearing three-one-zero degrees. We'll make forty-five knots if the sea doesn't beat us to death. That'll put you over the deck in approximately eleven minutes. Can you make that happen?"

"Affirmative," she said. "But I can't land this thing on a pitching deck at forty-five knots. You'll have to get her below ten knots."

The captain said, "We're coming up to speed now. We'll be on the foils in two minutes. If you need us at or below ten knots, we have to put some more space between us and those ships. They carry eight anti-ship missiles each. If they open fire, we can't out-run those missiles."

"You can shoot them down, though, right?"

"Affirmative," he said. "But that's going to get a lot of attention. Run northwest, and when we intercept, I'll bring us about and into the wind. You'll have two minutes or less to make your approach and landing."

"Roger, Captain. We're on our way." The exhaustion on her face morphed into sheer determination, and she said, "I have the controls."

I was the wrong man to be in the front seat, but Disco was already back aboard the ship, so Gun Bunny was stuck with me by her side in a race for our lives. If the patrol boats could take out a ship, taking out a chopper running on fumes would be a piece of Mexican cake.

Chapter 29
Carnival Ride

I could almost see the wheels turning inside Gun Bunny's head. The time, distance, and fuel calculations weren't terribly complex, but coupled with the stress of low-level night flying over the ocean, followed by a high-wind approach and landing aboard a pitching and rolling deck at sea, made the numbers more than a little daunting.

"You good?" I asked.

"Yeah, it's going to be close, but we can do it. Keep your fingers crossed for flat seas."

"I hate to break it to you, but that southwest wind has been blowing over eight thousand miles of ocean. Flat is not in the forecast."

She sighed. "Yeah, I know, but keep your fingers crossed anyway. We might get lucky."

"Yep, that's exactly how we roll. Leap, and the net will appear, right?"

"Something like that. I'm going to do a three-sixty to give the forward-looking radar a glance at those ships. Keep your eye on the scope, and feed me speeds and distance, will you?"

I said, "Sure, but why don't we have three-hundred-sixty-degree radar?"

She shrugged. "Because I don't have the authority to sign checks."

"After what you pulled off tonight, you do now," I said. "Whatever you want or need is yours. If the ship's budget can't bear it, I'll cover it personally."

She chuckled. "Oh, sure. Make big promises when we're being chased by the Mexican Navy into a howling wind toward a ship the size of a playing card in an overloaded chopper with a shot glass full of gas in the tank. Here comes the turn."

She banked to the left, and I pinned my eyes to the radar scope. As she turned through 180 degrees, the green returns appeared, and a data block populated beside each vessel.

I said, "They're at one-three-zero degrees at twenty-four miles, making twenty-six knots."

Some of the stress drained from her face, and she said, "I wonder what the range on those anti-ship missiles is."

"You don't want to know."

She tried to smile. "Here's a little tidbit to make all of this sound happier. We just painted a pair of warships with our piece-of-crap radar. Do you think they've got us locked up yet?"

"I'm sure the tone is ringing like a bell. Let's just hope they don't pull the trigger."

She gave me a nudge. "Now look who's crossing his fingers."

Back on course, I expanded the range of the radar and spotted six targets looming ahead. "Which one of those is ours?"

She pointed to the closest target. "That's the *Lori Danielle*, and I'm glad to see her." She pecked the fuel indicators with the tips of her fingers. "We're almost out of gas and time."

Our ship appeared on the horizon, and I jabbed a finger toward the windshield. "There she is!"

She called the ship. "Bring her about, Captain. We've got just enough gas to make the deck."

As we grew closer, the lights of the helipad made the perfect welcome mat. Captain Sprayberry turned into the wind and slowed to ten knots.

Gun Bunny adjusted herself in the seat and took a deep breath. "Call my distances inside fifty feet."

I leaned forward and let my eyes adjust to the lights of the ship. The same two crewmen who fueled the chopper on the quick turn were standing at the limits of the helipad, waiting to lock the skids down as soon as we planted them on deck.

"Here we go," she said.

As we approached, the helipad bucked vertically from front to back, and she said, "At least it's not rolling left and right."

"Fifty feet," I said, estimating the distance to the best of my ability.

She continued descending, and the deck kept pitching ten feet or more.

"Forty feet."

As we fell into the lee of the superstructure, the wind calmed, but the stability didn't. We rocked and jerked as she tried to match the rise and fall of the pad.

"Thirty feet . . . Twenty-five."

A gust of wind rounded the superstructure and blew us to port, and our seasoned pilot responded sharply, but it was too late. We were too far off centerline to continue the approach. She broke left and accelerated across the water to try again.

"That was exciting," Singer said.

Gun Bunny maneuvered us back on line and descended again. "Tell them to hit the deck when I come to a hover. I can't risk losing them if we have to wave off again."

I leaned toward our sniper. "When she brings us to a hover, she wants you guys to bail out and clear the pad."

He yelled back, "Roger."

"Call the distances," she said.

"Fifty feet."

The approach felt more stable, and the deck seemed to be calming down, even if only a little.

"Forty feet."

Again, we slipped from the headwind and into the lee of the superstructure. She handled the transition perfectly.

"Thirty feet . . . Twenty-five."

The deck rose and then plummeted as the ship crested a wave and dived down the back side.

"Twenty."

She said, "Tell them to go at the ten-feet call."

She continued the approach and ignored the pitching deck.

"Ten." I leaned toward Singer. "Go! Go! Go!"

Singer, Anya, Kodiak, and Ronda leapt from the chopper and landed with a roll onto the helipad. In an instant, they were on their feet and retreating into the hangar bay. To my surprise, Gun Bunny didn't wave off. She continued the approach, inching toward the deck with her eyes pinned on the edge of the helipad. As the front edge of the pad rose, she pulled pitch and maneuvered to avoid striking the deck too hard.

Everything inside of me wanted to take the controls and stick the Little Bird to the deck, but she was a far more experienced and capable chopper pilot than I'd ever be. I sat with my feet curled beneath my seat and my hands in my lap.

Trying to take my mind off the carnival ride I was on, I scanned the instrument panel and watched the fuel gauges turn from yellow to red. "We're outta gas!"

The front of the pad rose again, and she pulled barely enough pitch to keep the skids off the deck. As the ship slid down the back side of the wave, she followed it and stuck both skids to the pad, then rolled the throttle to flight idle.

I gave her shoulder a squeeze. "Nice flying."

She looked up with confusion on her face. "What do you mean? I thought you were doing the flying."

The deck crew anchored the chopper, and the captain brought our speed back up to outrun the approaching patrol boats.

Within seconds of shutting down the turbine of the Little Bird, the claxon sounded general quarters, and our speed increased even more. The captain whipped the *Lori Danielle* through sixty-degree turns submariners call "Crazy Ivans." I didn't know what was happening, but I knew how to find out. I made my way into the heart of the vessel to the CIC.

"What's going on?" I demanded as soon as I cleared the hatch.

Mr. LaGrange, the ship's weapons officer, glanced up from his console and announced, "Missiles in the air."

"The Navy is shooting at us?" I asked.

"Affirmative, but they're radar-guided missiles, and now that the Little Bird is on deck, we're as good as invisible. We're actively jamming, and we've activated stealth condition. If they hit us, it'll be pure luck."

"You're still tracking the missiles in case you have to shoot them down, right?"

"Of course," he said. "But probably not for the reasons you suspect. If the missile's radar locks up another vessel like a freighter or a commercial fishing ship, we can't let them sink an innocent."

I stepped behind Weps and looked across his shoulder.

He pointed to his screen. "That's missile number one, and I hope we've confused it badly enough to self-destruct. We'll know in a few seconds." He slid his finger across the screen. "And that's number two. I'm still a little nervous about that one. It seems to have a little better guidance system. That's the reason for the Crazy Ivans."

Number one vanished from the screen, and I asked, "Where'd it go?"

Weps said, "It's either in tiny pieces, sinking to the bottom of the Pacific, or it's skimming the waves. Either way, we're golden as far as that one's concerned."

Number two kept coming and seemed to adjust to our sporadic turns.

Weps said, "I don't know how, but it's still tracking us. If it breaks three thousand yards, I'll kill it, but I'd much rather watch it kill itself."

The captain continued his erratic maneuvers until Weps pressed a button on the console and said, "Close-in weapon system active. Recommend you stand on course and authorize the kill."

Our turn ceased, and Captain Sprayberry said, "Standing on course three-one-zero. Kill that thing, Weps."

"Aye, sir."

Four seconds later, missile number two vanished from the screen.

Weps made a pistol out of his thumb and index finger and blew imaginary smoke from the muzzle. "And that's how modern-day gunfighting works. Let's go home." He pressed the button again. "Splash both bogies, Captain. No more weapons inbound, and we're making twice the speed of the Mexican Navy vessels, sir."

"Nice shootin', Weps. Secure general quarters, and return to normal high-speed operations."

The fight was over, and the good guys prevailed. I should've been elated, but all I could think about was Clark lying in sick bay, fortunate just to be alive.

Dr. Shadrack met me as I stepped through the hatch and into his lair. "Good to see you, Chase. Come in."

"Thanks, Doctor. What's the word?"

He asked, "Which word? The hostages or Clark?"

"Both. But Clark first."

He said, "I thought that might be your answer. It's nothing short of a miracle. I have some concerns about his spine. The impact was obviously massive, but so far, I've only found one broken bone in his forearm and a few in his left hand and wrist. You know a little about those injuries."

"Oh, yeah," I said. "I know those injuries all too well. Is he awake?"

"He's in and out. Last time I checked on him, he was dozing off, but you're welcome to go in if you'd like."

I said, "I'd like to see him if you don't think it'll be too much."

He laughed. "I can't promise he'll remember you coming in. I've given him plenty of meds to put him in the spirit world."

"Thanks. How about the hostages?"

"They're a different story. They're in remarkable condition for what they've been through. A few cuts and bruises are all I could find except for exhaustion and dehydration. They're all on IV fluids, and I recommend a shower for all of them . . . soon."

I chuckled. "Hygiene in captivity isn't high on the priority list."

"I guess not. Make yourself at home, and if you need anything, don't hesitate to ask. There are two nurses milling about and managing things. I'm going to get a couple of hours of sleep."

"Thanks again, Doc. I don't know how to thank you for what you do down here."

He laid a hand on my shoulder. "None of us are in this for the thanks, Chase. You of all people know that."

I pulled back a curtain and saw Clark propped awkwardly on a pile of pillows with an IV in one arm and a splint on the other.

A nurse stuck her head through the curtain. "Is he doing all right?"

I shrugged. "I don't know. That's your department. He looks stoned to me."

"That's a pretty fair assessment. We'll set and cast his arm in the morning, but for now, we're letting him and his battered body catch up on some much-needed rest."

Clark stirred and opened one eye. "Hey, College Boy. Have you ever been shot down?"

"No, I can't say I have."

He yawned. "Let me tell you . . . it sucks!"

"It looks to me like you've got it made. Nurses and doctors at your beck and call, all the narcotics you can swallow, and a nice stack of pillows."

He groaned. "Yeah, well, this is the best part so far. Is everybody else alive?"

"All the good guys are. The hostages are safe and in good shape. The Mexican Navy shot at us, but we dealt with that, too."

He grinned. "You know what Confucius always said . . . It ain't a party 'til the Mexicans start shooting at you."

I shared a glance with the nurse and said, "That's always been my favorite of Confucius's words of wisdom."

Clark let his eyes drift around the room. "Yep, I knew that about you. Confucius is as Confucius does. Ain't that right?"

"You've never been more right, my friend. Get some rest. I'll check on you in the morning. It's good to see you alive."

"It sure is," he whispered as his eyes fell closed and the smile remained.

Chapter 30
Taken

As Clark drifted back into his narcotic-induced euphoric state of slumber, I slipped from the room and stepped through the curtain, into the area where the former hostages lay, soaking in their IV fluids and resting for the first time in weeks. My arrival stirred a few of the Americans, and one woman asked, "Are you one of the SEALs who rescued us?"

I smiled. "No, ma'am. I'm not a SEAL. I just came down to check on you. How are you feeling?"

"Are you a doctor, then?"

I continued smiling. "No, ma'am. I'm not a doctor, either. I just want to make sure you're feeling all right."

She was relentless. "Are the SEALs on this ship? It would be so nice to give them a hug and thank them in person."

The man in the next bed leaned up and stared into my face. "Wait a minute. You're the guy who gave me a rifle and told me to kill anybody who came through the door. You *were* out there. You *are* one of the SEALs."

"We're not SEALs," I finally said. "We're just Americans who came to give you a ride home. That's all."

All eight former hostages were now awake and shouting.

"That's some of the bravest stuff I've ever seen, man. How do you guys do that?"

Tears came from a few faces.

"How can we ever thank you? Are all of the SEALs okay? What about the crew of the helicopter?"

I patted the air with both hands. "I know you're excited, but the chopper pilot who was shot down is resting just on the other side of the room. He's injured but alive, and I'm sure he'd love to get some rest."

The first woman tossed off her blanket and stood. "I can't come to you, so please come to me. I have to give you a hug."

Tears were streaming from her face, so I took a step toward her before looking down at my clothes. "Ma'am, I'm filthy and covered in somebody else's blood. Maybe I should get cleaned up before..."

Her tears increased, and she reached for me like a frightened child, so I took another step and let her wrap me in her arms.

She said, "I don't have the words. I just can't tell you—"

I stepped back. "It's okay. This is what we do. You don't have to thank me."

Hers weren't the only tears in the bay, but I tried to camouflage mine.

"Who's Simms?" I asked.

A man toward the back of the bay raised a finger. I stepped beside his bed, and he asked, "Were you the one who sent in the note?"

"I was."

He reached up and shook my hand with both of his for a long time. He obviously wanted to speak, but the words weren't coming.

I said, "It's okay. You're safe now, and we'll have you home in a couple of days."

He choked back the tears. "I'm a meteorologist. I was just studying the desert climate. I didn't do anything wrong. Why would they take me?"

"I don't know, but you're safe now, and they'll never take anyone else."

"You killed them all?"

I nodded. "I need to ask you a question. When you answered my note, you wrote seven and eleven. What did the eleven mean?"

He almost laughed. "Have you ever seen the movie *Taken*?"

I shook my head. "No, sir. I have not."

He said, "It's a Liam Neeson film about a kidnapping. While I was being taken, I tried to remember what the girl did in that movie to help her dad find her. I know that's stupid and just a movie, but somehow, Neeson's character found out how many people there were holding his daughter, and that was an important piece of information. I saw eleven different people between the time I was taken and the time you flew the drone into my hands. Did it help?"

I gave him a broad smile. "It sure did. Thank you for that. Here's hoping you never have to use anything you learned from a kidnapping movie ever again."

Patti Baldwin was sitting on the edge of one of the beds with a man's hand clasped tightly in hers, so I stepped to the bedside.

She looked up and mouthed, "Thank you a thousand times."

I nodded, turned to the man on the bed, and offered my hand. "You must be Spencer."

His face was badly bruised, with a few lacerations across the cheekbones and forehead. He pulled his hand from Patti's and took mine. "Whoever you are—SEAL or not—I can't thank you enough. They would've killed us, you know. You saved all of our lives."

I pulled a rolling stool beneath me and took a seat. "I've got a lot of questions, Spencer. I know you were researching an upcoming piece, but we really can't wait for your article to hit the papers. We need to know what happened down there."

He glanced at Patti and then back to me. "Everything?"

"Yes, everything. But we don't have to do it here."

The ship slowed and settled from its foils, back onto the hull.

"What was that?" Spencer asked.

"The captain just reduced our speed. We needed to get out of Mexican waters as quickly as possible. Now we can relax. We'll be back in California in thirty-six hours or so."

He said, "So, your questions?"

"Why don't you get some rest and a shower first? We'll talk later today."

He nodded and returned his hand back into Patti's.

I stood and walked toward the hatch, but before I could leave the bay, everyone began to clap. I turned and raised a finger. "You know what? Hold that thought. I'll be right back."

I left sick bay and headed back for the CIC. When I'd assembled the team, had them don hats and tie bandanas to cover most of their faces, I led them back to the field hospital.

I brought the team through the curtain and into the bay, where the former hostages lay. "This is the brave team of men and women who pulled you out of Mexico tonight. The only one missing is the chopper pilot over there sleeping."

The applause returned, and so did the tears. The team spent half an hour talking with the former hostages and soaking in their gratitude.

I slipped away and shucked off my filthy clothes. Twenty minutes under the hottest shower I could stand felt like Heaven on Earth as the blood, sand, and grime washed from my skin and hair. I watched the stained water swirl around my feet and disappear down the drain, and I yearned for a shower that could do the same for my innermost place, where the horrors I've seen and committed fester and boil. I would pray. I'd spend hours talking with Singer. And I'd tell myself a thousand lies to justify what I'd done in the name of freedom. But I'd still bear the burden and the scars of the decisions I made so far from home and so far from my own humanity.

I fell asleep the instant my body landed on my bunk, and I dreamed of holding Penny's hand the way Spencer held Patti's.

* * *

Spencer met me in the small conference room beside the CIC just before noon. He was clean, shaven, and in good spirits.

"Thanks for coming, Spencer. Can I get you a coffee or anything?"

"Maybe a single malt scotch on the rocks. Make it a double."

I motioned toward a chair. "Have a seat, and you and I will have that single malt together when we're finished here."

He took the seat and crossed his legs. "I guess you want to get right to it, huh?"

"We can do this anyway you'd like. If you want to talk, I'll listen. If you want me to ask specific questions, we can do that, as well."

He cocked his head. "You sound like a shrink."

"In another life," I said. "Why don't you just tell me what happened down there? And start in Sacramento."

He touched his face where an adhesive strip covered five stitches just below his left eye, and he seemed to consider my recommendation. After a long moment, he looked up. "Are you sure we can't have that scotch now?"

I leaned back in my chair and mirrored his body position. "Sure we can. Just give me a couple of minutes. We keep the good stuff locked up. You know how sailors are."

He pretended to smile, and I stepped through the hatch and into the passage where Skipper waited with two glasses of beautifully golden scotch on the rocks. She held them up, shaking the first one. "Yours is tea. His is Glenlivet twenty-one-year-old."

I took both tumblers from her hands. "I'm jealous."

She lowered her chin. "You're on the clock."

Back through the hatch and in the conference room, I handed Spencer his tumbler of real single malt scotch. After settling back onto my seat and matching his posture again, I raised my glass to his. "Here's to freedom . . . newfound and enduring."

He touched the rim of his glass to mine and took his first sip. "This is spectacular. What is it?"

I took my sip and pretended to savor the rich aromas and complex flavors of my sweet tea. "It's Glenlivet twenty-one, and spectacular is the perfect description."

He placed his glass on the table. "Thank you."

"Enjoy," I said. "There's plenty more."

"Not for the scotch," he said. "For everything. Especially for getting Patti out of Sacramento. I never meant to put her in danger. I never dreamed this thing ran as deep as it does."

I was intrigued, but I maintained my blank expression, nodding occasionally.

He continued. "Before we go too far, did you bring back any of the weapons the cartel was using?"

My intrigue turned to the excitement of a boy on Christmas morning. "Why do you ask?"

He uncrossed his legs and leaned forward. "First, I have to know if you work for the federal government."

Honesty was the policy I chose in that pivotal moment. "Yes, sometimes, but I'm not an employee of the federal government. I'm a contractor of sorts."

"Of sorts?"

"Yes. I'm a private security contractor, but sometimes the government hires us for specific missions."

"Like rescuing hostages from Mexican drug cartels?"

I shook my head and uncrossed my legs. "No, I've never been hired to do that. We're doing this one out of our own pockets because we noticed the feds weren't interested in having anything to do with this operation."

"So, you're not working with or for the feds?"

"No. I told you we're on our own for this one."

He furrowed his brow and looked around the room. "A ship like this, two helicopters, and the ability to prosecute an operation like the one you pulled off last night. Everything about that screams government to me."

I pulled a hearing aid from behind my ear and held it in the air between us. "Then perhaps you're the one who needs a set of these. We are not feds. We're not working with or for the feds. We're here of our own accord and on our own dime. Ship, helicopter, and all."

Something caught his attention. "You said helicopter, singular."

"I did. The Huey that my partner rode to the ground, after being shot with an RPG, belonged to the DEA. You might say we 'borrowed' it when they weren't using it anymore."

He leaned back, obviously skeptical. "You stole a DEA helicopter to rescue me and seven other people?"

"It's the same helicopter they carried you in on last night. You were bagged and chained, so you probably didn't see it until it fell out of the sky."

"Really? How did you manage to acquire it?"

"The pilot who brought you to the camp last night was probably DEA. The cartel shot him in the face and set his body on fire after he dropped you off. We're trying to identify his remains now, but it's not easy to track down a DEA pilot in Central America." I took another sip, and he followed suit. I said, "Let me tell you what I know, then you can fill in the blanks."

He twirled the tumbler in his hand, watching the ice cubes on their liquid merry-go-round. "Okay, I'm listening."

I cleared my throat. "A group of Navy SEALs on leave in Cabo overheard a rumor about some Americans who'd been taken hostage by a local drug cartel."

"Los Toros?"

"Yes, Los Toros. Like the good patriots they are, the SEALs promptly reported the rumor to their chain of command, expecting immediate orders to return to Mexico and liberate the hostages."

"So you are SEALs," he said.

"No, not even close. But let me finish. Instead of getting orders to pull you and your fellow hostages out of the Mexican desert, they were ordered on another mission halfway around the world and immediately sequestered."

"Sequestered?"

"Yes, that's actually pretty common during the workup to the actual mission. The Navy will put the deploying SEALs on lockdown so they can focus on training up for the mission and getting in the right mindset to execute. Because of that, there was nothing suspicious about those guys being sequestered."

"Okay, I get that. But are you telling me you spent this fortune to come down here and rescue us because of something that's so easily explained away with a few SEALs being sequestered and deployed?"

"No, that's not what I'm saying at all. The SEALs are just one of the indicators that caught our attention. The more we looked into the rumor of kidnapped Americans, the more the investigation kept pointing back to an investigative journalist from Sacramento. Where were you before they brought you to that camp last night?"

"I don't know. They moved me every few days. Sometimes I'd spend two days in one place before they shuttled me somewhere else in the middle of the night. Sometimes I'd only stay a few hours in one location. It felt completely random, but I'm thankful they delivered me to that particular camp last night."

"So am I, Spencer. Now, tell me about the guns."

"They're American."

"I knew that the instant they started shooting back at us. There's no other sound like that five-five-six round, but how do you know they're American?"

He took another sip. "I found the purchase order from the California National Guard."

I dug my toes into the sole of my boot, trying not to react to the biggest bombshell I'd heard in years. "How did they get to Mexico?"

"That's the wrong question. The right question is, how are they still getting to Mexico? And I have the answer to both of those questions."

"Let's have it."

He drained his tumbler. "Have you ever heard of Air America?"

"Of course, but that was a CIA operation. I know people who were part of that network back in the day."

He said, "It's still in operation. Of course, the names have changed, and the players are a little different, but the business of illegal transportation of illegal goods and services to parts of the world we don't talk about in polite society is still booming. And just like the guns, I've got the proof."

I subconsciously glanced to the ceiling, where the microphones and cameras were nestled, capturing every word and move that Spencer Baldwin made. Skipper was undoubtedly running every piece of new information through every processor she could find.

Spencer Baldwin was a goldmine, and all I had to do was keep him talking.

I drained my cocktail and shook the empty glass toward his. "Would you care for another?"

"Would you?" he asked.

I lifted his tumbler. "I'll be right back."

Chapter 31
Scout's Honor

I stepped through the door of the CIC, and Skipper looked up with disbelief on her face. "Is this guy for real?"

"I think he is. What does he have to gain by lying to me?"

"This is golden stuff, but what are we going to do with it?"

"I don't know yet, but as long as he's talking, I'll keep listening."

"Absolutely, and I'll keep recording."

"Where's the scotch and sweet tea?"

"It's on its way. I couldn't leave while he was talking, so I made a call."

Anya stepped through the door with two fresh tumblers in her hands and gave me that smile no man can ignore. "It has been long time since I make for you drink, Chasechka. I am proud of you."

"Proud?" I asked. "Why?"

"You are now having only tea instead of alcohol. I left for you note on boat many years ago to tell you of drinking too much. Is good to know you are now better."

I took the drinks from her hands, and she let her index finger linger on my skin an instant longer than she should have. I thought about my wife and unborn child. "Thank you. Keep them coming, if you will. I'll be sure to tip the waitress at the end of the night."

She giggled—something I didn't know she was capable of doing—and I made my exit.

"Here you go," I said as I placed Spencer's drink on the table beside him. "So, where were we?"

"Air America."

"Ah, yes. Those guys."

He took a sip. "That's even better than the first glass. Thank you."

"Tell me about how the guns are getting into Mexico."

"Not just Mexico," he said. "They're going all over the world, and the new Air America is making it happen under the guise of humanitarian aid. You should see these things. Entire cargo planes packed full of rice and beans, medicine, pallets of water, and always a few crates of guns and ammo for the local warlord or cartel leader. Some of the pilots and crew openly justify it by claiming there's no other way to get the warlords and cartels to allow the humanitarian relief to get to the people. I call BS on that. I think it's the other way around. The beans and penicillin are being used to buy the silence of the locals."

"But why? Why would the U.S. be supplying arms for the people we claim to fight so hard against?"

He lowered his chin. "Don't be so naïve. When was the last time the government told anyone the truth about anything?"

"Touché. Let's change gears for a minute. Tell me about Robert Wells, your editor at the *Sacramento Bee*."

He didn't hesitate. "Bought and paid for. That's why the piece I'm working on won't go to the *Bee*. It'll go straight to the New York Times."

"He's dead," I said. "Apparent suicide, and his body miraculously disappeared from federal custody before an autopsy could be conducted."

Journalists must look at the world through an entirely different lens than the rest of us. Instead of asking about the details of the suicide or if I had any theories, Spencer asked, "Why was his body in federal custody?"

I snapped my fingers. "Now *you're* asking the right questions."

He didn't hesitate. "What about his secretary, Barbara?"

"It was Brenda Collier," I said. "She's been missing since Wells's apparent suicide."

He said, "I know her name, and now I know you knew her name. You may be a SEAL or whatever, but you're not the only one who can dig for information."

"Nicely done," I said. "But we're not SEALs. None of us has ever been a SEAL. Why do you guys keep assuming we are?"

He admired his scotch and swallowed another sip. "Because that's what regular civilians do. We believe what's presented to us without questioning the information or who's providing it. If hostages are rescued, it's either done by the FBI Hostage Rescue Team or the Navy SEALs."

"But you're not a regular civilian," I said.

"No, I'm not, but I am looking for indicators of misdirection and outright lies."

"I've told you none of either."

He shrugged. "Maybe, but you haven't been completely honest with me."

"Why do you say that?"

"If you've made no attempts to deceive me, let me have a drink of your scotch."

"How did you know?" I asked.

"It's basic chemistry. There's sugar in whatever you're drinking. The bubbles against the glass on the surface of the liquid mean there's sufficient surface tension in the liquid to maintain the structural stability of a bubble. There's no sugar in my scotch. If bubbles form, they pop very quickly. The higher the alcohol content, the faster the bubbles burst."

"It's sweet tea."

"Wells tried to convince me not to do the cartel story. I told him I didn't care what he thought about the potential fallout. I was doing the story, and I'd sell it to the highest bidder, or he could print it in his little hometown paper, the *Bee*. It's going to get me a Pulitzer, regardless of where it's published."

"It's going to get you a bullet in the head is what it's going to get you. You know that, right?"

"From somebody like you?" he asked.

"No, that's not what we do, but there are people who can get almost anything done for the right price."

He seemed to ignore the stab. "You haven't heard the best part yet."

Suddenly, my sweet tea didn't look so appealing, and Spencer said, "This thing goes all the way to the White House. Guess who was the commander of the California National Guard before becoming governor of California before becoming the president of the United States."

I stared into his eyes, desperately searching for any sign of a lie. "And you have proof?"

"Reams of it."

"Why?" I asked.

He raised an eyebrow. "Why is the president involved? Simple. It's all part of his anti-gun agenda. If he can convince enough of the American people that the guns we build and sell all over the country are ending up in the hands of über-violent Mexican cartels, he's one step closer to banning them in the U.S."

"But those weapons aren't AR-Fifteens. They're M-Fours, full-auto rifles."

"Over forty percent of Americans already believe AR-Fifteens are full auto even though thirty seconds of research dispels that myth. That brings us back to my theory on regular civilians. They're not rational thinking, logical people. They're sheep who want to be led to slaughter."

"Did Los Toros know who you were?" I asked.

"Oh, yeah, they knew. And they were planning to force me to write a piece on four other rival cartels, exposing their leadership, distribution routes, and operational tactics. That's why they were keeping me alive. They're no different than our elected so-called leaders. They all have an agenda, and they're willing to do whatever it takes to see that agenda in action."

I let his theory roll around in my head. "What about Patti? Aren't you afraid someone will get to her after you publish?"

"Sure, I'm worried. Weren't you concerned when you learned you were about to go head-to-head with the deadliest cartel in history?"

"Of course. But the reward of recovering American hostages far outweighs my selfish fear."

He took another sip. "You just answered your own question. If my story exposes the corruption all the way to the top, so what if I get a bullet in the head and Patti never gets her book published? Exposing corruption of this magnitude is worth my life. Wouldn't you agree, Mr. 'I'm not a SEAL'?"

"What if I can give you an avenue to expose the corruption without tying your name or Patti's to any of it? Is your Pulitzer so important that you're willing to die for it?"

"I'm listening."

"The people I work for most of the time are not elected officials or government employees at any level. They are a completely independent board of patriotic Americans who believe truth is more important than getting elected or reelected. They are extremely powerful men and women who pull a lot of strings most people don't know exist."

He said, "You're talking about Skull and Crossbones–type guys."

"Not exactly. It's not a secret society. It's a small group of people who truly believe in the principles on which our country was founded. They believe in freedom, rule of law, and perhaps most importantly, they believe our elected officials are not leaders. They're servants of the people."

He sighed. "It sounds like the Boy Scouts all grown up. I'm not buying it."

"It's an option. You know full well that the publication of your piece will result in grave danger for you and Patti, even if you disappear to some corner of the world no one has ever heard of. Powerful people have powerful friends who have powerful ways of finding those of us outside that ring of power and privilege. You'll be on the run as long as you live. I'm not trying to sell you on anything. If you want a way to make your point and hold responsible the ones who deserve it, I'll set up the meeting. If not, I'll help you find that unknown corner of the world, and I'll do my best to keep you alive. The third option is you walk off my ship, and you never see me or speak with me again. The call is yours."

For the first time, I believed Spencer Baldwin was speechless. He stared between his shoes and then hid behind his tumbler. Finally, he said, "You've got all of this recorded, right?" I nodded slowly, and he asked, "What are you going to do with the audio if I walk away?"

"Nothing. The audio is worthless without the proof you claim to have. I could play the audio for the whole world, and the White House would brush it off as some lunatic who has no idea what he's talking about."

"What if I gave you the proof?"

It was my turn to be speechless. When I finally found my words, I asked, "Why would you do that?"

He slid his tumbler toward me. "Because you're some kind of secret agent man with all the answers. If you'd run to Mexico and start a fight with Los Toros on a hunch, you're not the kind of man who could sit on information like I have. You wouldn't be able to sleep at night. You'd have to feed it to this mysterious board of yours because you're a Boy Scout."

Chapter 32
Philosophy 101

I stood and collected Spencer's glass. "Go talk with Patti and make a decision. I've got a lot to do, but when you're ready to continue our conversation, come back to this deck and pick up the phone beside the door to the Combat Information Center. We call it the CIC. Our analyst will answer and find me. Nothing that I have to do is more important than talking with you, so don't hesitate to have the analyst hunt me down."

He didn't stand. Instead, he said. "I've got one more question, if you don't mind."

I leaned against the table. "Sure, go ahead."

"Last night, when you brought the whole team into the medical center—or whatever it's called—there was a woman with blue eyes like a glacier. She wasn't American. Her accent was distinctly Eastern European. What was her involvement in all of this?"

"She's a very long story. But suffice it to say, she isn't admin or support staff. She's a frontline fighter like us. She was responsible for more than her share of dead cartel members last night and brings a set of skills to the team we wouldn't have without her."

"There were three other women. None of them was dirty, but they all looked tired, just like you."

"One was our analyst. The two in the flight suits were one of our pilots and a door gunner. Without them, the rescue couldn't have happened."

"That sounds like a story I'd love to write."

I pushed off the table. "Unfortunately, neither of them will talk with you. They're under nondisclosure agreements, and we can't risk having their identities revealed to the general public."

"Why aren't you hiding behind a mask like everyone else?"

"It's not hiding. It's protecting. What we do is dangerous, and the people we deal with are even more dangerous. If our faces make it onto the front page or the evening news, our careers are over, and so may be our lives. As for why I'm not wearing a mask, I'm finished."

"Finished?" he asked. "What does that mean?"

"This is my final mission. I'll step aside, and the work will continue without me."

He scowled. "But you're still young. Why would you retire so early?"

"I'm going to be a father in a few months, and I can't bear the thought of leaving my child without a father."

He stood. "You're a good man, Chase. Can we still have that scotch together later? Both of us?"

"I'd like that," I said. "We'll talk again soon."

My next stop was back in sick bay. Clark was clean, his arm was in a cast, and he appeared to be only slightly stoned.

"Hey, College Boy. I wondered if you were going to come see me."

"You're never going to believe the hornets' nest we kicked on this one."

He beamed. "Oh, really?"

Some of his beaming was from the painkillers, but mostly, it was his curiosity.

"According to Spencer Baldwin, this thing is a conspiracy that runs all the way to the White House, and it's about the president's anti-gun agenda."

He shuddered. "I'm not exactly sober here. You need to break that down for me."

"You can listen to the recording. It's pretty incredible stuff."

"I'll bet. Did I mention how badly getting shot down sucks?"

"You brought it up last night," I said.

"Last night? I didn't see you last night."

I chuckled. "You were a little out of it. We had a long, deep conversation about our favorite philosopher."

He shook his head. "I don't have a favorite philosopher."

"You did last night. And you were quoting him line-by-line. It was a special moment."

"I'm glad I could be a source of amusement for you."

I said, "I see they set your arm."

He held up the cast. "Yep, that sucked, too. I'm having an MRI sometime today. Doc said I may have done some damage to my already screwed-up spine."

"How does it feel?"

He groaned. "It hurts all over, but I'm an old man, and crashing helicopters is definitely a young man's game."

"That's not a game I want to play."

He threw back the blanket and lifted his gown. "Check this out."

I turned away. "Whatever you're about to show off, I don't want to see it."

He scowled. "I'm wearing boxers, you idiot. Just look."

I turned back to see his abdomen and both sides completely covered by an enormous black bruise. I tried not to react, but that was impossible. "That looks horrible. Has Dr. Shadrack seen it?"

"Yeah. He called it some big fancy medical word I can't remember. It was something about hematoma or something like that. He said it's not as bad as it looks."

"I certainly hope it's not. It looks like you should be dead."

"I *feel* like I should be dead. Now, get me out of this bed, and take me to wherever the interview tapes are."

I threw up my hands. "Easy, big fellow. Let's talk to the doctor about that before I drag your old butt on a field trip."

He tried to stand. "Let's not. You know me, kid. Like I always say, it's always better to ask for a hand in the cookie jar than to get forgiveness or whatever."

"See there? Philosophy by Conclarkus Johnsonus."

When he finally managed to force himself to his feet, he grabbed the bedrail. "Whoa. I wasn't expecting that."

"What?"

"The whole world started spinning."

I took him by his good arm. "Get back in bed. I'll bring the audio and some headphones, and you can stick your hand in the cookie jar all you want."

To my surprise, he obeyed and said, "I don't know what that means, but it sounds like a good idea."

Skipper transferred the audio to my tablet and pulled a pair of headphones from the bin. She said, "Don't let him slobber on these. They're expensive."

"I'll do my best, but no promises. You know how he gets."

I delivered the tablet and headset, as well as Skipper's admonition against slobbering on her shiny new headset.

Clark dived right in. It only took a few seconds for him to stop the audio and pull off the headset. "Is this guy for real?"

I laughed. "That's exactly what Skipper asked, and I have to say he is. Listen to the whole thing, and then we'll talk about it. I'm going to check on our other patients while you listen."

He pulled the headset back in place, and I stepped across the bay. Everyone was clean and awake, and most were holding telephones to their ears.

Captain Sprayberry stepped into the bay a few seconds after me. "Ah, there you are. I've been looking for you."

"I was checking on Clark. What's up?"

He said, "The XO briefed everyone on the necessity of confidentiality, and we have a stack of signed, witnessed confidentiality agreements from everyone. Whether they live up to those agreements remains to be seen, but everybody was so happy to be free, I think they would've signed anything we handed them. What you did out there was really something, Chase. You should be proud."

"Do you mean that part when I outran and outmaneuvered a pair of Mexican Navy patrol boats? Oh, no . . . wait. That wasn't me. That was you. Thank you for getting us out of there."

"That's my job," he said.

"And we did our job on the ground. We're quite a team, Captain."

"Indeed, we are. I hope you don't mind, but we handed out satellite phones so everyone could call home."

"Of course I don't mind. That was very kind of you."

"Hey, College Boy! Get back over here."

Captain Sprayberry shot a thumb across the bay. "I think you're being summoned."

"Let me see what he wants, and then I'll come find you if you still need me."

"No, no. I just wanted you to know about the confidentiality agreements and our ETA back to San Diego. We'll be home in less than twenty-four hours."

"Thanks, Barry. I'm sure these guys will be anxious to get their feet back on American soil, even if it is Californian soil."

"Oh, yeah. That's the other thing. How are we going to get these guys through customs?"

"I'll get Skipper on that."

He said, "Good enough. Go deal with Clark."

When I stepped behind his curtain, Clark shook the headset at me. "Do you have any of the proof Baldwin claims to have?"

"I've not seen it yet, but he swears he's got it."

He said, "Get it before he gets off this ship. We have to pass it to the Board. We don't have a choice."

"That's what I figured. I'll see what I can do, but first, I'd like to call a team meeting. Can you stay awake for another fifteen minutes?"

"I've told you a thousand times. I'm a Green Beret. I can get by on ten minutes of sleep and a hundred calories a day."

"You can't get by on a hundred calories per hour," I said. "I'll get everybody together, and we'll have our chat in here so you don't have to miss it."

By the time I rounded everyone up and got them down to sick bay, Clark was sound asleep, but I didn't let that stop the meeting. It was time to make my official announcement.

I said, "I'll keep this short. Some of you have already heard the rumors. They are true. I've loved every minute of working with every one of you, but now that Penny and I are having a baby, I've made the decision to hang up my boots and become a full-time father."

A chorus of sighs and moans came, and I couldn't resist allowing my eyes to fall on Anya. She looked as if I had crushed her heart.

I continued. "Nothing will change except me being part of the team. Bonaventure is still our home and where I think you should be. The op center is yours. The airport is yours, and of course, the training facilities are yours. I'll be there to consult if you need me, but I won't deploy with you. The baby and Penny will be my priorities, and I'm sure all of you can understand that. We're family, and that won't change."

Everyone seemed to have something to say, but I held up my hand. "This isn't goodbye. It's just a change in team structure. It makes sense to me for Mongo to become team lead, but that's up to all of you. You'll also need to add another knuckle-dragger, so think about anyone you know who's looking for work."

My sat-phone rang, and I pulled it from my pocket. I didn't recognize the number, so I pushed the button, silencing the call and sending it to voicemail. A few seconds later, it rang again from the same number.

I read it out loud and asked, "Does anyone recognize that number?"

No one spoke up, so I sent it to voicemail again. Whatever and whoever it was could wait, but before I could continue my announcement, Skipper pulled her phone from her pocket and said, "Chase, it's the same number. Maybe we should answer it."

"Go ahead," I said, and she stuck the phone to her ear.

"Hello." She paused to listen and then said, "Yes, who's calling, please?" Skipper stood and stuck the phone toward me. "Chase, you need to take this."

I lifted the phone from her hand. "Hello, this is Chase."

A calm voice asked, "Is this Mr. Chase Fulton?"

"It is. Who is this?"

"Mr. Fulton, my name is Dr. McElroy. I'm with the trauma team at Cedars-Sinai Medical Center in Los Angeles. There's been an accident, and your wife, Nicole Thomas Fulton, was brought here to our trauma center."

Penny's real name sounded foreign to me. I'd never heard anyone call her Nicole, and somehow, that made me believe it wasn't real.

I said, "Who?"

He said, "I'm Dr. McElroy."

"No, not you. Are you talking about Penny?"

He stammered. "I'm sorry, Mr. Fulton. You are married to Nicole Bethany Thomas Fulton, aren't you?"

It finally hit me. "Yes, yes! That's Penny. She's my wife. What's happening?"

"Your wife has been in a serious automobile accident, Mr. Fulton. We need you to come to the hospital as soon as possible. If necessary, we can arrange for transportation for you."

"What about the baby? Is the baby all right?"

His calm, measured tone continued. "Mr. Fulton, what's important at this moment is for you to come to the hospital. How long will it take you to get here?"

I suddenly lost all ability to understand the passage of time. "I don't know. I'm in the ocean. I'm on a ship. I'm . . ."

Singer leaned toward me and held out his hand. "Give me the phone, Chase."

Something about his quiet confidence made me lay the phone in his palm. "This is Jimmy Grossmann. I'm an associate of Mr. Fulton's. He's visibly upset. Can you tell me what's happening? I may be able to help." He listened and said, "It will be several hours. We're offshore, but we'll have him there as soon as possible." There was more silence as Singer listened. "His blood type is A-positive. Why do you ask?"

The silence felt endless, and I was shell-shocked and in a fog.

"Stand by." He covered the phone with his palm. "Chase, Penny's been in an accident, and she has to have a liver transplant from someone with blood type O-negative."

I was frozen but managed to say, "I'm A-positive."

Singer said, "I know, and no one on the team is O-negative. Do you know anyone who is O-negative and would consider donating part of their liver? This is extremely serious, Chase. I need you to think."

Everyone I knew well was sitting in front of me, and I couldn't think of another living soul who might consider giving up part of their liver to save Penny's life.

As I sat drowning in a sea of helplessness, Anya said, "I am O-negative."

Chapter 33
Part of Me

I've lain in the dirt and mud and blood all over the world, with hordes of men pouring fire onto my position, and trembled as I came to terms with my own mortality and the probability of never returning home. But I'd never known terror like I felt the moment I learned my wife lay dying in a hospital hundreds of miles away, with no way of getting to her quickly.

I shook myself from my haze and became the calm, rational battlefield commander my team believed me to be. "Skipper, find Captain Sprayberry and order maximum sustained speed for San Diego."

Without a word, she turned and vanished through the curtain.

I turned to our chief pilot. "Disco, get on the phone with the airport, and have the *Ghost* fully ready when we arrive. Mongo, the team is yours. I need you and Skipper to compile the proof Spencer Baldwin claims to have about the U.S. involvement in arms distribution to Mexican drug cartels. Do *not* let Baldwin off this ship until you have every piece of proof he has. It's all going to the Board. When Clark wakes up, brief him on what's happening, and coordinate the briefing for the Board."

He turned for the door. "Done."

A nurse walked past, and I grabbed the sleeve of her scrubs. "Where's Dr. Shadrack?"

"Is everything okay?" she asked.

"No, I need Dr. Shadrack now."

She stepped past me to Clark's bedside, concerned for her patient.

I said, "He's fine. I need the doctor."

She took my hand. "Have a seat, sir. I'll bring him to you."

"No, you don't understand. Take me to him."

"Follow me."

We found the doctor in his small office adjacent to sick bay.

He looked up and said, "Come in, Chase. What can I do for you?"

"I need you on the phone with a Dr. McElroy at Cedars-Sinai in L.A. He's on the trauma team. Penny was in a wreck, and she needs a liver transplant. One of us has the same blood type, and we're willing to give a portion of our liver. I need you to coordinate that."

The ship accelerated sharply and rose from the water onto her foils. I could imagine how it must look to anyone in the vicinity to see a five-hundred-foot ship rise and soar across the waves at sixty knots.

Without questions or hesitation, he lifted the phone from his desk.

While he was dialing, I said, "I also need Clark awake and alert. Can you make that happen?"

He stuck the phone to his ear and looked up at the nurse. "Wake him up, and postpone any more pain meds until this is resolved."

"Yes, Doctor."

What came next was a conversation I never could've dreamed would happen.

I pulled Anya into a storeroom and caught my breath. "Are you sure you're willing to do this?"

She took both of my hands in hers and pierced my soul with the most sincere expression I've ever seen from anyone. Her Russian accent I loved so much softened, and she spoke straight to my heart. "My Chase, I have loved you from moment you first touched my hand so many years ago. I can now save life of woman you love. This is for me a beautiful gift, and I would never hesitate to do this for you and for Penny."

"It is so much more than a beautiful gift you're giving us, Anya. It's . . ."

She frowned. "No, Chase. Is not gift *from* me. Is gift *to* me to be able to do this thing for you. But what about the baby?"

I swallowed the lump in my throat and squeezed her hands. The words wouldn't come, so I just shook my head as she released my hands and took me in her arms.

"I will forever love you, my Chasechka, and now there will always be part of me with you."

I held her in my arms for a moment, digging as deeply into my heart as I could reach, but there were no words to express the gratitude I felt or the debt I now owed to the woman who could've been my ruin.

She whispered, "I have taken so many lives. I cannot count this number, but I can now say I have also given life and not only taken it away. Love her, Chase. Love her the way I have so often dreamed of having you love me."

I wiped the tears from my eyes. "I need you to talk with Dr. Shadrack. He'll explain what's going to happen and answer your questions."

"I do not have questions."

"But this is a complicated thing, and there are risks involved. You need to understand what could happen."

She smiled up at me. "This does not matter. Is not decision made while considering risk. Is decision made of love."

I led her to Dr. Shadrack's office, where we found him with the phone still pressed to his ear and a legal pad beneath his active pen. Nothing on the pad was legible to me, but that didn't matter. He looked up and stared at Anya. The look on his face said he didn't believe what was happening before his eyes. He motioned to Anya, looked back at me, and mouthed, "Her?"

I nodded, and he pointed to a pair of chairs.

Anya sat, but I did not. I wanted so badly to say something—anything—that rose to the level of true expression of my gratitude, but she pressed her finger to her lips. "Shhh."

I found Skipper in the CIC, with Spencer and Patti Baldwin by her side, in front of a pair of computer monitors.

When I walked in, she said, "It's all here, Chase. You're never going to believe it."

I sank onto a chair. "Today, I can believe anything is possible."

"Are you okay?" she asked.

"I don't know. I'm numb right now. How fast are we going?"

She turned to a third monitor. "Sixty-two knots. I didn't know the *Lori Danielle* was capable of this kind of speed."

"How long until we're in San Diego?"

"Eight hours, and the jet's ready and waiting."

"That's too long," I said. "There has to be another way."

Skipper leaned back and stared at the ceiling. "I've got an idea. Give me a minute."

I watched as her fingers flew across the keyboard, and map after map of the west coast of Mexico appeared and disappeared time after time.

After several minutes, she said, "Got it. If we can find a flight crew to bring the *Ghost* to Ciudad Constitución Airport in Baja California Sur, we can fly you and Anya on the Little Bird to meet the jet. If everything went well, you could be in L.A. in a little over three hours. It's risky, though. If you get detained at the airport, it could be days before you get out of there."

I drew the map in my head and played through the likelihood of the Mexican authorities putting together a task force to intercept us on the ground. "Make it happen."

I sprinted back to sick bay, where I found Anya and Dr. Shadrack still in his office.

"Change of plans," I said. "We're arranging for someone to fly our jet from San Diego to Ciudad Constitución Airport in Baja California Sur. Anya and I will fly there in the Little Bird and take the *Ghost* to L.A. It'll cut the trip down to a little more than three hours."

Anya said, "I do not have to go with you. If Dr. Shadrack harvests part of my liver, you can take it with you inside icebox."

I turned to the doctor, and he said, "She's right, but there's risk. I'm not a transplant surgeon. I'm a board-certified general surgeon. But I can do it. If I don't harvest enough of the liver, or if I harvest the wrong portion of the liver, it would mean the organ wouldn't be viable for transplant. It's much safer to have the transplant surgeons at Cedars-Sinai harvest the portion they need."

Rapid decision-making is a skill developed over a lifetime, but it took only an instant for me to weigh the risks and potential benefits of each option. "You're coming with me. How soon will you be ready to go?"

The ship changed course beneath us, and we were headed for the coastline off Baja California Sur.

Without asking, I snatched the phone from Dr. Shadrack's desk and dialed the CIC. When Skipper answered, I asked, "Did you find a crew?"

"They'll be airborne in twenty minutes. I'm working out the rendezvous timing now. How soon can you be ready to go?"

"We're ready now."

She said, "Meet Gun Bunny in the hangar bay. And Chase . . . we've got this."

I looked up to see Clark dragging himself across the deck by his heels in a wheelchair and said, "That's not a good look for you."

He ran his hand through his hair. "I'm afraid it's the only look I've got right now. I hear you're leaving us."

"That's right. Anya and I are flying to meet the *Grey Ghost* at Ciudad Constitución Airport."

He screwed up his face. "What? You're running away with her? What?"

"No," I said. "We're meeting the jet to take us to L.A. so Anya can donate part of her liver to Penny."

"When did this happen? The nurse told me you were retiring. She didn't say anything about a liver transplant."

I caught him up on what he'd missed during his slumber and said, "Skipper has the proof you wanted from Spencer. As soon as we're off the ship, I'm sure she'll be ready to brief you and the Board."

"That part makes sense, but I was way behind on the liver thing. Is Penny okay? What about the baby?"

"We don't know about the baby yet, but no, Penny is not okay. She's going to die if she doesn't get the liver transplant."

"What do you need from me?"

I said, "Grease the wheels in L.A. so we can get through Customs and Immigration."

"No problem. What else?"

I said, "Deal with getting our guests back into the U.S. legally without making headlines."

"I can do that. Have you talked to Singer?"

I furrowed my brow. "About what?"

Clark rolled his eyes. "About getting a little help from above."

"Add that to your list if you don't mind. We've got a chopper to catch."

Disco, Anya, and I headed for the helipad, where Barbie was waiting with the turbine running and the blades turning. We climbed aboard and took off into the afternoon sun. When we turned east toward the coast of Mexico, the headwind we fought running from the patrol boats became a tailwind for us, and our ground speed hit 130 knots.

We flew in silence for an hour until the coastline passed beneath us and the airport at Baja California Sur came into sight. The timing was perfect. The temporary flight crew put the *Grey Ghost* on the runway only minutes before our arrival. They stopped on the runway and taxied back to the approach end, where Gun Bunny was aiming. We touched down a hundred feet from the nose of the *Ghost*, and the three of us leapt from the chopper.

The airstairs came down, and we ran up them and aboard our jet. We were climbing northward before we had time to buckle our seat belts, and seventy-five minutes later, the wheels touched down at Santa Monica Airport with Disco in the driver's seat.

The thrust reversers roared, and the brakes strained to stop the Gulfstream on the short runway. A black Suburban met us at the bottom of the airstairs, and Anya and I raced away in the back seat with no sign of a customs agent anywhere in sight.

Dr. McElroy met us at reception, and I immediately asked, "Can I see her?"

He sent Anya away with another surgeon and said, "I'm sorry, but she's already prepped for surgery. I'll have a nurse take you to the surgical waiting area, where you'll have a private room to wait."

"How long will the surgery take?"

"After we determine that the donor liver is compatible with Mrs. Fulton, we'll begin the surgeries simultaneously. By the time

I've removed Mrs. Fulton's damaged liver, Dr. Jenson will have harvested the partial from the donor, and I'll begin the transplant. Depending on how much abdominal damage I find, the entire procedure will take between six and twelve hours."

"What do you need from me, Doctor?"

He laid a hand on my shoulder and turned me toward a desk where a young lady sat, obviously awaiting my arrival. "We have some documents for you to sign, and I have to explain the risks so you can give fully informed consent."

"Dr. Shadrack explained the risks, and I have no objections. Do the surgery."

He said, "I have to go scrub in, but before I go, I want you to know that your wife is in very good hands, and we will do everything in our power to make the procedure a success. There is one more thing you should know . . . The fetus did not survive the accident, and I will perform the procedure to remove its remains during the liver transplant."

I lowered my chin. "*Her* remains. She was a baby, not a fetus."

I signed a thousand documents without reading them, and someone parked me in the waiting area in a relatively comfortable niche that looked more like a hotel room than a surgical waiting room. All that remained for me to do was the thing I most hated, and that was wait.

I cried, I slept, I paced, and I drank a gallon of coffee that tasted like boiled dirt. Hours passed like eons, and I ached to see Penny and hold her again.

Eight hours into my wait, the door opened, and I leapt to my feet. As badly as I wanted to see Dr. McElroy come through the door, I wasn't disappointed when I saw my team—my family—file into the waiting room.

Once everyone was settled, I told them about losing the baby in the accident . . . and I cried some more.

Epilogue

Four months later, I sat in an Adirondack chair inside the gazebo, looking out over the North River and holding Penny's hand in mine. We'd spent every day since coming home from Cedars-Sinai just like that. Some days, we sat in the house, others we spent on the settee aboard *Aegis*, but no matter where we sat, we held hands.

"The doctors say I can do short walks," she said.

I grinned. "You want to go see the horses, don't you?"

She gave me the puppy dog eyes I couldn't resist. "It has been a long time since they've seen me."

"Oh, so it's about them, is it?"

"Of course. They miss me."

We took the short walk down the path that led to the barn, where she kept her demons that hated me almost as much as I despised them. She was right, though. They had apparently missed her, and it was easy to believe they somehow knew to be gentle with her.

She rubbed their faces and nuzzled their ears. "I've missed you guys."

They neighed in response. And who knows? Maybe she *could* understand them. At least it looked like she could.

After the grand adventure with the horses, we slowly made our way home, and I flipped on my preferred television news channel.

The anchor laid out the details of the impeachment proceedings against the president of the United States following the investigation of a scandal that had come to be known as Gun Gate. The unexplained slaughter of an entire cartel known as Los Toros remained a mystery, even though three rival cartels had claimed responsibility for the brutal slaying of nearly fifty cartel members, making it the bloodiest single event in cartel history.

As time passed, Penny grew more restless and stricken with cabin fever. "We've got to go somewhere, Chase. Sitting at home is killing me."

"Have you ever been to Switzerland?"

She cocked her head and smiled. "Not yet."

Two days later, we crossed the icy North Atlantic in the *Grey Ghost*, with the cabin full of the people we loved, and landed in Château-d'Oex for the International Hot-Air Balloon Festival. Over a hundred brilliantly colored balloons filled the air every day, and we all grew more mesmerized by the minute.

The grace and beauty of enormous bags of hot air carrying perfectly woven gondolas of fascinated fliers across the unearthly beauty of the Swiss landscape was the very antithesis of the world in which I'd spent my adult life. No one fired a shot. No one drew a knife. And no one threatened to initiate an international incident.

On the seventh day of the festival, I arranged for Penny and me to have a private ride in the most beautiful balloon at the event. We rose from the earth and into the breathtaking beauty of the cloudless sky, with the Swiss Alps shining in the distance. I opened my coat and let her snuggle against me as we braved the cold, lost in each other's arms and the most gorgeous surroundings imaginable.

The abrupt roar of the fire overhead when the pilot pulled the chain activating the burner made her jump and nuzzle even closer.

She gazed out over the landscape too perfect to be real and sighed. "Thank you for this. You have no idea how much I needed this getaway. Maybe you could learn to fly a balloon."

I stared up into the massive bag of hot air above our heads. "Maybe I could."

We floated on the gentle breeze, and I felt Penny's hair brushing against my face. She reached up to tame it, but I pushed her hand away.

"Don't waste your time," I said. "You can't control it, and I love it."

She squeezed me as if she were never going to let go. "Now that the baby isn't coming, you're not retiring, are you?"

Author's Note

I usually start these notes with a confession that I made it all up, but I can't do that this time. Some of this story is true. I'll leave it up to you to determine what is fiction and what is fact. The frightening part of that determination for me was that the real part is harder to believe than the stuff I made up. We live in a world gone mad, but I still believe there's hope. I pray that you share my hope and are willing to hold the line against what we know is wrong. Now, let's talk about the story.

When *The Diamond Chase*, book #23 in the series, ended, I was just as shocked as you to find out that Penny was pregnant. I had no idea what I was going to do with a baby in the series. To help you understand why the ending surprised me, I have to tell you about the craziest possible way to write a story.

Good writers, serious writers, writers with something meaningful to say, start with an outline and a plan of how their novel will flow and bend and rise and fall, and definitely how it will end. That's the so-called correct way to write a novel. Here's the first confession of this note. I'm not smart enough to plan or outline. Even if I were, that sounds like the most boring, torturous, tedious job in the world. I would lose my mind if I tried to turn my career into such an organized endeavor.

Here's the crazy way to write a novel. Sit down every day of your life and write what the bizarre cast of characters in your head does and says. Listen to your imaginary friends, and no matter how insane the storyline appears to be, don't question it. Just write what they do and say . . . every day. I've now done that thirty-one times, and so far, every one of those books has become an international bestseller. I can't explain it. I don't understand it. And to be completely honest, I have no desire to understand it. I love everything about the experience. It's like watching a movie in my head and writing it down. Everything that happens surprises me. Every time Clark screws up a common phrase, I laugh out loud. Every time I get somebody hurt or killed, I feel like I've been kicked in the gut. Being your personal storyteller is the most wonderful job I've ever had and the only job I want for the rest of my life.

Here's the truth about the cartel I named Los Toros. It doesn't exist. It has never existed. And I hope it never does. It is, however, based on a conglomeration of Mexican drug cartels I pieced together to create a particularly scary bunch of bad guys. I think it worked, and I think I'd never want to meet those guys in a dark alley.

I chose the desert north of Cabo San Lucas as the setting for this story because that's where I found it. That's where I unearthed this one. I have no idea if a cartel has ever operated in that particular stretch of desert, but if you'd like to get a feel for the terrain, you can Google Cabo San Lucas and zoom in just north of the city. You'll find the dry riverbed I described in this story. You'll find a ranch exactly where I put the Los Toros camp. You'll find the airport where I landed the Huey and got the pilot shot in the face. The airport is now used as a car racing track called Hipodromo El Sauzal. The geography is all there, and it's all real. To my knowledge, though, none of the events I described in this story have ever happened there, but the geographic features I described all exist where I put them in the story. I hope you'll take the time to have a look at the aerial photos of the area provided by Google.

We've talked about the *Lori Danielle* before, but I need to reiterate that it is fictional. No such ship exists, and it's likely that it could not exist. The foiling technology exists and is, in fact, now used in the America's Cup sailboats, but I'm not aware of any ship of the size and displacement of the *Lori Danielle* that has the ability to achieve the speeds I describe in my stories. I know it's farfetched, but I love the ship I dreamed up, and I'm keeping it around. Here's an interesting little tidbit you may not know: I named the ship after my niece, because just like her, the ship is not what it appears to be. Both she and the ship are remarkable, surprising, and unforgettable. Although I temporarily named the ship *Arctic Explorer* in a previous book, it'll always be the *Lori Danielle*.

You knew this part was coming, so here it is. The government conspiracy portions of the story are fictional, for the most part. I have no idea if a revised Air America is delivering weapons and ammo to cartels and warlords across the globe, but it worked for the story, so I put it in. I don't know if there are politicians willing to sacrifice lives and freedom to press their agendas forward. Okay, so maybe I do know such politicians exist, and I believe they should be flushed out of local, state, and federal office as quickly as possible. Just like I state in this story, elected officials were never meant to be our leaders. They were meant to be our servants, and somehow, in our two hundred fifty years of existence, we've forgotten that. *They* have forgotten that.

I have to clear up a couple of lies I told about the feds. The Residential Reentry Management facility in Sacramento exists, but I have no idea if they have a morgue in their basement. There is no logical reason a body would be taken there, even if they had one. I needed a convenient way to have Wells's corpse disappear, so I picked on the FBI. The Congressional Security Bureau does not exist, but it sounds official and plausible on the surface. That's the best part about writing fiction. It doesn't have to *be* real to *sound* real.

The heartbreaking loss of the unborn child is, by far, the saddest element of this story, and I must admit it brought a tear to my eye when it happened. I had no idea how I was going to include a baby in Chase's and Penny's life, but I trusted the voices in my head to work it out. I did not expect the result that happened. For those who've lost a child, the agony must be unthinkable, and my heart cries for your loss. I don't know why the pregnancy and ultimate loss of the unborn child happened in the last two books, but if I could go back and remove it, I would. My editor taught me that every line of every story must accomplish one of two things: It must either further the plot or develop a character. Perhaps the heartbreaking event will serve to develop the characters of Chase and Penny. I suppose, in time, we'll find out together.

What happened inside Chase's head when he thought Clark had perished troubled me greatly. I didn't like it when I wrote it or proofread it, and I don't like it now that it's in print. However, I understand it. As mentioned earlier, there's never a plan for my writing. It unfolds before my eyes, just as it does for the reader.

In the early chapters, Chase expressed concern that it might become necessary to employ extreme violence involving knives. He struggled with the idea of any member of his team having to resort to that degree of barbarism. His understanding of Anya's ability to both apply and survive that level of violence was his justification for including her in the operation. When writing those early passages, I assumed it would be Anya who wore the blood of their enemies and not Chase, but I was wrong. (I'm wrong a lot, so it wasn't a surprise.)

When Chase watched the Huey fall from the sky after the RPG attack with Clark at the controls, his rage and unquenchable lust for revenge drove him to cross the line he worked so hard to keep his team from having to cross. The event set up my favorite passage of this book and gave us an opportunity to have a look deep into Chase's heart and mind. Although my stories are thriller/action/adventure fiction, I try to include elements of humanity, especially when they display a flaw or weakness in a character. Superhero characters who never make mistakes are dull to me. I greatly prefer relatable characters who screw up and learn from their mistakes. Chase has certainly done more than his share of that in these first twenty-four books of the series, but this installment may be what leaves the most enduring impression on his character throughout the rest of this series.

I enjoy writing the psychological consequences of war. Those are often the longest-lasting and most painful scars our brave men and women wear for the rest of their lives after protecting us from the evils in the world. Those scars are unseen by the world but deeply painful for those who must bear them for the remainder of their lives, and those wounds are the elements of my stories I hope will be the most memorable for the reader.

If you happen to be curious about my favorite passage from this story, this is it:

I slipped away and shucked off my filthy clothes. Twenty minutes under the hottest shower I could stand felt like Heaven on Earth as the blood, sand, and grime washed from my skin and hair. I watched the stained water swirl around my feet and disappear down the drain, and I yearned for a shower that could do the same for my innermost place, where the horrors I've seen and committed fester and boil. I would pray. I'd spend hours talking with Singer. And I'd tell myself a thousand lies to justify what I'd done in the name of freedom. But I'd still bear the burden and the scars of the decisions I made so far from home and so far from my own humanity.

I'd like to quickly mention the cover, because to me, it's quite humorous. I write the back cover descriptions of every book before I've written a word of the actual story. That's further proof of the insanity of my writing process. However, that's not where it ends. I select a cover photo and layout before either the description or the story is written. When we chose a hot-air balloon for the cover, I had absolutely no idea how that would fit into the story, and the more I wrote, the more I believed there would be no way to squeeze a balloon into the manuscript. When it finally happened in the Epilogue, I couldn't resist pulling my fingers from the keys and laughing at the bizarre nature of this out-of-control process of mine.

I've droned on long enough with my self-indulgent author's note, so I'll leave you once again with my deepest appreciation for the indescribable kindness you continue to show me by supporting my work, emailing me to share your experiences, and sharing my stories with your friends and family. The gift you've given me is beyond my ability to describe in its precious value to me. Sincerely, I thank you for letting me be your personal storyteller. There's nothing I'd rather be.

—*Cap*

About the Author

Cap Daniels

Cap Daniels is a former sailing charter captain, scuba and sailing instructor, pilot, Air Force combat veteran, and civil servant of the U.S. Department of Defense. Raised far from the ocean in rural East Tennessee, his early infatuation with salt water was sparked by the fascinating, and sometimes true, sea stories told by his father, a retired Navy Chief Petty Officer. Those stories of adventure on the high seas sent Cap in search of adventure of his own, which eventually landed him on Florida's Gulf Coast where he spends as much time as possible on, in, and under the waters of the Emerald Coast.

With a headful of larger-than-life characters and their thrilling exploits, Cap pours his love of adventure and passion for the ocean onto the pages of the Chase Fulton Novels and the Avenging Angel - Seven Deadly Sins series.

Visit www.CapDaniels.com to join the mailing list to receive newsletter and release updates.

Connect with Cap Daniels:

Facebook: www.Facebook.com/WriterCapDaniels
Instagram: https://www.instagram.com/authorcapdaniels/
BookBub: https://www.bookbub.com/profile/cap-daniels

Also by Cap Daniels

The Chase Fulton Novels Series
Book One: *The Opening Chase*
Book Two: *The Broken Chase*
Book Three: *The Stronger Chase*
Book Four: *The Unending Chase*
Book Five: *The Distant Chase*
Book Six: *The Entangled Chase*
Book Seven: *The Devil's Chase*
Book Eight: *The Angel's Chase*
Book Nine: *The Forgotten Chase*
Book Ten: *The Emerald Chase*
Book Eleven: *The Polar Chase*
Book Twelve: *The Burning Chase*
Book Thirteen: *The Poison Chase*
Book Fourteen: *The Bitter Chase*
Book Fifteen: *The Blind Chase*
Book Sixteen: *The Smuggler's Chase*
Book Seventeen: *The Hollow Chase*
Book Eighteen: *The Sunken Chase*
Book Nineteen: *The Darker Chase*
Book Twenty: *The Abandoned Chase*
Book Twenty-One: *The Gambler's Chase*
Book Twenty-Two: *The Arctic Chase*
Book Twenty-Three: *The Diamond Chase*
Book Twenty-Four: *The Phantom Chase*
Book Twenty-Five: *The Crimson Chase*

The Avenging Angel – Seven Deadly Sins Series
Book One: *The Russian's Pride*
Book Two: *The Russian's Greed*
Book Three: *The Russian's Gluttony*
Book Four: *The Russian's Lust*
Book Five: *The Russian's Sloth*
Book Six: *The Russian's Envy* (2024)
Book Seven: *The Russian's Wrath* (TBA)

Stand-Alone Novels
We Were Brave
Singer – Memoir of a Christian Sniper

Novellas
The Chase Is On
I Am Gypsy

Made in the USA
Coppell, TX
02 June 2024

33045026R10163